REALMS

BY ALEXA SUAREZ V.

Disclaimer

Read upon personal discretion as this book does touch on topics such as mental health, abuse, and the use of profanity.

This is a work of fiction. Names, characters, businesses, places, events, locales, and incidents are either the products of the author's imagination or used in a fictitious manner. Any resemblance to actual persons, living or dead, or actual events is purely coincidental.

This book goes to those who have supported me.

To the readers who have been made fun of for their passions and whimsical likeness.

To the ones struggling in any way, whether physically or mentally.

Lastly, to those who like me, who ever felt like they didn't belong.

May all of you enjoy the ride into the realms.

1

Greetings

"I'll fix this. I'll make it right." Isa rips parts of the fabric of her clothes and wraps them around his disembodied waist.

There is so much redness.

It was everywhere.

She applied as much pressure as she could. But. It. Wouldn't. Stop.

Hold on!

Oh my! Do my eyes deceive me? Ha! A newcomer?

Nice to meet you. Though, I don't think meeting someone like me is a pleasure.

What are you? Part Fae? Vampire? Sorcerer? Seer?

I know! You are one of those Dreamers. Yeah, you're one of *them*.

Oh, you don't know what a Dreamer is…right.

I see.

Well, I guess that doesn't matter now, does it?

I'm assuming you're here for a story.

It's not much of a happy one.

Let that be known before you continue.

In other words, I suggest you scram somewhere else.
Especially if you don't want to ruin your boring ordinary human
life with this tragedy. Not everything will be sunshine and
rainbows.

Go on then. Travel to a different story.

No?

Wow, you're pretty stubborn. A common quality of a
Dreamer.

Very well…since you won't be leaving anytime soon,
let's bring this story to the beginning, shall we?

Ahem.

Before the Kidnap

Isabel's day went terribly.

She wanted to die.

(Not in a literal sense…at least in this part of the story.)

She knew she was a little too rested for she could almost feel the sunrise poking out of the crevices of her darkened curtains. Shadows of the trees waved at her to open her eyes. She yielded to them, and mumbled a curse under her breath, already dreading her day.

Blinking, out of pure temptation, her blankets clung to her body, soothing her worries for a while until she had to shove them away.

Checking her phone, Isa sighed at the time. She had an eerie feeling in her gut as it twisted and turned inside of her. She, of course, ignored it assuming it had to do with her exam.

(She was wrong. Extremely wrong, dear Dreamer.)

In the cluttered kitchen, eating their classic whole grain cereal, all four of her brothers spotted their big sister storming out of her room with a hairbrush stuck to her curly hair. In sync, they smiled evilly and whispered among themselves chuckling.

Isa, of course, glowered at each of them, slamming the front door behind her, and tossing the brush to the ground.

The little monsters had messed with her alarm again. This time they were extra sneaky about it. Isa knew it was their doing. But why? Usually, their antics would be out of spite of something she had done to them, like when she threw water balloons at them during the winter.

Whatever.

Isa didn't need to think about that. She'll deal with them later.

As Isa made her way to the front yard, she spotted her abuela with the very thing Isa needed. She held the keys to her car in the palms of her hands along with a rosary.

At first, Isa asked her abuela to hand them over, but her abuela refused. Isa asked again, this time with more urgency in her voice. Abuela declined and tightened her grip on the keys. Having no other choice, Isa uses force and attempts to pry them away.

Her elderly hands were rough and firm as they tightened and wrapped around the holes of the metal ring keeping the keys together. When she managed to rip them out, Isa took the opportunity to quickly open her car and fly into the passenger seat, locking the doors.

Relief had yet to wash over her. Isa knew that all too well. Her abuela was no weak old lady.

As Isa was inside her car, abuela came around the corner and stepped in front of the Lexus slamming her arms and chest onto the hood. Isa yells at her through the window, honking with such force, she could've sworn she would've needed another horn.

"Look I'll talk to you after class! I need to leave!" Isa turns on the engine and switches the gear in reverse, bidding no mind to the disapproving stares of her neighbor.

"Quédate por favor!" she said raising her rosary to the sky as she removed herself from the vehicle.

Glancing at the time, Isa backed the car in reverse and blasted the speakers with the sounds of her favorite indie music.

Under her breath, the grandmother cursed as she failed to stop her granddaughter. There was only so much she could do.

So, she prayed.

Upon arrival, Isa's mouth curved downwards as if she had eaten something sour.

She recognized the figure approaching her as she tried to weave her way directly to her classroom building.

(Who is that figure you may ask?)

Dylan.

Her ex.

Ex-boyfriend.

Ex-fiancé.

A Cheater.

A narcissist.

The anti-cupid.

The heartbreaker.

"We get it!" Isa growled throwing her hands up in the air.

(Okay, okay sorry! Jeez, and don't ever break the fourth wall again. I'm the one telling the story remember?)

"Fine. Now get on with it."

(Very well.)

Anyways as I was saying, had she followed her dreams and moved away to New York, she would not have needed to face the dilemma of hiding from him until graduation. Much more, she would be far away from her demeaning, cruel, and vengeful cousin, Lyra.

Her whole situation seems almost laughable as if it came out of one of those Telenovelas her mom watched every night. Nothing about Isa's life was remotely normal. There was always something happening.

Peace and quiet were two words gone from her dictionary.

Isa hated every minute.

Every second.

And every day of her life.

"Do not talk to me, I am late for my exam, and I don't need my day to be any worse than it is," Isa said while glancing past the parking structure she left. Her head pounding with resentment fighting each of his words with great effort.

"I've tried contacting you Isa, I didn't mean all this to happen." Dylan stepped in front of her. Swiftly, he grabbed her hand and gave her a small tug, pulling her closer to him.

"For what to happen? For you to cheat on me with my cousin and throw away four years of our relationship down the drain? By the way, congratulations on the engagement. You'll both make a lovely couple."

"But Isa,"

"GET OFF OF ME!" she shouts, breaking away from him. "Don't you ever touch me again!"

On his finger glistened the engagement ring Lyra had given him after they found out she had been pregnant. The ring Isa tossed out when she saw him cheating.

Her ring. The one she bought for them.

She was such a fool.

"You guys are so alike. If it makes you feel any better, I always thought of you when I was with her." He reasoned, grasping for Isa's arm.

His touch was a symphony of old memories that quickly etched her skin. It was the touch of a predator, forceful and vexing.

Isa screams loudly, thrashing herself away from him. Marks started to develop on her wrists. Marks he had once left before.

He releases her and tells Isa to calm down.

"No! Leave me alone!"

"If you would just listen to me!"

"That's all I've been doing! Listening to YOU!" Isa snaps. "I'm done! If you want someone to listen, go to Lyra."

Lyra.

The perfect person in her family.

The person who had it out for her.

She had it all.

She had friends, athletic skills, the support of her family, and most important of all, she was normal. Something Isa always struggled with and was often reprimanded for.

Unlike Isa, Lyra didn't have freak accidents or visions that kept her up at night. At least when Lyra received attention, everyone was willing to give it to her. Meanwhile, if Isa were to mention one of her visions or mess up in any shape or form, she would be reprimanded by her entire family.

"Attention seeker," is what they would call Isa.

Lyra was the perfect child Isa never could be even if she tried. And she did. Multiple times.

It

Was

Never

Enough.

When Isa was admitted to UCLA, no one was there for her. They were there for Lyra.

"Lyra should've been admitted," Her uncle would comment under his breath peering at Isa in the hallway, holding her cousin's rejection letter.

Her mother smacked him on the head, and they continued to reassure Lyra. She cried and cried, but Isa knew none of those crocodile tears were real.

Having enough, Isa stormed away from them and began to change into formal clothes.

At the time, when Dylan had been himself (before his ego caught up to him), he took Isa out to dinner to celebrate. He paid for all the food and invited Isa over to his apartment. Upon arrival, he gave Isa her favorite flowers and a new leather journal.

Those were the good times.

Now she wished they'd never happened.

Despite the various times Isabel denied taking him back, he would not give up. He went as far as memorizing her schedule and like today, ran to her side when he spotted her on campus.

The restraining order against him wasn't enough.

"I know how much you need me. You can't possibly think you can do things alone, can you? I'm the only person who has been there for you Isa. You can't shut me out." He retorted, almost as if he expected his tactic to be enough for her to slide back into his arms.

Thankfully, it didn't.

While he was with her cousin, Isabel took it upon herself to find her self-worth so he could never threaten her with his company.

She found herself a new love, kickboxing. During her classes, she punched away with all her anger and previous insecurities that once prevented her from leaving him in the first place. She made new connections in the class and found a love for her independence.

"Enough!" Isa shouts, her heart quickened.

Hands clenching and lifting ever so subtly, Isabel stopped in her tracks and spun quickly, punching Dylan in the face.

The Isa she was before, would never dream of laying a hand on someone, but the version of Isa standing in front of him, saw how much he deserved it, especially of how he had previously degraded her.

Taking deep breaths, Isa recentered herself, drawing back any wasted efforts.

"Let me get one thing straight, I don't need you or anyone for that matter. I have been fine on my own, and I will keep it that way. You should be ashamed of yourself if you think I will be crawling on my knees for us to be together after everything you've done." She said calmly, almost too calmly.

He blinked and snapped back to earth at the sound of her voice. The passion and fire they once had, were gone to ashes, and he knew it.

She stopped fighting for *them*.

Calling Dylan's name underneath some trees stood Lyra waiting hand and foot. Shooting daggers, he didn't move an inch.

Isa bid her little to no mind. Instead, she turned on her heels and made her way to class. She knew if she reacted now, it would give her cousin some satisfaction.

Isa would much rather perish than do that.

Lyra wasn't going to get under her skin this time.

3

The Kidnap

Much to Isa's disappointment, her endeavor to take the test did not go as planned. She arrived far too late as she entered the classroom with no one but the professor there.

She made a pitiful attempt to make a bit of small talk in hopes of smoothly convincing him to let her take his test.

It horribly failed.

"But Professor,"

"I'm sorry Ms. Poblete. I don't make exceptions. It would be unfair if I bent the rules and allowed you to retake the exam." Professor Simons states, compiling the tests that were lying on his desk.

"Professor, if you could just-"

"I don't want any excuses." He cuts her off, turning his back to her, collecting the tests in a hurry.

Mouth slightly ajar, Isa attempted to make some sort of response. No sound came out of her mouth as she tried to articulate other phrases to persuade him. Right then and there as he turned back to her, she realized how futile it was. He was stern as he was strict.

"Now, if you can excuse me, I have a meeting to attend." He says, walking out the door with a stack of exams, one of them not being Isa's.

Frustrated, Isa leaves the classroom and storms towards the end of the building where no one would bother her. It was secluded and offered shade underneath the rising sun. Sitting there with her heels touching the floor, she took a deep breath and slouched.

Isa couldn't help but feel trapped in the back of the building. She was overcome with the reality in which all the control she had once fought for these past few years faded in a matter of seconds. Almost as if every single attempt she made to repair herself went down in ruins. She was stressed beyond compare. She wanted to scream to the clouds that dared to be free as she wanted to be of her fate.

Not to mention, every inch of heartache she had towards her ruined relationship was drowned out by her need to focus on her grades, writing, fashion, kickboxing, and her part-time job at a local cafe shop.

It worked for a while until it didn't. Life had other plans that got in the way of her pursuit of something better.

As the eldest daughter in her family, she took it upon herself to help her abuela and her siblings while her parents worked. She spent whatever was left of her paycheck to pay the tuition bills when she could.

Given all these responsibilities and pressures, it drained Isa. She felt used like a playground doll as each child took a turn to her beating. It didn't help that she was recently diagnosed as a prediabetic, which added more to her worries.

So much has happened to her, but none of them broke her as much as something like getting a C.

In a feeble attempt to make herself feel better, Isa hauls out a book she kept stowed in her backpack. Skimming the pages to find her favorite line, a single teardrop falls onto one of them.

"Let yourself dream, even if it is not real, it's still yours." Isa read aloud to herself. The wind carried her voice and fizzled it out to the expanse of the beyond.

She kept those words with her for the longest time, as it reminded her to stick with her dreams. She could almost, just almost, imagine a life of ruling a kingdom of her own and fighting off bad guys such as the characters in her book.

Aside from reading, Isa designed and made outfits in her family's garage. She would proudly craft them, picturing herself wearing each outfit in her desired fantasy land. She wanted to share her designs with the world to make it a little more magical than it is. Sure, she was made fun of from time to time, but other people like her, who wanted to escape reality and run in ballgowns in the woods, loved her designs. So much so that she had one chance in New York to intern with designers like her.

And she blew it!

She threw it all away to stay with her ex-fiancé, now her cousin's fiancé.

It chewed her to pieces thinking about each day she could've been spending in New York instead of L.A.

Although LA had its scene for fashion designers, it was hard to keep up as everyone was trying to stand out and stick with the trends. You would think she would thrive, but it was quite the opposite. This only made Isa feel worse.

"If only I could teleport myself into the pages." She thought to herself while reading the last page where the two protagonists achieved their happily ever after. Her mind replaces herself as the protagonist.

(Funny enough, that was who she was just about to become. You'll enjoy this, dear Dreamer.)

Closing the book, what posed to be a galactic black hole with colorful sparks surrounding it, started opening right next to Isa. It was almost as if her wish had been miraculously granted on-site.

One by one four figures stepped out of the portal dressed like cosplayers from a renaissance fair. Three out of the four were male, one of them had pointed ears, and all of them appeared to be right around Isa's age. They seem to be arguing, barely noticing Isa sitting on the floor right next to the portal they had stepped out of.

"God not this realm! I hate dealing with Hues and the way they make fun of us." The one with grey eyes, tanned skin, and pointed elf ears grumbled.

"That's because three out of four of us blend in, Will."

The second guy with curly hair and a muscular figure, pulled on Will's elf ears, proving his point. He was tall as a tree and had freckles near his nose area. They were subtle but present against his olive complexion. On a single ear, he wore a golden spiral piercing around his helix. His voice rolled off his tongue with such smooth suave.

The last male who was laughing at the other two, wore glasses that perfectly framed his sharp facial features and stood out with his bright blue short hair.

"Come on Jack, give poor Will a break."

While they bickered, Isa grabbed her backpack and started getting up, moving away from them. As she turned, something struck her shoulder blades, completely paralyzing her.

"You guys are idiots," The fourth member swore with a deep feminine voice. The sorceress shook her head unamused.

"Also, I may be blind but I'm not deaf sweetheart, if you were trying to run away you should've been quieter and made fewer movements." She scoffed at Isa, tightening her grip.

Isa yelps and remains still under the binding. Its hold on her was that of steel as her elbows crashed into the sides of her waist.

In front of the human girl, is the sorceress. To put it simply, the sorceress had deep jet-black hair falling down her waist in a long thick braid covered by a series of flowers and stems. With the slightest tilt of her head, she was looking directly at Isa, intentionally showing her own pair of brown eyes. Its interior was slightly clouded and remained locked in place, giving little to no movement.

In the sorceress's hands was a sleek black leather whip quickly shifting into an elongated staff. The previous whip in the sorceress's hands is what was used to paralyze Isa. All the sorceress needed to do was push the button on her whip to release its potent venom.

With her shifted staff, she used the tip of it to feel around where Isa's body had fallen. The tip of the staff is a sharp gem. When she reached her body, the sorceress smiled with pleasure and patted Isa's head shushing her.

"Hello, we got company over here!" the sorceress yelled loudly enough for all three of the men to turn.

"Who?"

"Your aunt." replied the sorceress, sarcastically snapping at the curly-haired man. She lifted her staff as if she were to whack him in the head.

"The joke is your mom. Not your aunt, Vero. Get with the modern Human Realm." He corrects her unfazed.

"Whatever! For fae sake! Get the girl!" Vero curses, stomping the butt of her staff. Her braid sways and a few colorful petals fall to the ground underneath her polished leather loafers.

"Jeez, not my fault you're so outdated. I bet you don't know how a phone works." He smirks, and the sorceress scowls at him.

Stopping their conversation, the three flashed their eyes at Isa, examining her with curiosity. It wasn't every day they encountered a human, much less kidnap one.

She lacked any special qualities they normally expect from their realm. Her teeth were no wear near fanged and her ears were perfectly round. There were no horns or spikes sprouting at the top of her head. She lacked claws and colorful features aside from her reddish hair. She was very much human, but was she too human?

Together, all four sorcerers carry Isa's paralyzed body and place her in what resembles a large potato sack.

"I bet she's the Seer we're looking for," she said sternly.

"You think?" Will questions, observing the sac with curiosity. He lifts a finger as if he were to touch it.

"Oh yeah, the portal definitely led us to her." The curly-haired one smirks and lightly pats the sack.

"She's far too *different*."

'Different? She looks like a normal Hue."

"She may have lost her traits along the lines of this realm. I too can feel myself fade. My abilities don't seem to be working too well. We must leave before we become like them."

Isa's heart began to race. She assumed the worst had been to come. Her body couldn't move, and she had no idea what they were going to do to her.

Elder Arthur

All three of the sorcerers kept their guard up as they made sure no humans would spot them. They were surprised they managed to catch their hopefully new teammate so soon. Usually on missions, they would have to yield to a battlefield as they carry on their tasks. Granted, this was the Human Realm. The one realm where most magic ceases to exist in comparison to the others.

"Okay Jack, drag her carefully." The soft-spoken blue-haired male with glasses said. He hovered his hands over the sac as he cautiously kept Isa's body upright.

The man with curly hair and freckles, whose name is apparently Jack, wrapped his arms around the sack Isa was in. He lifted her to his shoulders bridal style and walked into the newly opened portal.

"Wait! What if she is just a normal Hue, she'll die if she goes to our realm. Human bodies can't handle it." The female with the deep feminine voice warns as she slams the butt of her staff, shifting it back into a whip. With a quick extension of her wrist, the whip catches Jack's ankle, preventing him from taking another step closer to the portal.

"Great! If she lives that means she's a Seer or a sorcerer like us, and if she dies, she was a Hue all along!" Will rolls his eyes, seeming a little too on edge than usual. In his hands is a small item he keeps hidden.

"Yikes Will, have some morality. Vero is right, we need to think about this carefully." The one with the glasses and blue hair agrees as he simultaneously scrutinizes Will's behavior.

"Well, we better think fast. If a Hue catches us, we will be in great trouble. We don't want to repeat what happened last time."

"I said I'm sorry!"

"Say that to the government agent."

"She had it coming! If our presence is reported to HQ, our team would've been suspended."

"Yes, because you injured a human being. We're not supposed to interact with this kind."

"I thought it was a Jinn of some sort."

"It was a costume. They dress up for a festive holiday they call Halloween."

"They don't teach us this in our realm!"

"Yes, they do! In Realmology 103A. You were too busy hexing your pencil to pay attention."

"Enough! Just throw her in."

"No!"

"Yes!"

"No!"

All at once, they argued with one another while Isa slowly but surely regained momentum. Her mouth was sealed shut; lips frozen in place as the rest of her upper body. She twisted and moved her knees, shifting herself in the bag. All she needed to do was to fall and wiggle herself out of the sack without getting noticed.

In her attempt to escape, Jack notices Isa moving in the sac and throws her straight into the fluorescent portal.

"JACK!" All three of the sorcerers reprimanded him.

"Elder Arthur is going to be pissed," one of the sorcerers' comments under their breath.

'What! She tried to escape." He shrugs and hops right into the portal after Isa.

"Best hope she's alive." The half-elf muttered, tucking his dagger into the pocket of his waist belt.

As she was in the portal, Isa felt sick to her stomach. Being in the sac while moving inside the portal was a roller coaster of its own as she was tossed back and forth. It didn't help that her glasses had slid off her face and most likely broken somewhere in the sac. It felt like she was in the ocean as the tides kept trying to drown her out. All she could see from the top of the sac hole was a wave of colors.

When she made it out to the other end, all Isa could feel was the grass below. It cushioned her fall leaving a few bruises on her.

Using the little movement, she had left in her arms and legs, Isa slowly weaved herself out of the sac. Once she was out, she felt as if all her energy had been sucked out of her, which made her sick to her stomach causing her to puke.

"Hello? Are you okay?" Jack said right behind her. He patted her shoulder and held her reddish brown curly hair back as the others materialized out of the portal.

"Do I look okay?" Isa answered bitterly while gasping for air and moving away from her vomit. Beside Isa was a bush full of orange berries and colorful flowers. None she recognized except the pink roses.

"I think she looks just fine." snickered Will as he dusted his leather vest.

"Shut it, elf boy." Isa snaps, breathing heavily. "Oh god not again."

Isa lurches, clutching one hand over her stomach, her body shaking.

"Someone didn't like the portal," The blue-haired one said trying not to look at the pile of puke Isa left on the ground. He then went next to Isa and handed her a pouch holding water as she was lying on the grass.

"Jack you're an idiot!" Vero angrily shakes her staff to the side striking at Jack's shoulder blade.

"Ouch! We all make mistakes! Chill Vero. Drink some rosewater."

"Well could be worse, at least the Hue is not dead," Will uttered, sparing a quick glance at Isa.

"Excuse me? What did you just call me?" Isa hisses and spouts out insults in Spanish. None of which he and the other sorcerers understood.

Will ignores her and proceeds to listen to the rest of his members talking around them.

"Considering she isn't dead, that means she must be a Seer, right? Possibly one of us." The one with blue-hair glances at Isa, returning his eyes back to one of his team members.

"One of us? Are you guys some sort of cult?"

"No," replied Vero.

"I mean we are part of an organization," Jack said, placing a finger on his chin.

"We are not a cult Jack!"

"Cult or not a cult. I'm not interested. My name is Isabel Poblete. My parents are from Mexico, and I am a Mexican-American citizen. Take me home and I promise not to say a word. I'll pay you whatever you want, just let me go." Isa said without a stutter to spare.

"Oh honey, money isn't what we need. The fact you are not dead means you're not who you think you are. Don't worry we'll have a chat with one of our elders and then maybe you might be able to go home, okay?" Will said, lifting her chin with the tip of his finger, his face inches from hers. Bewildered as if he got stung by a bee, he shoves Isa away from him.

"Ouch!" Isa exclaims. "What the f- "

Vero flicks her hand and forces Isa to eat a berry she plucked off a bush.

After their interaction, the half-elf, unmistakably troubled by Isa, relentlessly receded his head to the sky as his eyes caught hers from time to time. It wasn't his usual behavior, for when his teammate Jack observed him, he would slightly lift an eyebrow questioning Will.

"Can you walk?" asked the one with blue hair. He was far kinder than the rest.

"Uh-" Isa says, swallowing the berry.

"Don't worry Haru, I got this! Just place little Miss Fox-haired over here." Jack laughs while flexing his arms bulging against his shirt.

"Considering you almost killed me, I'll pass," Isa replied, narrowing her eyes. As she twists her neck to move a strand of hair away from her eyes, Isa spots a creature lingering at the side of a bush.

The creature munches on a berry and stows the remainder of it into its pouch. The creature was as miniature as a squirrel and possessed the body of a kangaroo. It wasn't anything like the creatures that would frolic in her realm.

Her gaze followed the creature to a river sweeping over the hill they were on. In the river were colorful fish and frogs swimming in its clear waters. Unbeknownst to Isa, it took her a few blinks to recover from the phoenix flying past her head, causing the curls of her hair to drape slightly close to her chin.

Swiftly, Vero pulls a rope from her satchel and hands it to Jack.

"I'll handle this now that we're back in the Celestial Realm. Just tie her up."

"Watch your hands, I will bite." Isa threatens.

"I like this girl." Vero grins pointing at Isa.

"She's as demeaning as you."

"Wouldn't be surprised if she had rabies with that behavior." Will comments and Haru chuckles.

"Wouldn't be surprised if you can hear miles away from here with those ears," Isa retorts, writing small inscriptions with her finger on the dirt.

Jack swoops in with the rope and smudges the words Isa wrote on the ground.

"Hold still." He clamps his hand on her shoulder. Isa did not like his touch on her skin as she could recall the sensation of Dylan fondling her.

Noticing her fallen expression, Jack softens his hold and waits for Isa to stop struggling. When she does, he lightly maneuvers himself, draping the rope on Isa.

Within seconds Isa was no longer on the grass, rather she was lifted three feet from the ground almost as if she was lying on an invisible cloud.

During the walk, everyone stayed quiet as Vero kept her concentration on Isa so she wouldn't fall on the ground and used her staff to prevent her from tripping into anything. Sounds of chirps from various birds and wild rabbits rustling in bushes flooded their ears.

Once they arrived at a large cottage, they all stopped at the door, Isa still tied up and floating close to a tree branch.

"Who is it?" grunted a gruff old voice inside the wooden cottage covered in flourishing plants.

"It's us Elder Arthur. You know the ones you sent to find a Seer?" said Haru, the now-named blue-haired and glasses-wearing guy.

"Who?"

"Elder Arthur, it's Will and the team you old geezer. We went to get the Seer."

"Oh!"

Inside the cottage were sounds of rustling such as what could be potions clinking against each other, pieces of paper being scattered, and the slightest sound of footsteps from the floorboard.

Appearing at the door stood a tall elderly large man wearing a dark emerald green silk cloak, smiling directly at Isa. In the middle is a gap between his teeth.

"Ah yes! Come on in."

Official Seer

As the elderly man widens the front door to his quaint cottage, Vero lowers Isa's body to the ground. At her chin is a small grassy welcome home carpet. A whiff coming out of the cottage was the sweet scent of a bakery.

"A little help here?" Isa yells, struggling to lift herself up and escape her binds.

She slithers across the floor until Elder Arthur helps to escort her inside.

"Untie the poor girl, she is a visitor and no visitor of mine will be in such conditions, besides it's not like she has anywhere to escape to." Elder Arthur mutters the last part and situates a few items in his living room while they sit down and untie Isa.

The living room had just enough space for everyone to have a seat whether it was on the sofa on the left or right side. On the right side were Isa, Vero, and Haru, while on the left side, on a separate couch, were Jack and Will. Elder Arthur sat in the top center of the wooden living room with his makeshift chair. In his hand appeared to be some type of blue herbal tea. Steam escapes his cup as if it were to be freshly made.

As Haru and Vero untied her, Isa distracted herself. She couldn't help but notice all the different and unusual objects surrounding her. The table in front of them had various gems and jewels laid out, which most of Isa tried to identify such as clear quartz or opal. On the left side, next to Jack and Will, was a small display of different weapons, they all seemed to be hung up as if they were trophies along with potion bottles.

Covering the walls were photos of Elder Arthur and his fellow Seers who wore the same emerald cloak as he did, except that each person had a different patch on their cloak. Their patches had a Roman numeral, most had two, while a woman with a braid and Elder Arthur had the Roman numeral three. At the edge of the photo was a man with a blurred face and antlers. He was the only person with a four.

Why is this man blurred? Why can't I see it?

Touching the face of the man, Isa's finger sizzles.

"Agh!"

"Careful. It has a hex."

"A warning would've been nice."

"You wouldn't have needed a warning if you didn't touch something that is not yours."

"Sorry," Isa mutters, her cheeks turning pink.

"Much like those you see there, depending on your level, you'll be able to wear one too." Elder Arthur said to Isa, stroking his beard.

Embarrassed, Isa kept her eyes on the frame, recognizing the woman.

Isa was sure of who she was.

"What's your name, young one?" He gruffed.

"Isabel, but I prefer Isa," she said confidently and with more mobility. Whatever paralyzed her began to wear off.

"I'll call you Isa then," he gives a small smile, putting his hand out.

Isa doesn't move. She noticed the shift in the expressions of the people near her and clenched her fists tightly.

"May I have your hand?" he says, keeping his arm extended in the same position.

Isa pursed her lips and leaned away. There was something about the way he presented himself. He was overtly an open book yet, Isa sensed something different about this man. He wasn't human. At least not in the same way she was. She was afraid that if she touched him, her soul would be stolen right out of her body.

"Why?"

"You'll see." He grins, patiently waiting for Isa to comply.

"I'll see?"

"Yes."

"Will you kill me?"

"No."

"Are you going to hurt me?"

"No."

"Then why do you require my hand?"

"You shall see. My you are a stubborn one!"

"I get that a lot."

"I can see why."

With great hesitation, she clamped her hand over his and moved closer to him. Elder Arthur suddenly closed his eyes and magically so did Isa's.

In that second, Isa awoke in a dark space where it was only her and Elder Arthur. Above them were stars and constellations cascading the sky as if she entered a planetarium. It was beautiful and frightening at the same time as the stars above were the only sign of light in the abyss they walked in. Isa tightened her grip and followed him.

He reminded Isa of a mouse she once experimented on in her biology research internship. The mouse would be put in a vastly large maze and with little to no struggle, it found its way to the end. Similarly, Elder Arthur gaits his way into the darkness until the two reach a white door.

It illuminated enough light for Isa to make out Elder Arthur's silhouette. Isa expected Elder Arthur to open the door but when he grabbed the knob, it refused to turn all the way. He tugs the knob hard, and the door remains unscathed. When he realized it would not open to his command, he turned to Isa.

"Here is where you'll find the visions you'll need. I cannot access them. Only you can." Elder Arthur gruffs, no longer smiling. "You will have to find this on your own. Whatever you see and feel here, you'll feel out there do you understand?" His voice deepened in a serious tone.

Unable to comprehend what was happening, Isa stayed silent. The only sense she could make out of all this was they were possibly in her mind and whatever was behind that door is the visions she will eventually see and need access to.

While Isa did indeed get visions when she was younger, they were nothing major other than seeing what her grade was on an exam or what would happen that day. When she told her parents, she was sent to her local priest and was prayed over. The only one who listened to her was her abuela.

"Abuela," Isa mutters to herself.

Isa recalled the photo of Elder Arthur and the other individuals in their cloaks.

The woman with a long colorful braid she saw had to be abuela when she was younger. This almost made Isa laugh because who would've thought someone in her super-religious Mexican family had been affiliated with brujeria?

As Isa stood there thinking in silence, she lifted her eyes back up to Elder Arthur and said, "Not really, but I'm sure to figure it out. I have one question though. What does that mean?" Isa said, pointing at his patch with the Roman numeral three.

"You have a keen eye, Isa. I'll give you that. It's my rank. Level ones can only see visions that will occur in a short period such as seeing an event that will happen in a few days or a couple of hours. Second-level Seers can see visions for a longer duration and most of the time give important visions. Then they're people like me, level three, we can see the visions level ones and twos see, and as a plus, we can see what is on your mind and how you truly feel." He explains and spectates Isa as if she were his daughter learning the basics of riding a bike.

"And four?" Isa questions, revisiting the frame with the blurred face.

His smile vanished, his jaw clenched, and his eyes were no longer seeking into Isa's.

In a deep sulking voice, he quietly said, "Genocide. There's no more of them, and I hope you do not ever meet their fate. A Seer's rank is not born but created by the individual's mind." He adds the final part speaking a little more clearly.

"I think I understand," Isa finally said, processing the rankings and all the information given to her.

Elder Arthur smiled at Isa, and within another blink, they were back in the room with everyone staring at them.

"Are their eyes still closed?" Vero asked aloud unable to make out their expressions.

Before any could answer, Elder Arthur responds.
"Not anymore, congratulations you found your official Seer!" he exclaimed, grinning ear to ear, lifting his beard.

Kate

Blinking, Isa's sudden assignment of her newfound role brought a rise of emotion in Isa and not the happy kind.

"Hold up! I am not joining ANYTHING until I get answers. I haven't even gotten visions since I was like ten, I'd probably be a level one Seer at most!" Isa exclaims to everyone, ripping her hands away from Elder Arthur. Her mouth gaped wide open into a frown.

She didn't want another responsibility.

Another role.

Another weight placed on her shoulders, a weight heavier than her self-hatred.

In an effort to escape, Isa horribly wobbles to the door. Making little to no noise, Will lifts out of his seat and blocks the doorway with a heavy sword.

"Going somewhere?" He twists his head, slightly taunting Isa.

Isa raises her hand to punch Will but is caught midway by the force of strong air pulling her from the door and then her body onto the couch. Jack lets out a small chuckle from using his ability.

Isa curses under her breath huffing out her frustration.

"Language."

"Don't tell me you guys didn't tell her." Elder Arthur's eyes shift to the others, his voice rising slowly with anger. All of them came off as guilty as they avoided his gaze.

"Did any of you introduce yourself to her or at least have the decency to talk to this young lady before tying her up and bringing her here!" His voice rumbles into a growl.

Silence filled the air among the sorcerers, answering his question.

"To be fair she was running away from us, and it was Jack who suddenly tossed her into the portal!" Vero slouches into the couch crossing her arms and blowing a loose strand of her hair from her face.

"Oh, Hades no! You are not pinning this on me! At least I'M not the one who paralyzed her!" he grumbles, standing up from the couch. Vero retaliates by whipping Jack in the back, without using the paralyzing venom.

He turns to her and slices the air. Water escapes from a container in his pocket and splashes directly onto Vero. The color of the couch darkened as it soaked up the excess around her.

The two rise out of their seats and break out into an argument as they shout at each other for a good five minutes. Haru decided it was enough when Jack took out his ax and Vero positioned her hand with the whip. With a flick of a wrist, Haru moves his hands to control Vero's and Jack's shadows. His blue hair glowed brightly, and his eyes turned black.

In their shadow form, you see them both still as they are at the moment. Their expressions remained non-existent under

Haru's trance. As Haru twirls his fingers, the two rotate their bodies as reflected in their shadows and return to their original positions. At the snap of his fingers, they both went back to normal.

"All right, it was all of our faults." This time Haru talks and gives a big sigh when he tries to reach for Vero's hand, which she declines and pushes away.

On the other side of the room, still not facing Isa, was Will sulking and muttering something under his breath. Although Isa couldn't make out what he said, it seemed like Elder Arthur completely understood because he abruptly placed his teacup down. While speaking he gives a glare directly toward Will, which causes the tip of his elf ears to go red.

"It doesn't matter how you have met Isa or treated her. It's much too late to apologize. What matters is I want you all to treat this girl kindly as you treated Kate. She is your official Seer and one that I approve of after you all forcibly tried to include the previous Seer despite my advice." Elder Arthur huffs out in the end.

At the mention of Kate, Will removes himself from the couch and leaves the room shutting the door forcibly.

"I'll go talk to him," Haru gets up from the couch leaving Isa, Vero, Jack, and Elder Arthur in the room.

Elder Arthur gave him an unspoken nod before waving him off, his forehead creasing and pressing his hand against it.

"I'll make dinner. Jack, if you can show Isa to her room and explain everything to her? That would be delightful. Vero I'll need your help catching our dinner for tonight while I bake the dessert." Elder Arthur finally says before turning around and walking to a wooden door leading to what's supposed to be the kitchen.

"Yes sir," Jack and Vero said simultaneously.

Isa wanted to ask about what he had meant about catching their dinner but decided against it, given the circumstances.

Jack apologetically smiles at Isa and leads her down a hallway.

"Are you by any chance single, foxy?" He says with the corner of his lips lifting. Slightly moving closer to Isa right behind her, his hands hovered around her for if she were to fall, he would catch her.

"Don't push it. If I were human, I would've been dead after you threw me into the portal." Isa replies, walking slightly with each step.

He had offered Isa to hold onto his arm, but Isa was quick to decline.

"Yeah, sorry about that... hope you can forgive me." Jack sighed while placing a hand on the back of his head, his hand accidentally producing flames.

It wasn't much of a walk considering they lived in such a small cottage, and there were only three rooms, one being Elder Arthur's, another being a spacious bathroom, and lastly a small bedroom Jack and Isa walked into.

"It's not much but okay for the meantime. Usually, we all use our portals to get to our dorm but considering you puked last time, I suggest you spend the night here. Plus, we also need to register you into the Celestial facility for you to get your room at the dorms." Jack adds the final part as Isa situates herself on the bed.

Judging by Isa's eyebrow raise and unamused frown, it was more than crystal clear to Jack she had no idea what he was talking about. From the sound of it, the Celestial Facility sounded either like a university, or a magical form of the FBI. As intriguing as it is, Isa was much too ill-tempered to care. Her head was fuming with vexation. Perhaps if she was politely asked to come with them rather than attacked, she would be more compliant.

"Right, you're not from here. God, where do I start….my name is -uh Jack and I'm an elemental sorcerer…." He pauses, moving his mouth to one side. He thinks to himself while his hand rests on top of his head.

Although Isa didn't have her glasses, from up close she was able to see how nice and fluffy his short brown curly hair was. It wasn't necessarily overtly curly since the top of his head was wavy and the ends fringed out in curls. The freckles on the bridge of his nose against his olive complexion made him appear charming despite his strong physique.

"How about explaining why I'm here," Isa interjected, getting straight to the point. If she were to stay here, she needed to know what she was going to be dealing with. It's "chosen one" protocol she had seen all too well in the books she's read. She didn't have time for all the introductions, she needed answers.

"Right, um, so… there is this mad evil sorcerer. This sorcerer is killing off and taking away Seers because she wants to find these relics that allow you to travel into different dimensions and grant you wishes. Certain Seers can find these relics because they see them in their visions. Usually, if their visions permit, mostly level three Seers can locate and predict where these relics are." Jack explains, waving his hands around.

"And what does that have to do with me?"

"Well, the thing is, Seers are being killed left and right because of this evil sorcerer lady, Seer Slayer for short. Since so many are being attacked and killed, many are in hiding and don't really wanna help us, sorcerers, in our mission to stop her. The thing is, we sorcerers can't stop this lady without a Seer because, well, only Seers can predict her whereabouts and where the next relic is. Here's where you come in,"

"Finally," Isa moves her hands to her hips, defensive as ever. When deep down she did all these mannerisms to hide the underlying fear that crept down her spine.

Isa, this time listens more closely, waiting to see what is in store for her, and if she is willing to contribute.

"So, when I, Will, Haru, and Vero were put on this mission since we are deemed as powerful sorcerers in the Celestial Facility we train at, the only Seer we technically could rely on was Elder Arthur. He didn't have any new visions, and at the time, we also had an additional member, Kate. She wasn't necessarily a member per se, but we treated her like one because she was Will's girlfriend and Vero's BFF. She was always there at our training and joined us in our quests. Plus, she was a Seer, so it made sense for her to join us, right?"

Isa bobs her head taking mental notes of her new potential opponent, Kate. From the tone shift in Jack's voice, this girl must've been no good.

"The thing with Kate is that Elder Arthur always thought she was suspicious because she would always ask him about his visions and would get mad when he would say he hasn't had any. Sadly, Elder Arthur was right because when he finally had a vision of the next relic, Kate went off to find it and gave it to the Seer Slayer. There are only two more relics and if the Seer Slayer finds them, we're going to be in big trouble. No Seer has been able to find these relics, and too many are already dead or captured...." He pauses for a bit, slightly biting the inside of his cheek.

Isa's eyes widened. If Elder Arthur had been right that she indeed is a Seer, she is completely screwed. What is she gonna do? Somehow use her mediocre kickboxing skills against toned and magical bad guys? Yeah right.

"It wasn't until earlier today out of all Seers, it was Elder Arthur, who finally had a vision, and it was of you. Essentially what he saw was you leading us to our next relic." Jack finally comes to a quiet stop. Judging by how Jack said Kate's name very quietly, it seemed like the betrayal still stung the group as they all had been close to her.

"In other words, you're telling me, I am here because Elder Arthur saw me in his vision to help you guys stop the Seer Slayer?" Isa speaks slowly as she is trying to take everything in like a last-minute study sesh before her final exam. She decided it would be wise not to ask about Kate in the meantime and to just focus on what she was supposed to do so she could go back home.

"Yeah…"

She had to be dreaming, right? She knew all the tropes and disasters the main characters go through. She would much rather possess a less important role, so she wasn't so tense. She definitely couldn't be the comedic side character, because Jack perfectly fits that description. Haru seems like the mysterious kind with his blue hair and sudden lightheartedness. The other girl, Vero, owned the badass role, which Isa was positive she could not reach the potential of. Then there's the half-elf.

He was an odd one, Isa knew that. He clearly had a disdain for her, and the feeling was essentially mutual on her behalf. Sure, he was appealing to her eyes, but his pretty privilege can only take him so far.

"Okay, okay. I have a question. What is the difference between realms and dimensions?" Like if this Seer Slayer manages to find these relics because I can't see any visions, what is she going to do?"

For a moment Jack pauses before his eyes light up and resumes his explanation.

"In other words, realms are like different worlds. You're from the human realm, well I don't know now because you are alive in this realm so you're definitely not a Hue, aka a human. You might qualify as a Dreamer, in this case." His eyes move up and down analyzing Isa's features that could possibly distinguish her away from regular humans.

"Dreamer?" Isa mutters to herself, twisting her face. She did like to sleep if that's what he is referring to.

"Anyways, other examples of realms are: the Aquatic Realm where it's all water and merpeople, the Vampiric Realm where vampires roam, the Celestial Realm where you are right now where the population is mainly sorcerers, and many more. Meanwhile, dimensions are worlds where there are other versions of us."

"Okay, so realms are like different worlds, and dimensions are an alternative universe where there are various versions of me. Maybe, in another dimension, I'll have blonde hair or be evil." Isa reiterates in the simplest way possible.

"Correct!" He smiles and rests his hand on the wall leaning against it. "While it's unclear what her motive is, seeking these relics is a major red flag. She can corrupt these realms and cause an all-out war between realms and dimensions if she wants to, especially with that type of power. It's pretty messy the more you think about it." He lets out a small laugh as if he were making a punchline.

"If I end up not getting any visions and no other group of sorcerers with their Seer stops the Seer Slayer, does that mean we're all doomed?"

"Pretty much," Jack replies. We're kinda counting on you foxy," he says, gesturing at my reddish curly hair.

We are so doomed.

7

Processing it All

Before Jack left, he handed Isa the potato sack she had once been in and patted her shoulder. Inside the sac was her phone, backpack with her books and school supplies, and at the bottom sat shards of her broken glasses with the frame completely bent. Everything inside the backpack seemed fine, with the exception that her laptop wouldn't turn on and her phone had a cracked screen.

Isa's phone was filled with phone calls and voicemails from her mother yelling at her to pick up the phone in Spanish. Prior to leaving the room, Jack had told her that phones and the internet don't exactly work in this realm so when Isa tried to call her family, both her text messages and phone calls were dropped, and the only thing she could think of was taking a photo of the room.

"Yeah, as if someone sane would believe this." Her sarcasm spouted out, providing Isa with some sort of sense of reality.

If and when Isa returned to her realm, she would have a lot of explaining to do. She was praying that her family wouldn't try to kill her upon arrival.

Thinking back on the portal, it was then everything suddenly started to dawn on Isa. Her fingernails dug into the palm of her hands which would surely leave a mark when she pulled them to their original positions. The pain reminded Isa that she was in fact not dreaming. She pinched herself just to be sure.

Sudden rage hit her like a baseball bat as all she wanted to do was punch the walls and tear apart the small but nice cottage. The sight of miles of forest outside of her window only fed into her frustrations as she realized she couldn't escape even if she wanted to. She didn't know how to survive in the wild, much less navigate a possibly deadly forest with magical creatures. It had upset her, even more, when her stomach began to growl. She felt so weak that she needed to stay lying down on the wooden bed filled with knitted soft sheets.

Searching the room, inside the drawers were feminine clothes as if they had expected her arrival. They were similar to the ren fair attire they had worn earlier which Isa wasn't fully used to such as corsets and various belted leather attire. Present on most of her blouses and tops was a mysterious eye symbol sewn into them.

It felt very cult-like.

The second drawer had leather pants and short overlays fit for making a frock as the fabrics were loose and comfortable. With the right materials, Isa would be able to make an entire gown out of various fabrics of clothing. Picking at the clothes, she set aside her favorite combinations and moved to the closet.

In the closet were large men's clothes, possibly for one of her teammates when they stayed over. Set aside was a small corner filled with armor.

On the bookshelf next to the small desk are a pile of miniature purple succulents, Venus flytraps, and a few other plants to contribute to the cottage aesthetic. Some pots were hung on the ceiling with the plant's roots and vines sticking out.

Hungry and feeling drained, Isa then pulled out some emergency snacks she carried in her backpack for whenever she felt her sugar drop. Isa was thankful that at least she didn't need insulin just yet to survive, but she was getting to that point.

Sitting in the room by herself and eating a protein bar, Isa couldn't help but wonder when she was ever going to be sent back home. Like some of the stages of grief, missing a few steps, she went from angry to somber quickly. She didn't necessarily hate being in the Celestial Realm, yet she also didn't feel like fighting off some crazy magical serial killer.

Though, if she was honest, she felt excited yet terrified. It made her feel like she was special for once instead of some girl who spent all her life drawing and designing clothing in her parents' garage until she was forced to go outside.

Coming into this realm meant a fresh new start, no more Dylan, no one telling her what to do, no more responsibilities, and most important of all, she was finally able to live her life the way she always wanted to, even though deep down she felt her guilt telling her to go home.

Isa had been so buried in her thoughts and possibilities, that it didn't take long for her to fall asleep, especially since she had been exhausted and living off coffee the last few days. When she did fall asleep, she was once again back in that dark space Elder Arthur had taken her to.

For a while, Isa walked around in the dark still gazing at the stars above her. It was surprisingly calm yet at the same time scary. It reminded Isa of the times when in grade school, she had been thrown and locked in a dark bathroom that was at the rear end of her school away from the playground and the teachers. She would try to open the door but somehow her bullies had managed to lock it every time.

This frequently happened to Isa where she would somewhat have an unhealthy routine, she would start with having a panic attack until she finally calmed herself by holding a book like a teddy bear. During that time, she would be let out by Dylan who notified the janitor to open the door.

~~That's when Dylan was still Dylan~~... *"but it didn't matter now because he was old news."* Isa reminded herself.

Anyways, pivoting her focus to her new reality, Isa had finally spotted the door she had been seeking. Like last time, it was a glowing white light within the dark. The door was freshly painted white and appeared to be completely untouched.

Putting her hand on the knob, Isa felt it glide to her touch, turning ever so smoothly. Just as Isa was about to open the door and peek inside, all around her Isa heard sounds of knocking which woke her up.

Frustrated and groggy Isa begrudgingly stomps her way out of bed and opens the door.

Standing there was Vero with her walking stick touching the foot of the door. "Wake up, food is about to be ready soon." She smirks.

"Thanks for the heads up," Isa replies groggily, fixing her bedhead. She sits there expecting Vero to leave but she doesn't.

"Is there something you need from the room?"

"No, I just…"

"Yes?"

"Ugh, how does Jack do this," Vero complains inside her head unable to figure out a way to apologize to Isa. Usually, when she attacks someone, the last thing she'd consider is apologizing, but this scenario is very different.

"Can I come in and have a quick chat with you?" Vero blurts, coming out of her mouth more like a demand than a question.

"Sure?" Isa said awkwardly gesturing for Vero to enter the room and take a seat.

Observing Vero up close, Isa couldn't help but admire her complexion as it was as if the night glossed over her dark skin, completely clear of imperfections. Her eyes, despite being dark brown, were eye-catching as they made you want to look inside to see what was going on in her mind.

She had all the right curves in all the best places Isa wished she could have in comparison to her slender body shape (having been compared to her cousin all the time who also had the right curves).

Vero's hair was additionally smooth enough to comb through as if were water despite being in a long tight braid reaching barely past her hips.

Her outfit hugged her body as she wore flexible dark tights with a belt holding all her items in a series of pouches and a holder for her staff/whip. Her shirt had an elastic to be off the shoulders and in between was a red velvet corset that had fine detailing of black jewels embezzled in it. Tucked in the leather harness in her thighs are small vials Vero kept on her for if she accidentally poisoned herself with her whip.

Both girls sat on the opposite side of the bed in complete silence until Vero spoke again. "I'm sorry for paralyzing you. I get excited like that sometimes." She attempts to reach for the vial but stops at Isa's reply.

"It's okay I'm back to my normal self," Isa claims, not knowing what more to say to her. The two pause in silence and Vero begins again.

"You know, it's okay to ask me questions, right? I'm an open book. Think of me as your new big sister." Vero smiled yet there was a hint of sadness lingering as she said, sister. It didn't take much to assume she was most likely reminiscing and referring to Kate.

"I can ask you anything?"

"As long as it's not stupid." Vero clarifies, recalling the time Jack asked her if she could tell the time of day, it was when they had first met.

"Okay, um what are you? Like, are you guys' magicians? Wizards?-"

"Sorcerers," Vero cuts in. "All of that other stuff is fake and created by you Hues and your weird imaginations about us. I'm a telekinetic sorcerer, like most I can move objects here and there but it's a little tricky. Although I'm partially blind, I can see the world through the energy around me and of course, my convertible whip that paralyzed you. For example, on a windy day, you can feel the wind against your skin, right?" She paused, waiting for Isa to nod before continuing.

In comparison to everyone's energy, Vero found Isa's to be interesting. She could detect the Seer energy from her as it stood out strong and clear. It brought out a new curiosity for Vero, which rarely happens.

"It's like that but in terms of energy. When you moved, I felt a shift of energy in your direction, that's when I uh- attacked you…" Feeling embarrassed, Vero places her hand on her head kind of slapping it.

Isa laughs which lightens up the room and allows Vero to lower and relax her shoulders.

"So, you guys don't use wands?"

"Heaven's no." Vero scoffs.

"If a person wants to, you can use a staff. It helps to yield a person's ability, same with any weapon depending on the person's ability and how they harness it." Vero touches her staff handing it over to Isa to examine.

"Plus, these are much cooler," Vero adds.

Isa flicks the staff to the side to transform it into the whip that hits her. She was careful not to press the button on the handle as she didn't want to accidentally paralyze herself. She flicks it once more and returns the magical weapon to Vero

"What about the other guys?" Isa returns the staff.

"Those idiots," Vero mutters before explaining to Isa. According to Vero, the semi-curly-haired with freckles named Jack has elemental abilities. He can move water, throw a boulder at you, float in the winds of air, and produce fire in the palm of his hands. The catch with his ability is there needs to be elements of these near him to use them unless it's fire, which is what he produces.

"Then there's my soulmate, Haru." She smiles softly.

"Wait soulmate in a literal sense or metaphorically?" Isa interrupts, sounding extremely interested. Her voice rose to a high pitch. Isa had always fantasized about having a soulmate, of course, that idea ceased as she grew older and dated Dylan.

She was so sure he was the one, but he had other plans. Isa wasn't sure if she was ready to completely move on, but she also didn't want to miss out on finding her actual magical soulmate.

"In a literal sense," she says pointing at a small tattoo of a black rose with a pair of hands cupping it almost as if it is protecting it. "I'll explain after."

Vero then proceeded to talk about the blue-haired one with glasses called Haru. Aside from being her soulmate, he was the sorcerer of shadows. In the living room, he used his ability to control her and Jack to stop arguing by using their shadows. Vero emphasized Haru was a caring person but when he uses his ability, then it becomes another story.

"What was it like? Like being controlled only by your shadow." Isa questioned.

"It's like everything goes numb and dark. At least with my vision, I can kinda make out figures, and everything is just blurry. When my shadow is used, it's all just pitch black, and you feel nothing. No sadness. Happiness. Nothing." she says calmly.

Last but not least was Will, the one with elf ears. He is a sorcerer of creation. A type of sorcerer with the purpose of grabbing anything and making it into a weapon, chair, or whatever the person wanted. Though, the item in his hand had to be equivalent to the one he wanted to make.

He was the one who made Vero's convertible staff that shifts into a whip.

Vero then giggled when she mentioned his elf background. She often teased him about being able to talk to animals since it's another ability their kind has. She found it funny as it reminded her of a sort of animated princess she saw in a movie.

Though, after the whole Kate incident, it left Will quite upset, and as Vero would call it, he was essentially emotionally unavailable.

Isa took on the possibility that Will is taking out his frustrations on her as the team's new Seer. Either that, or he is an extremely irritable elf.

"Was she, his soulmate?"

"You would think by the way they were always together." Vero sighed, her chest rising and lowering in deep underlying scorn.

"Sadly, Will was not able to participate in the soulmate ceremony because he is part elf. Half-breeds who tried the ceremony died in the process, so we don't allow it anymore despite it strengthening our sorcery. Kate, on the other hand, had a soulmate but didn't tell Will until the day she went off stealing the relic and trading it to save her recent partner." Vero explains, replaying the night it all happened in her head.

She could still recall the last conversation with Kate. She knew there was something off with Kate as she held onto Vero a little tighter than usual when she hugged her. Yet, Vero would've never guessed Kate would go this far.

"Don't feel too bad for him, Jack also has his bad luck since he hasn't passed his sorcerer's written exam to do the ceremony and has his fair share of failed relationships. He never learns."

Isa nods her head recalling her own failed relationship. Perhaps it was a blessing in disguise for it taught her a lesson about love, no one is safe from heartbreak.

Once again, the room went silent with only the sounds of the kitchen pots and pans clashing. Neither one turned to the other nor felt the need to. They both had heavy burdens and were exhausted by the events of today. In the silence, their stomachs created sounds of rumbles and the mating call of whales as their noses captured the sweet smells of the food.

"Dinner's ready," Jack shouted from the living room. Quickly both girls got out of bed and made their way to the backyard where everyone was waiting.

The table was completely filled with food, few familiar to Isa. Everyone sat in their personal chair leaving Isa to have no other choice but to sit at the bottom corner of the table next to the irritated half-elf, Will. In front of Isa, was Jack who handed her a plate while giving a not-so-subtle wink.

"I hope you like unicorn," Vero said sitting next to Haru and Elder Arthur looking a little too excited with a knife in her hand.

Unicorn Dinner

Unicorn tasted like sweet and spicy fried chicken with the consistency of beef. The way Elder Arthur had seasoned it, the taste and smell were immaculate as everyone had gotten seconds, Isa included. The piece of the meat fell off ever so simply making it easier to eat it off the bone.

Vero used the unicorn's horn as a skewer to form her own shish kabob. The rest of the members each got a leg of their own to munch on.

(Now before y'all complain, Isa had no other choice but to eat unicorn, the poor girl was hungry, and you got to do what you got to do to survive. Plus weren't you also curious about how it tasted, dear Dreamer? Exactly.)

On an additional note, unicorns have been known to be invasive species throughout the realms, hence why every realm has some sort of knowledge on unicorns, and in the Human Realm, narwals exist. The non-invasive species these sorcerers do not eat are pegasi and the average noble steed.

As the sun had gone down, Jack lit the lanterns with his pinkie, and the fireflies began to show their light. Above them were the skies cascaded with stars and lights with bright colorations of purple, blue, and yellow like the northern lights in her realm. The Human Realm, or the Hue Realm the sorcerers like to call it.

At the table, the team groaned and reclined into their chairs. Their glasses filled with their drinks, began to produce a gentle radiance. It was as if someone had poured the inside of a glowstick into their drinks.

It all felt so surreal to Isa.

As Isa soaked in her surroundings, there over their heads she saw animal spirits glide through the clouds and dance freely in ways she wished she could. The cooling wind blows them in a general direction and Isa watches them flee to their next adventure. With them followed small pixies bidding no mind to those on the ground. They were small and delicate as a dandelion.

Enchanted, not much can ruin it other than the Seer Slayer and the constant glares shot by Will.

"If you can't keep your eyes to yourself, I'd gladly take them from you."

All the sorcerers and Elder Arthur stopped their conversation and shifted their attention to Will and Isa.

"My eyes are fine. Last time I checked, your eyes were defective ones. You were wearing glasses, weren't you? Or are you lying about that? Who knows if we can trust you? Your kind loves to lie, Hue." He continues to slouch in his seat with his hands folded.

Isa stands from her chair and leans over to Will grabbing a table knife.

A dark force spiked within her. She did not like being called a liar. Not when she was the truthful one and was the victim of a lie. A lie that broke her heart. Her trust. Her relationship.

She points the tip towards him holding it stiffly. Her eyes darkened like never before. The sensation inside of her stomach twisted outward and expanded to her lungs.

It was new.

"Wait a minute. I did not lie about anything! None of you guys let me speak before kidnapping me against my will, and I didn't even know what a Seer was before meeting Elder Arthur!" Isa responded feeling a little more annoyed at Will. Will stands from his seat and turns over to Isa, grabbing her wrist and twisting it so she drops the knife.

"I suggest you learn how to use a knife before I use it against you."

"Is that a threat?"

"Well, it isn't an invitation that's for damn sure."

"Language," Jack says, taking another bite from his filled plate.

"Is damn a bad word?" Vero asks Elder Arthur over the table while playing with a firefly in her hand.

"Yes."

"Fine. Be like that, sour my mood with your so-called wannabe tough guy act. I know you're only acting like this because of Kate. Don't need to drag all of us down with you." All the sympathy she had for him went down the drain like fine wine wasted.

He glowers leaning towards Isa, trying to intimidate her. His stance reminded her of the kind her ex would make when he felt a little too overtly conceited. Confident in his intentions to overpower Isa.

Trying to scare her.

To intimidate her.

Taking the challenge, Isa leans closer to him whispering in his ear in a low voice. "Caught your attention, did I? Know your place *Will*, and I'll know mine. Don't call me a Hue either, I have a name and it's Isa." She grabs Will by the collar of his shirt forcing him to come closer to her face. The corner of his mouth twisted upward, intrigued by her temper and mention of his name on her lips.

He was enjoying this a little too much. Isa saw no hope in convincing a man who was not willing to listen to her, much less feed into his coyness of hidden secrets behind those grey-clouded eyes.

"I suggest you learn it since we'll be spending so much wonderful time together since who knows when I'll be back to my normal life." Isa was no longer speaking to Will but rather was presently glancing over to Elder Arthur who seemed to be irritated by the way his eyebrow was raised and his forehead crinkled.

"Vero you got a run for your money," Haru whispers to her, she too begins to find the interaction to be amusing.

"Is it me or is it getting hot in here?" Jack comments.

"Very well *Isa*, next time you threaten me, I suggest using a different weapon and picking a number. Also, if this is your way to flirt with me, you're not doing a good job at it." Will emphasizes her name mimicking her pronunciation as if he was teasing Isa, her hand still gripping his shirt.

"Ugh, you sick bastard! As if I'd flirt with you out of all people. I rather sacrifice myself to Hades."

"Language." Vero asserts as the firefly flies from her hand and into the neighboring trees of the forest.

"Does that mean I still have a chance?" Jack asks jokingly.

"No! And why should I watch my language? We're all adults here! "

"Yes, but we're all not sailors or pirates," Haru adds. "We have manners."

"Wouldn't be surprised if she was one," Will boasts as he is having fun toying with Isa. Perhaps he was a sort of sadist judging by the scars reaching his forearms.

Glaring at him, Isa releases her grip from Will's shirt and stabs a fork next to his plate. She returns to her seat exchanging her attention with Elder Arthur.

She needed to calm herself down and not let him get to her. Otherwise, she would be the one to look like an idiot. More than she was already. Her past relationship was a perfect example.

"Well? When am I going home?"

"You'll go home when the Seer Slayer is stopped. Heaven knows when that is if your visions are far too weak to find the relics due to your human counterpart."

"But that's going to take forever!" Isa exclaims, her head thinking about all of what she will miss in her realm.

Sure, it may have sucked, but the fantasy life she wished for didn't have possible death on its roster. All she wanted was a happily ever after.

"Well then, I insist you start getting comfortable." Elder Arthur gruffs, stroking his beard intensely.

"Speaking of getting comfortable, I suggest you sleep early because tomorrow at dawn we will be going to the Celestial facility to get you your room and training schedule."

"And what if I don't? I'm clearly not helpful."

"It's not an option."

"There's always an option," Isa replies taking out her irritability and short temper on the palms of her hands with her nails. A small stream falls near her thumb which she usually picks at.

"Not everyone with your abilities does!" He bellowed, slamming the stable with his fist. Everyone looked at him with wide eyes as no one, including Will, had ever seen him this upset. "Options do not come to Seers!"

"I am not a Seer!"

"Yes, you are! The sooner you can accept that fact the better it would be for all of us. Think of how your grandmother would feel if you were to reject who you are."

"I am nothing like her!" Isa raises her voice into a shriek.

"You're right. You're like your grandfather." He retorts, clearing his throat to a rumble.

Isa didn't know whether it was a good thing or a bad one. She didn't know anything about her abuelo, much less his name. Abuela always refused to talk about him as it would often cause her to weep in silence. She would isolate herself and fall asleep into the next day.

Elder Arthur then spares a glance at Haru who started picking up their dishes and putting away glasses into a small wooden basket. He made his way next to Isa and whispered in her ear "I suggest you get on good terms with Elder Arthur. He can be exceptionally terrifying."

Isa gave a small nod relaxing the tension on her knuckles and helped him with the dishes as the other sorcerers left for their dorms at the Celestial Facility using the portal. He kissed Vero lightly on the head, sending her off with a smile.

It hurt Isa a bit and arose a tang of jealousy within her. She wasn't jealous of them as individuals, but substantially of their relationship as a whole. It was a quick reminder of the years she had wasted and the loneliness that plagued her.

In the kitchen, she took it upon herself to put away her senseless emotions and proceeded to load the rest of the dishes into the sink.

"Did you like the food?" Haru passes a wet plate for Isa to dry and uses his elbow to move a strand of his blue hair out of his face.

Despite its roundness, he had firm cheekbones, and the bridge of his nose seemed to curve nicely. He wore glasses, something Isa deeply needed now since they were in bits inside the potato sac.

In terms of clothing, he had on a navy-blue elbow-length shirt that had poofy yet thin breathable fabric. It needed some patchwork to be done. Despite being the slender one in the group, he definitely had some muscles to spare under his shirt. It was essentially one of those renaissance fair shirts a common farm boy would wear with a slight open in the front.

"It was good. I didn't expect unicorns to taste like that, or to actually exist." Isa grabs the plate and uses a thick rag to dry it.

He makes a small chuckle and mentions it's Vero's favorite dish of Elder Arthur's. He informed Isa about his hobbies such as when Elder Arthur isn't with the team or having visions, he mostly spends his free time running a small cafe and helping at the cafeteria at the Celestial facility.

By the time the two had finished washing plates, Isa felt a sort of comfort from Haru she didn't expect from a person with his ability. As he was drying his hands Isa noticed the same tattoo of a black rose with a pair of hands cupping it on his wrist. Haru noticed Isa looking at the tattoo and began to explain how he got it.

While every realm is different, here in the Celestial Realm, after you graduate from the sorcerer academy, you are able to apply and move into the Celestial facility.

The Celestial facility is essentially a magical version of a university, and the only place you get to participate in the soulmate ritual. It's customary for sorcerers and Seers (unless they are half-breed creatures like Will).

They all go into this room in a circle, and above them is a rose quartz crystal that will give you the tattoo using a beam of light summoned by a leader. As you get the imprint, it will also magically display on your soulmate's skin, and all you have to do after is to find them. The symbol itself will have significant meaning revolving around their relationship.

It was mostly encouraged since your power doubles whenever you are near your soulmate. The only catch is if your soulmate dies, you die as well unless you break the bond by saying some sort of vow or falling in love with another person.

"Did it hurt?" Isa asked.

"A little, it feels like a little laser zapping the mark on you. Though I don't regret getting it at all." Haru smiled tracing his tattoo.

"Is that how you met Vero?"

"No, I knew her since we were kids, but we didn't get together until after we got the mark. We were best friends and for the longest time, she had a jerk of a boyfriend named Ash. It wasn't until she had the mark appear on her after I got mine, she dumped him, and we got together. It's quite the story." He laughs lightheartedly, pressing his hand to the back of his head.

After their chore, Haru opened a portal using something in his hand and left Isa there in the cottage with her and Elder Arthur. At first, she thought about going to her room, but she also felt the need to get answers.

Otherwise, how on earth would she be able to sleep with such thoughts clouding her head.

She recalled the picture frame and returned to the living room to retrieve it from the wall. Confident not to step on Elder Arthur's toes, Isa took a deep breath and searched for him.

Perla and Beau

With the picture, Isa knocks and opens the door of what she believes is supposed to be Elder Arthur's room. It might as well be for a vampire since there was little to no light in his room except for a small glowing mushroom on his desk.

"You should be getting some rest or at least getting ready for bed. You'll need it for tomorrow." He said, coming out of his small walk-in closet, startling Isa.

"I will, once you tell me about her," Isa says, handing him the picture frame. "Please?"

Without hesitation, he takes it from her hands and peers at the picture, his eyes squinting. Right as he realized what the picture was, his gaze began to soften, and his frown turned into a small tender smile. He didn't take long to disregard the photo but when he did, he moved to the corner of his room and sat on what seemed to be a fluffy rug, patting the space next to him.

Cautiously, Isa makes her way into his dark room trying not to knock any glowing objects over using whatever eyesight she has left.

"Still hung up on this picture huh? That young lady you are referring to is the lovely Perla. Though, I figured you know her."

Elder Arthur chuckles tumultuously as his round belly rises and falls greatly.

"She was a talented fighter and Seer. We were good friends, not soulmates but very good friends. Her soulmate was the man you saw with the level four patch, Beau. He said the unmatching vow before they had him and all other level four Seers executed so she too would not die if he died." Elder Arthur went as far as telling Isa about their heartache.

The two lovers were practically inseparable, it was as if they had been joined by the hip. Although they didn't like each other at the start, they eventually saw eye to eye.

Beau was a man of great pride and loyalty. He would rather die alone than bring his love into this and so when he had been imprisoned, he went ahead and said the vow. Though, despite the bond being gone, she was still his world, his spirit, and his joy. If he could, he would rip the world apart just so she didn't shed any more tears that were in her eyes.

"Even if she and Beau were no longer soulmates, their hearts were still intertwined." Elder Arthur added, stroking his beard.

Right then and there at the prison, the two were forced to say goodbye with one last embrace and an exchange of a few sweet words. They were only given a matter of minutes to speak with each other, and they did the most they could. They held hands like they had been glued to each other. He would caress her face as he tried to wipe each tear falling on her cheek. If the bars weren't between them, he would kiss each tear away and hold her until he couldn't.

As much as Perla wanted to stop the execution, she was far too weak and vulnerable as she had been expecting twins. She had led rallies and protests to save him and the other level four Seers, but nothing worked.

Elder Arthur did not want to tell Isa what a level four Seer was, and Isa hoped she was nowhere near that rank for she too would meet her grandfather's fate.

After Perla was forced away from Beau she ran over to Elder Arthur's cottage and told him what had happened. Perla had expressed to Elder Arthur the painful sensation sinking in her heart as both of their tattoos vanished from their skin.

It wasn't the tattoo disappearing that hurt her the most, it was the realization that the only things she had left of him were her memories and unborn twins. To comfort her, Elder Arthur offered her food, but she refused to eat and drink. The least Elder Arthur was able to do was to give her a place to sleep. He let her stay in the guest room Isa had settled her things in.

Not once did Elder Arthur hear a peep. So much so, that he didn't notice she was gone until guards were knocking at his door. They were sent for him to break Perla out of prison for stopping the execution and the slaughter of the Celestial soldiers.

It was revealed when Perla had gotten into her room, she fled to stop Beau's execution which was supposed to be held at sundown.

By the time she arrived, he was gone. Not just gone in the sense he had been moved somewhere else, but the feeling inside Perla told her they had executed the level four Seers much earlier behind the scenes. Above her, the speakers shouted the cancellation of the execution for the public to watch and that's when Perla had indeed lost every sense of peace she had left.

They killed her lover, so she killed them. Every. Single. Person. Involved.

When Elder Arthur found her in the prison cell, Perla was sitting on the floor soaked in blood from head to toe. Tears in her eyes burned with anguish as she had one small object in her dirty hands, it was the necklace her lover once wore.

"After the execution and her prison release, Perla came to me once again but with such anger in her eyes. It was as if she had been possessed by some sort of demon. She mentioned leaving this realm like all the other supernatural beings that are now in your Human Realm, but I had to decline." Elder Arthur tells Isa, his voice becoming nothing but a whisper.

"Is that what you meant about not having a choice?"

He nods his head, swaying his beard up and down. "We can try to change what we will see, but it's not always possible. A change cannot happen without consequence."

There was more to the story on his end, but it seemed like the storm in his eyes was too much to explain in words. You could tell solely based on his change of voice when he mentioned Perla, how much he had loved her.

In the midst of it all, Isa couldn't help but wonder how different things would be if her grandmother had never fled this realm or if they hadn't been so cruel to execute Beau.

This explained so much as to why her abuela never had photos and why her mother and uncle never spoke about their father. It's no wonder why they both wanted such big families, it's because they hardly had any.

Knowing her background made Isa regretful about all the times she had argued with her parents about her family and the struggles she faced being the oldest. It didn't excuse how she was given responsibilities at such a young age and the pressures of being the golden child, but there was some sort of understanding on their end.

Speaking of family, if what Arthur had said about "a Seer's rank is not born but created by the individual's mind", that must mean if Isa was capable of being a Seer, so had her uncle, mother, and siblings. This explained so much about her experience but left so many questions yet to be answered.

After a pause, Elder Arthur cleared his throat, grabbing a teacup next to him that Isa had not noticed.

"That's when I had last seen her. It wasn't until I had my vision of you, I immediately recognized her features. You do indeed have human blood from your human father, but the rest is Seer blood in your veins. Not all those with some human blood have the capabilities. In fact, not all Seer descendants are Seers! They're just normal people living in the Celestial Realm. As I said, a Seer's rank is not born but created by the individual's mind."

"What about a sorcerer?" Isa questioned thinking back to her current crewmates.

"Their sorcery is hereditary, but the strength of their abilities relies on them." Elder Arthur then finally puts down his teacup after sipping from it and guides Isa to the door offering her a small tart, he had pulled out of the sleeve of his cloak. Hearing a yawn escape from his lips, Isa didn't feel like disturbing him anymore.

After they have said their goodnights and farewells, Isa enters her temporary room feeling as exhausted as ever. She took it upon herself to use the restroom and at least wash her face with some water and what seemed to be a bar of lavender-scented soap.

"Hopefully, this doesn't break me out." She thought to herself, reflecting in the mirror.

Despite her attempts to clean herself to appear much more suitable, Isa frowned at her reflection. Her mid-length reddish-brow hair was all over the place, the bags under her brown eyes seemed darker than usual, and her legs and arms were full of scrapes from when she had been tossed out of the portal.

When she got to her room, a small portal opened on top of her bed. Two items plopped right out, one being her clothing design journal, and another was a full-body black jumpsuit with the design of an Egyptian-looking outline of a singular eye at the front chest area and golden lining on the sides of the arm traveling to the legs. The back of the jumpsuit had some patterned mesh at the top exposing enough to be modest but flattering. Soon after the portal was closed, Isa went to inspect what was placed on her bed.

Isa first grabbed her journal to see if any of her designs had been missing. While flipping through the pages, on the page of the design where the jumpsuit was on was a little note.

Here's your suit. I took inspiration from your little journal you left out while you and Haru were cleaning dishes. Should be good enough for tomorrow's training. I won't go through your stuff anymore, ~~Hue~~ Isa. Let's call it a truce. Though, it doesn't mean I'll go easy on you."

At the bottom was Will's name in surprisingly nice cursive.

10

Weapon Room

Isa is not a morning person. She hated waking up to the sun hitting her eyes or her relatives rushing into her room as they all tried to make her weekend mornings a living nightmare. She was greeted by loads of chores Lyra had neglected to do and did so while fighting away her brothers. For the most part, it would usually take her two whole cups of pure coffee with some creamer to keep her sane.

That was not the case for today. In the dark morning when the sun had barely started coming out, Elder Arthur pounded on Isa's door to wake her up. Isa grumbled and stayed in her bed hiding under the sheets.

She was exhausted beyond belief. Aches and purple bruises covered her body as they swelled and slowly became filled with last night's mosquito bites. Although Isa didn't have any visions or dreams, she had hoped by the time she woke up, she would be in the comfort of her own bed and on time for her test.

She was definitely not.

Isa tugged the quilt tighter to her body and crawled deeper into the covers of the bed. Her eyelids felt heavy, unmovable. When she attempted to move her arms, a sharp pain struck her head, approaching a migraine.

Elder Arthur's beard sways side to side in disapproval. He opens the windows of the room, allowing the breeze to conquer the warmth of the room. He hoped the subtle gesture would be enough to cause Isa to surface.

She did not. This only made Isa sink and preserve the remaining comfort she had in the sheets, tucking any possible openings for a breeze to enter.

Running low on patience, Elder Arthur passes the task to someone less courteous.

"All right, you've given me no choice. Vero! Go ahead!" Elder Arthur shouts down the hall. He leaves the room and tends to his kitchen duties.

Following his orders, quietly, the sorceress sneaks into Isa's bedroom. Much like most of her prey, she wanted to surprise Isa.

Undetected, reaching the foot of the bed, Vero raises her hand pulling Isa's leg out of the covers, hanging her upside down in mid-air away from her bed.

"Okay! Okay, I'm awake! I get it! I'll get dressed. Put me down!" Isa shouts feeling incredibly annoyed. Her hands spun around, flailing to grab anything in her reach.

"Will you really?" Vero crosses her arms.

"Yes!"

"Say it like you mean it."

"Vero!"

"Say it!"

"I'll get dressed!"

Satisfied, lowering her hand using a strange motion, Vero plops Isa on her bed. She lets out a laugh before leaving her room saying, "Breakfast will be ready soon!"

Isa grunts, slamming the door behind Vero. She eyed her bed sheets, debating on whether she wanted to wear them as clothes out of spite. Picking a few accessories from her drawers and the jumpsuit Will made her, Isa was out of her room in an instant and met everyone outside where they were having breakfast. Shivers crept up her spine as a puff of hot air escaped her lips.

"Morning sleepy head. Got any visions last night?" Jack smiles as he pats the seat next to him gesturing to Isa to sit. On the other hand, he toasted a slice of bread with the warmth of his fingertips. Isa was not in the mood to argue and was eager for warmth, so she begrudgingly slumped in the seat. He was her one-way ticket to a portable heater.

"Yeah, any new reports?" Haru said, passing a plate of pancakes and a bowl of berries to them.

"Hate to burst everyone's bubble but no. Maybe if I had gotten more sleep, I could've gotten a vision. Also, anyone got coffee or anything with caffeine?" She responds by taking a bite of the wondrous fluffy pancake Elder Arthur had made.

It took her every urge to not add more chocolate spread and sweetness onto her plate, as she knew her body would tremble under her pre-diabetes. She would often have to battle her sugar cravings and stick to a healthier diet. Her body was too sensitive for a sugar spike.

"Someone slept on the wrong side of the bed. Was it too uncomfortable for you? Did you need someone to fluff up your pillow?" Will remarks to Isa.

Isa glowers at him and returns to her food, searching the table for a drink.

"What happened to keeping a truce?"

"I am keeping a truce. All I did was make an observation." He raises his hands at his sides defensively.

"In that case," the corners of Isa's lips lift. "I have an observation as well."

"And that is?"

"Not only do you like to push people's buttons, but your ears also turn red whenever you're angry or embarrassed." Isa takes a bite from her plate and gleefully smirks.

At the table, Vero spits out and chokes on her drink. The flower crown on her head falls to the ground and Haru picks it up.

Will rolls his eyes and takes a sip out of his cup defeated. His ears turned red at the tips as Isa predicted.

"Wow, you really got him on that one Isa." Jack harks raising his hand for a high five, anticipating a reaction. Isa goes ahead and returns the gesture, widening Jack's smile. His downturned eyes glistened in delight, recognizing the small achievement.

"I have three younger brothers and a house filled with judgmental people. Insults are far from new."

Elder Arthur then comes out with two water pitchers, one in each hand. The one on his right though, didn't look nor move like water. He pours one of them inside Isa's cup. "Don't drink it fast, it will burn your throat," Will said, in a not-so-keen tone.

Isa peers into her cup skeptical of Will's remark as if he had been suspiciously precautioning her.

"He's right, but it should help you," Haru adds bringing some sincerity to Will's warning.

For a moment Isa eyed the honey-colored liquid in her cup, mindfully regretting asking for coffee. Putting the cup to her lips she detected the sweet drink slowly but smoothly sliding down her throat. It smelled like a combination of fruits, flowers, and honey and tasted like how it smelt. Isa made sure not to drink it fast as Will recommended, but it was very addictive. Her body felt much more substantial and almost as if it was burning inside a sauna but in a good way.

It took a lot for Isa to not chug the whole thing down but judging by everyone watching her, she soon put the cup down. When she did, Jack took the cup and gave it to Vero who seemed less angry at him than yesterday.

"What is this?" Isa said, still warm to the touch.

"It's nectar from the godly realm. Jesus had it delivered to us by Hermes since Jupiter made an extra batch from a previous mission." Jack casually mentions knowing well enough it was going to confuse Isa.

"What you said made no sense. Jupiter? Jesus? Hermes?" Isa questioned raising her eyebrow and taking another bite out of her pancake.

"Wouldn't be the first time you know nothing."

"The godly realm has all the types of gods you can think of, Greek, Roman, Catholic, etc., and most cultural creatures and demons like the Japanese yōkai. We often help them with the yōkai problem so we're familiar with the Godly Realm." Vero and Haru explain alternating.

Although this wasn't mind-boggling to them, it was something Isa had a tough time wrapping her head around. She wasn't going to question anything else in the meantime and decided it was probably best to enjoy her breakfast.

It's too early for this.

After everyone had finished eating, they decided it was time to leave and go to the Celestial Facility. Isa had already gotten herself packed, but the issue was going through the portal again.

The first time she had gone into the portal, it felt like her insides were about to explode and her brain wanted to burst. It might've been because she was inside the sac or because her human body had been new to the whole thing, either way, she was just about to find out if she could handle it.

"Is there any other method?" she asks Vero.

"You could try walking for miles until you reach the facility."

"Miles?"

"Miles. We don't have a carriage and we don't have any horses. It's either the portal or on foot."

With her potato sac in her hand, Jack opens the portal by tossing a small cube with swirls and inscriptions into the air. Behind Isa, she could hear Haru asking Will to make two plushies out of his jacket.

"Right now? Why?" He said as he was making his way to the portal.

"Yes, right now, hurry before you go," Haru urged placing the jacket into his hands.

At the palm of Will's hand as if it was some magic trick, spawned two plushies, one was a hippo, and the other was a small red fox with a button nose.

Smiling happily, Haru grabs the plushies out of Will's hand and lets him go into the portal, turning to Isa and Vero.

"Here you go. I hope hugging this plushie might help. Also, how could I not get one for you as well my love," he said handing the fox to Isa and the hippo to Vero who shrunk and placed the staff in her hand in her pocket so she too could hold the plush and the other to hug Haru. Both enter the portal leaving Isa and Elder Arthur alone.

"Are you coming?" Isa asks him.

"Not yet, I have a few things to attend to. Go on child," He huffs out slowly walking Isa toward the portal until she has been completely immersed.

Stepping into the portal, Isa felt a sense of relief as it was like walking into one of those bounce houses her parents rented for birthday parties. Except you walk into a rainbow spiral and it feels more of a sloshing back-and-forth motion. She was happy Haru gave her a plush since it felt nice having something to grab onto. Usually, Isa didn't have many plushies since most were for her younger siblings, so it was a nice change to finally have one to hold.

By the time she made it to the other side, she had stood right in front of a glass skyscraper building. The front windows had a gradient effect which was clear from the top and gradually turned into a tinted black window at the bottom. From the inside, there were tubes people used as a slide to go down to the level below them rather than elevators. Most of those people wore those renaissance clothes her team was wearing, and others had knightly attire. They proudly displayed their emblems on their chest plates and carried their shields and swords with them.

Passing the modern building were the usual cottages, small shops, and mythical beings walking around. In one of the small shops, there were posters Isa could hardly read. At her feet, she caught a similar poster reading WANTED LEVEL FOURS. She quickly discarded it into a bin and waved to a small boy with butterfly wings. He waves back at her and flies away.

As she stood in awe, admiring her new world, her team members all looked back checking if she had passed through the portal. When they spotted her, they sighed with relief.

"Thank heavens she isn't dead," Jack assured.

With haste, they ushered Isa inside where more magical individuals roamed around wearing metal armor and doing basic sorcery. A man with green skin and orange hair used his telekinetic ability to sign a few documents as he sat there filling out paperwork.

Haru, with Vero still holding his hand, walks up to the receptionist. Vero places her plush on the counter and asks her to send the plushy to their room.

"Of course." The receptionist smiled.

The receptionist had short red hair and bright icy blue eyes with the intention of piercing into anyone's soul. She also wore a formal suit having the effect of the world being more "normal" and modern to Isa.

"We're here to have a Seer registered, Elder Arthur recently approved. We'd like to start with the weaponry room." Vero tells the receptionist.

With a quick hand motion, suddenly Isa floats over to the receptionist against her will. She grabs Isa's arm and puts a red band on her wrist.

"Her room should be ready by lunch. She's free to use the training center, but because she's new and based on the report Elder Arthur submitted, she will have to need a guide and free-of-passage certificate from one of the Elders if she wants to participate in the soulmate ritual." This time she turns to Vero and goes to wink at Isa or at least attempts to. Two of the three of her eyes blinked.

"Very well." They both say to the receptionist. Isa was somewhat able to read her name tag spelling Cindy.

Making their way to the elevator past the lounge, were doors in the color of orange, purple, blue, and red.

The same doors were there when they had gotten off the elevator with the exception these doors had different symbols.

The orange one had a spear pointing upward, the purple one had a pen and notepad, the blue one had a lightning bolt, and the red one had an eye design matching Isa's jumpsuit.

The first door they entered was the orange door at the end of the hallway. Coming into the room, it was evident there were weapons EVERYWHERE. Any type of mythical or regular weapon you could think of was in this room.

Will then said, "Go ahead and choose."

Isa turns her head as if she assumed he was talking to someone else.

"Me?" Isa points to her chest.

"No, the door. Yes, you!"

"Any?"

"Yes!"

"For me?"

"Who else?"

"You guys do know I'm broke right? I can't afford anything right now." Isa pats down her pockets

"We know." All of them say simultaneously.

"Just choose your weapon so I can customize it for you! Without one, you might die. So, choose." He gestures, pulling out a small dagger from one of his belt pockets. He then swings the dagger in a wide stride causing it to turn into an elongated silver sword.

"Show off." Jack coughs under his breath.

Following Will, everyone else pulls out their weapons, displaying them proudly to Isa. Vero's convertible whip turned into an elongated wooden staff with a small pointy gem at the top creating it almost into a spear. Haru carries a large disk that transforms into a powerful and deadly scythe. It was a sharp enough weapon to slash a person in half. His was strapped to his back.

Isa hadn't noticed the weapons because, like everyone else, they were convertible.

(It was mainly Will's doing when he created these weapons so no one could complain to him about how heavy their weapon was.)

In terms of Haru, considering that he was a sorcerer of shadows, it was very suitable for him. To open it, all he needed to do was pull out the small disk from his back and throw it in the air for him to catch his immediate scythe.

Jack had a classic axe. The special feature of his axe was that it could harness his elemental ability. With a click of a button, it could shrink to fit in his pocket into a mini version of itself. If Jack wanted to, he could mold and bend his weapon to the shape of his choosing.

Impressed and excited, Isa walks around the room looking at the different weapons there are. She considered something like a spear or one of those flails she saw hanging on the wall. Before she thought of grabbing the flail, something in the corner of the room caught her eye. It was a perfect blue bow with limbs of steel and had the centerpiece where the scope should be. The arc of the bow had metal gold wrappings poking out a bit as if it had wings.

Next to it were its arrows that had gold tips while the rest of it was steel.

"I want something like this," Isa said, holding the bow in her hand. It felt almost natural, a little too natural and warm in the palm of her hands. The tip of the arrows was sharp enough to prick the tip of her finger, which they did. Not wanting to have her blood on these items, she then puts them in their original place.

(Sure, it was a basic and standard weapon, but it made Isa feel special. After all, I bet most of ya'll at some point wanted to know how to use a bow and arrow. I'm right, aren't I?)

"Do you even know how to use a bow and arrow?" Will makes a slight snort.

"No, and I don't know how to use any of these other weapons either, so regardless I'll have to learn to use one. Granted, the only real weapons I had were my taser that was in my car, and my hands when I took kickboxing classes but even then, I'm still a beginner, to say the least," she replied.

"What's a taser?" Jack quietly asks Haru, whispering into his ear.

Will clicks his tongue, unimpressed. "Seriously? This is who I-we have to work with."

"Hey!"

"No way." Vero smiles sinisterly.

"Vero. I know that look."

"Oh, come on! If you don't tell her, I will."

Isa frowns. "Tell me what."

"As our second archer, you will be joining Will."

"I beg your pardon."

"Will just refuses to use a bow and arrow cause it's a stereotypical elf thing. He mostly uses the sword for training but rarely in battle. Some of us have multiple weapons, like how I too use a dagger, but my main is this baby right here." Jack laughs swinging his ax.

"None of us are skilled with the arrows so he'll be training you."

"You've got to be kidding me."

"Nope."

"Great, I'll pick something else then." Isa retorts as her finger oozes a bit of blood from where she had pricked it.

"Too late, the weapon chooses the individual, not the other way around. Kinda part of the room and its effects. Will will make your weapon, whether he likes it or not. Besides if you want a second weapon, he could make you that too." Haru said as he was ushering them out to the door.

After making a decision, Isa soon saw what Haru meant about the weapon choosing the person. All the weapons started to disappear like holograms until it was only them and the bow and arrow left in the room. Behind them, a door opens, and Will enters by himself.

"Give me a few." He mumbles going into the room while the rest leave through where they first entered.

11

Your Darkness is My Darkness

While Will was making Isa's weapon, they quickly took the elevator to the floor above. There were only two doors on this floor, and both were simple white heavy doors you would open when you go and see a doctor.

Inside the room was a mini hospital that had classic blue curtains, plain hospital beds, and monitors beyond Isa's knowledge. Some bottles were healing potions or elixirs of some kind, one Isa seemed to recognize was a small bottle of the nectar she had.

All of the potions were inside the clear glass medicine cabinet. Right at the entrance was a small front desk with a girl with long neon green hair, purple eyes, and a ghostlike complexion.

"Hey, Jessie," Jack said giving her a wink.

Jessie rolls her eyes and responds with "What do you want? Don't tell me you need me to heal someone again. I told you to leave the freshman alone." She scolds him and excitedly rushes to Vero when she spots her.

"Girl, it feels like forever since I last saw you! Can I give you a hug? Hello to you too Haru." She chirps and jumps up and down excitedly.

"Always." Vero smiles hugging Jessie.

She then shifts her gaze over to Isa who was awkwardly just standing there like a five-year-old on their first day of elementary school.

"And who is this?" She smiles before holding out her hand for Isa to shake. "I'm Jessie, I heal all minor injuries. If you got any headaches, sprained legs, splinters, bumps, and bruises, you can come to me!"

"My name is-"

"Foxy" Jack cuts in jokingly.

"Isa. My name is Isa, and you need to stop calling me that!" She corrects and glares at Jack giving him a light kick to his side.

Jessie smiles as she too glares at Jack. "Careful with that one, Jack is quite the handful and player. I seriously don't know how his soulmate will manage him whoever they are."

"Hey! Anyone is lucky to handle all of this! You should be careful with her too, Isa. She's a sneaky half-fae. She once stole ten higles from me."

Jessie rolls her eyes at Jack's remark and shifts her eyes to Isa who had a tad of blood on her index finger.

She gently reaches for Isa's finger and cups it in between her hands. She eyes the injury and swiftly blows on her finger. Isa felt a cooling sensation like when you put on aloe vera for a sunburn.

When Jessie had finished, Isa noticed the slice on her finger was no longer there. It was almost as if it never happened.

On her finger was some glittery residue that disappeared when she rubbed her fingers together.

"Woah…"

Jessie gives a smile and hands her a lollipop as she moves to her desk.

"Does the lollipop do anything I should be aware of?" Isa questions, eyeing the candy.

"Nope just for emotional support. My favorite is the blueberry-flavored one. Now let's get a move on to the library." Vero replies, throwing away the one she finished at the trash can by the door.

Everyone says goodbye to Jessie and makes their way to the elevator. They return to the floor below them where the four colorful doors were at.

So far, what Isa understood, the orange door with the spear symbol is the weaponry room and the purple door with the symbol of a pen and notepad that they are opening at the moment is the library. There were only two more doors left that they hadn't yet gotten to.

Taking her first steps inside, Isa fell in love. The décor and details of the library took her breath away as it was like nothing she had seen before. The shelves had golden linings with intricate designs of celestial symbols and occasional gems planted here and there. It was incredibly spacious as there were elevators taking you to the floor above as part of the library.

The tables where students were supposably studying were perfectly clean and had no sign of chipping. All seats looked like miniature thrones as they all had cotton armrests and fluffy pillows. Shelves were fully stocked with books big and small and made the room colorful as they were organized by the gradient of their section. Each of the backings had gold foil to easily read the title of the book and the author's name. On the sides of the room, there were whiteboards filled with writing and study rooms that had a full-blown sofa to rest on. The large window panels had red drapes providing the right amount of sunlight to let all the gold lining glimmer.

"Here is where you're gonna find all the information you'll need. We have books about the different realms, medicinal plants, and any important information that may be resourceful for us. They also have a nice braille section." Vero said.

Out of nowhere, Haru pulls out a book from a shelf and hands it to Isa. The title of the book was almost hidden since the cover was black and the lettering was almost engraved into the book cover. It was called "Dimensional Relics 101". As cheesy as the title was, Isa couldn't help but feel slightly intimidated. This book held all the information she needed as to what these relics were.

"I suggest you read this, so you know what is at stake."

"Good recommendation Haru." Jack elbows him in a fun-loving manner.

After Haru grabs more books to recommend Isa to read, the wristwatch Jack had on starts beeping like a timer. With a quick look at his watch, he saw a message from Will.

It said in simple words: **Everything is ready. Come over here. -Will**

Seeing the message, Jack charmingly attempts to take some of the handful of books Isa was carrying and tries to guide everyone out. Isa leers at him, defensively carrying her books and stowing some of them in the potato sac she had been carrying around. Jack raises his hands in defense leading the group out of the library. Haru couldn't help but lift his mouth at the interaction, stifling a laugh in the tail end of his throat.

The weaponry room, like before, had no weapons around in sight other than the two Will had in his hands as he walked out of the rear-end door that slid open and closed behind him. Inside the backroom, it had everything a blacksmith would desire including tools to repair or sharpen weapons if needed. It was always handy for Will but, like everything, he too has his limits.

The new bow and arrow set he made for Isa took a lot of energy from him. It was similar to the original blue one but this time it was red and had a silver lining instead of gold. The arrows for the bow looked like something Cupid would have. If someone were to get injured by these arrows, it would possibly match the color of the tips, making little to no difference between the victim and the arrow.

A significant detail Will added on his own accord was a pair of new glasses that could hook and fold into a scope to use with the bow. He went as far as creating a pair of gauntlet gloves with a pair of shin guards for Isa to use, as he had remembered her mentioning being a kickboxer. The metal gloves had an elasticity from the bottom of her hand and the top was the metal part so she could easily use the bow and arrow while wearing them.

Carefully putting the books on the floor beside her, Isa puts on the gauntlets, shin guards, and new glasses. Isa wondered how on earth Will was able to get her prescription right along with the details of everything else. When Will handed her the weapon, the original copy vanished from his hands making the room completely empty with just them and the weapons Will made her.

"Wow." Isa gasped breathlessly.

"I made it red just to piss you off, foxy," Will said having the corner of his lips slightly go up.

"Very charming of you. Truly Will." Isa says sarcastically. "Wait until I beat your butt in archery."

"Hey, foxy was my idea, get your own nickname," Jack replies slightly offended.

"Very well. Considering that Red said she hasn't used any of these weapons before, I'd like to see you try." Will responded this time giving a small grin that he was clearly fighting. Meanwhile the others, especially Vero, cringed.

"Red? For someone who is the sorcerer of creation, you sure lack creativity in comebacks." Isa rolls her eyes smiling slightly. She continued to admire how well everything fitted in her hands.

"Must I remind you; I just made your weapon and I'm heavily exhausted. A simple thank you would be nice."

'Thank you."

"Doesn't sound sincere but I'll take it."

Ignoring Will, Isa returned her attention to her new weapon. Isa had no idea how she was going to use it, but she did feel comforted that she had them.

Especially if the Seer Slayer decides to try to come for her next.

Vacating the weaponry room, the woman at the front desk named Cindy stood outside the door waiting for them. She quickly flashed her eyes at Isa's red band and reluctantly gave her an apologetic look.

"Your room is ready," she said to Isa, giving her a keycard. She then makes a hand gesture to follow her as they go on the elevator to the thirteenth floor.

When they got off the elevator and into a hallway, Isa noticed there were many doors. Each door had its distinct feature as if the owner living in that room had decorated it to their own accord. One door was painted with stars and moons, another had stickers of cute mythical creatures, and some of them had welcome mats and shoes waiting by them. Next to the door was a handprint scanner along with a swiper mechanism to swipe your keycard.

After passing countless doors, by the time they had reached the very end of the hall, right in front of them was the one with little to no sign of decorations or imprint of someone living there.

This was it. This is the room where Isa was going to potentially live.

Cindy gestures for Isa to swipe her card on the wall and place her hand on the fingerprint scanner. Isa does so, and within seconds she hears the door unlock.

Stepping into the room, Isa's jaw dropped, and her eyes widened in awe. This room wasn't any ordinary dormitory she was used to. Unlike the dorm she once lived in, she had a clean fully functioning kitchen all to herself, the fridge was loaded with fruits, vegetables, and items Isa would most likely try and hope it doesn't kill her.

Connecting to the kitchen was a small but cute living room that had the nicest couch Isa had ever seen. If she had taken this couch to her realm, it would've been severely scratched, stained, and worn out by her family in seconds. It was soft and the color of burgundy with small pillows containing golden tassels on its corners. The table in front of the couch was most likely made up of glass.

On the table were two remote controls, one of which Isa snatched and pressed a button. Right there and then, the chandelier above her turned on and gave the living room a nice glow.

The other remote that Isa then pressed had turned on a hologram that acted as a TV. Each channel seemed to broadcast news from a different realm.

"It's like watching a child on Christmas," Will snickers watching Isa intently.

"Hey, in my realm, this is considered the nicest thing I got. I don't expect you to understand. You're probably jealous." She replies as everyone follows Cindy to show her the simple bathroom by the hologram TV.

"Jealous? Considering that I will make all your things as the sorcerer of creation, I beg to differ. Most of the clothes you have in your closet are made by me. If you have any other needs or desires from here on out, you'll need to take them up with Cindy." Will replies.

After viewing the bathroom, Cindy then leads them to her room at last. The bed was nice and spacious in comparison to the one Isa had in her realm. It was simply decorated with red bedding and a few white pillows. Above the bed was a window that shined enough light to brighten the room. The room also had a closet, drawer, nightstand, and a simple wooden desk. In the closet was her new set of clothes that Will had made, most of it either worn for a knight as some had metal plates in the clothing or a series of jumpsuits like the one, she was wearing. Deeper in the drawer were more outfits she had designed in her fashion journal. This made Isa's eyes light up, as she was happy to see some of her creations come to life.

"If you need anything you can give me a call with your watch," Cindy comments as she then pulls out a small watch everyone has on. From a glance, it looked like one of those digital watches. In the contact section of the watch was the name of everyone on the team, Cindy, Elder Arthur, and surprisingly Jessie.

When Isa pressed Cindy's name it gave the option to send a message or make a phone call. The watch also had various times of the different realms, one of them being the Human realm.

"You know foxy if you need some company, I'll be more than happy to give you some," Jack says resting down on Isa's freshly made bed.

Vero lifted the staff she was using and whacked Jack's exposed stomach with it.

"OW!" Jack said, lifting himself out of the bed. "No need to be jelly, there's plenty of Jack to go around."

"Ugh, stop being a creep, Jack. We get it, you're lonely but geez, don't scare our new Seer away." Vero remarked. If Isa wasn't paying attention, she wouldn't have seen the way Haru looked at Vero. He loved her fire. Though, he was scared his darkness would one day fizzle her flames.

Haru was not scared of anything, except himself. Being a sorcerer of shadows had its price no one should pay. On the darkest days, his ability would take over him as if he were drowning in an ocean of tar and ink. In the worst way possible, it was as if bit by bit every single negative thought would sink him deeper into the depths of his mind.

When he was in too deep it was as if he had been gone and a soulless version of him took over him. His eyes would turn completely black and so would his veins. To drive him out of that state, he would need to find some sort of joy and calmness. He would often need to meditate and find his way to resume control using every positive thought he had left, which was quite difficult without Vero.

At one point in his life, it had gotten so bad that he locked himself in his room for days, constantly trying to shut out the repeating mean words kids in his class had said to him. They were terrified of him, and he was terrified too. He didn't mean to hurt anyone or control them in such a way. It just happens. He killed the one friend he had.

The day he left his room was when Vero had come over to check up on him. At the time she was new in the classroom, transferred from who knows where. She heard about Haru and was curious enough to come close to him.

From then on, it had been Vero to be the one to pull him through as she had held him tightly whenever he had his episodes. Not afraid, not scared.

Even when he tried to hide his internal struggle from the others, behind the bookcases, fake smiles, and attempts of optimism, the only one who could see behind all the faces was Vero. That's what made him love her unconditionally. She didn't judge him by his ability despite the others warning her, because she too knew what it was like to be judged for something that they didn't ask to have.

He fell fast and hard, yet what held him back all those years of adolescence was the uncertainty of whether she felt the same. He didn't want her to think that he had taken her kindness the wrong way. After all, she always had a line of potential suitors waiting for her.

Comparing himself to them, he felt terrible when they were matched because who would want to deal with someone with his ability? With his mentality? His kind of sorcery was frowned upon and deemed a curse for whoever inherited it.

He hated it.

He hated how it got worse every time he used his ability, and how he grew addicted to the feeling of control. He would never wish upon his ability to anyone, especially since he fears one day his ability would overcome him and hurt Vero.

On the day he received the mark and found Vero was his soulmate, he immediately offered her the chance to move on and say the unmatching vow for her sake. He was certain she would say it, except, to his surprise, she instead grabbed his face and kissed him.

"Your darkness is my darkness," she replied holding him tighter as he wept in her arms.

If only Haru had understood that regardless of the tattoos shown on their wrists, Vero would've always picked him. She had simply been waiting. She loved him for he was the first to see her as a person instead of some girl who saw the world through telepathy. He was the first not to cross the line. The first to treat her like a person unlike her family, (but that is a story for another occasion, a very soon occasion.).

12

Dreamer

Parting ways to their rooms (mostly it was Vero and Haru kicking Jack out), alone in her dorm, Isa decided to take it upon herself to read the books Haru had recommended to her. She didn't know which to choose from as they all had been tempting her to open the pages. Right on top of some of them was the fox plush Haru had given her lying on her bed.

As much as Isa wanted to sleep, she knew she needed more answers, especially about the world around her and what are the relics she is looking for. She put the backpack of her belongings down and went straight to the books.

She grabbed them and laid them out on the crystallized table in front of the Television. She turned it on as a way for her to concentrate as she often was used to operating under the loudness of her household. Sitting in her empty dorm, the silence was more than enough to drive her insane. On the TV, an anchor was speaking about the weather of the different realms.

Picking up some random books from the pile, Isa decided it was best to start with understanding the Celestial

Realm she was in. It read more like a story than it did of a history book.

Centuries ago, the Celestial Realm had no idea about the other realms until one day a scientist used forbidden spells and classic gems to build a small device that soon opened the portals we nowadays travel to. A small device was given to each realm for when they needed to do some type of exchange. This led to an entire era of using portals among the realms. Sorcerers from the Celestial Realm were famous for using portals as they completed tasks in return for currency or a trade of some sort.

Everything has been peaceful as one realm has been mindful of the other. It was not until someone had taken the journey of finding five relics that would change history. United together, the relics are capable of opening portals across dimensions, and if the person desires, it would grant them wishes as long as the relics were assembled under an eclipse.

While it grants three wishes, the relics united kept the dimensional portals open. This created complete and total mayhem as people tried to kill off the other version of themselves as a way of survival. To this day we don't know who is from the other dimension and who is the 'original' individual. Other outwardly entities too came passing through these portals and terrorized the realms around them. In turn, it is a sorcerer's job to maintain these entities.

To unopen the dimensions once and for all, a person must break apart these relics by hand under the eclipse, otherwise, these portals will remain open until the next date on which the eclipse occurs, allowing months, days, and/or years for dimensional beings to cross over. If these relics are broken after being assembled, a price will come in return for the destroyer.

"But what is the price?" Isa questioned as she flipped through the pages and found no further details other than what the relics were. A few seemed to be torn out of the book.

According to what was in the remaining pages, all five relics together formed a genie lamp, (which explained the whole make-a-wish aspect). The five pieces were the handle, the lid, the bottom part that makes it stand, the core piece, and the funnel tip. As Jack mentioned, only a Seer can find each piece.

Although there weren't any pictures in the book, it had described it as a golden lamp with blue and purple hand-painted designs completely embezzled in jewels. The lamp can only work at night when a full lunar eclipse takes place. If the pieces are assembled without the eclipse being present, it will not work.

It sounded very ominous, but Isa decided not to question it any further considering nothing about this was normal. When Isa was done reading about the relics, she then proceeded to pick up the book next to her about the different realms.

The Hue/human realm was deemed to be the realm that 'normalizes magical beings. Most go to the Human Realm to live a 'normal' life or to seek refuge during the days of the multi-dimensional war.

A common side effect is that magical offspring, also known as Dreamers, often exhibit the compulsive need for escapism such as through shifting and maladaptive daydreaming. The blood in their veins containing other realms thrives and rushes to their brain, causing them to excessively daydream.

The worst case reported had been of a girl named Alice. Alice had imagined a world of wonder. She believes it existed, which it hypothetically did. It was the Random Realm, a realm of inconsistencies run by a wicked Queen.

In the end, she was sent to a mental hospital in the Human realm and was never heard from again. She spoke too much of her hallucinations and was deemed mad.

It has been reported that Dreamers can additionally experience the inability to blend in with the human realm, have trouble belonging, experience loneliness, depression, and/or display signs and behaviors that indicate their blood-borne realm. For example, those who often dream of flying or wish to fly are most likely descendants of the fae.

However, they may never know of their true identities as the longer they remain in the Human Realm, the more they become 'human'. Once the Dreamer neglects their ability, they are doomed to never obtain the ability again.

"This explains so much!" Isa said out loud, almost as if she intended for it to be heard by her family in the human realm.

Isa had always felt like she was prevented from a life much more magical. She always found herself constantly daydreaming an abnormal number of times and spending hours making whimsical clothing in the middle of the night. Both things made her feel alive.

Everything she had once pushed aside so she wouldn't be sent to a mental hospital was explained within the pages of the book she was holding. All those times she was able to predict her test scores and the minor mishaps in her life were no Deja vu. It's no wonder why every little piece of fantasy felt comforting and all the friendships she had made in them, hit close to home.

She was a Dreamer. She had the blood of a Seer running through her veins. She was not entirely human. Her team was right and so was Elder Arthur.

"I'm not crazy!" The thought repeated in her brain over and over until she couldn't anymore. She didn't know whether to smile or to frown as her lips wavered.

Isa thought the last mental breakdown was going to be when she failed the exam but boy was, she wrong. For a moment, she wept, not for her test, not for Dylan, but for herself. The tears that poured out of her eyes were filled with the years she had been picked on and for every time she questioned her own delusions. Anger. Joy. Happiness. It all came out as she held the book tightly in her hands.

When Isa was able to compose herself, she carefully turned the page to the next chapter on the Celestial Realm.

The Celestial Realm is where sorcerers are originally from. In the Flialight forest across the valley of Milway, lived otherworldly individuals who chose to live in that realm such as elves, fae, wolf folk, goblins, and many more.

The Celestial Realm is the perfect realm for many and all outsiders to find a place they belong. In the Celestial Realm, payment can be done in trades, tasks, or higles (celestial coins).

Aside from sorcerers and mystical folk, Seers additionally contribute to the population of the realm despite their rarity. Among the Seers, it is those who are level four who are arguably more powerful than sorcerers of shadows.

Right as the book was about to talk about the level four Seers, Isa noticed a page of the book had been ripped out. The pages after were filled with chapters and maps of the other realms and their own set of information.

In the midst of her reading, Isa heard a voice causing her to set her book down. Peering into the peephole she saw that it was Jack. She stood there shifting his head to the sides as if there was someone else in the halls with him.

When finally took it upon herself to open the door, there right at her doorstep stood Jack and two men wearing the Seer cloaks similar to Elder Arthur.

Isa took a step back and quickly grabbed something she hid behind her.

"Hey Foxy, got a second to spare?" Jack asked as the two other men sharpened their eyes behind him.

13

Seer Slayer Attack

"Uhhhhhh"

"We're not going to hurt you, Isa, we are just going to ask a few questions to decide your Seer rank." The man who has a long ponytail says, smiling at Isa while the other Seer remains still and analyzes Isa from head to toe. He scoffs when she spots her attire.

Agreeing to follow them, they lead Isa down into an elevator that takes them to the floor she was on before with the different colored doors. Jack took the fun route and used the tunnels at the side of the building, sliding down to the level below. Awaiting in the halls, Isa tensed at the door they stood in front of. It was the door with the red eye.

"I'll wait out here, I'm not allowed in. I only came to give you emotional support." Jack said, opening the door for them. The two Seers nod in approval and walk past Jack, gesturing to Isa to enter.

"Thanks." The side of Isa's mouth lifts. She pats Jack's shoulder on her way inside, prompting as a small gesture to show her gratitude. (She's rarely a touchy type of person, so this is a big deal.)

Jack's eyes lit up in joy as if it made him feel as though he was getting somewhere with her. When he first met Isa, he noticed how tense and slightly wary she was. Granted, the kidnapping could make any being upset, magical or non-magical. In an effort to relieve the situation, he did the one thing he was best at, flirting.

When he had made attempts to jokingly flirt with her, she managed to lower her guard a little. He liked how she felt comfortable enough to talk to him. He much preferred to have Isa snap at him than for her to ignore him.

He also found her tempter to be extremely adorable as she was smaller than him and reminded him of a feisty little fox he raised at his farm, hence the nickname he gave her.

(Though, I would say her temper is more like a chihuahua, but I don't think Jack knows what that is.)

He felt bad about almost killing her with the whole portal incident.

It ate him to bits.

From that point on, all he wanted to do was protect Isa as he would for anyone on his team. Even if they all got on his nerves, (especially Vero), he still cared for them and was additionally hopeful that someday he would be able to be enough for everyone. Part of him would like to think that when he is able to pass his exams, he will find someone who could banter with him and spend late nights cuddled up in blankets.

He wanted someone who understood him behind the playboy façade everyone made him out to be. Though, he was far from a playboy. It was always Jack who got heartbroken and cheated on for a couple of laughs.

He was waiting for something real.

Walking into the room, Isa noticed how incredibly dark it was despite the candles that were lit here and there. The sounds of chimes and waves played in the background while everyone sat on their pillow seats and had their eyes closed completely unbothered. There were people who wore their cloaks and some who didn't, like the blue-haired figure in the corner of the room whose hair slightly glowed. Sitting on the floor with a pillow and surrounded by a circle of candles was Haru.

Like the Seers, those who were sorcerers of shadows had used this room to meditate to best manage their ability. Seers meditated in hopes of bringing out visions, while sorcerers of shadows meditated to keep control of their inner demons.

Haru had to do this daily as it became part of his routine since he was young. He often trained with the shadow of the candlestick or worked with his mobility in the dark from going from one side of the room to the other.

Hearing the door open, he too noticed Isa and gave her a reassuring nod and wave. Those around them began to whisper as they curiously broke out of their meditation to see what the new Seer was like.

"That's her?" A Seer with purple hair asks under her breath.

"She's supposed to find the next relic. What a joke."

"I heard she's from the Human realm."

"What's with the jumpsuit?"

"Where's her cloak?"

Like a thousand raindrops sounds of whispers filled the room, most of which Isa caught on to. At the sides of her hips, she clenches her fist, taking a deep breath. She told herself to bid them no mind.

Walking past Haru and deeper into the room the two Seers led her into another door to an area more secluded. Inside the room is a simple table and a series of scented candles making the room smell like gingerbread. Taking a seat, the man who was kinder looking started asking questions, skipping away their introductions.

"When was the last time you had a vision?" He asked.

"Uh, maybe since I was a kid?"

"Lie." said the serious-looking man.

"How did he know that?"

"Because I can read your mind and emotions," he responds.

"John here is a level three Seer. Think of this as one of those lie-detector tests. He can tell when you are lying as well as what you are thinking. Now please answer honestly." The Seer urges Isa and proceeds to take notes on a piece of paper.

"Fine. The last time I had a vision was about three months ago when I saw Dylan, my ex, cheat on me with my cousin. I haven't had any more visions besides that."

"She's telling the truth," John said.

"Thank you for your honesty. Now, have you had visions of the relics or anything revolving around the Celestial Realm?"

"No," replied Isa.

John nods his head, and the other Seer proceeds to ask her questions about the duration of her visions and how frequent they may have been. They were surprised by her results considering that the human world usually suppresses them to the extent that people simply experience Deja Vu.

Since Isa was able to have somewhat stable visions, the two Seers in front of her had concluded that she might be either a level two Seer or a level three who had not yet gained abilities such as mind reading. They believe that if Isa does the soulmate ritual, she will reach the potential of being a level three Seer once and for all.

"I'll think about the ritual," Isa responded quickly. John must've listened to her thoughts because both men did not pressure Isa anymore. They simply reminded Isa of what is at stake.

"Last question and then you may return to your room. It's part of the protocol."

Isa nods her head and listens to the question.

"Have you seen any spirits?"

"Spirits? Like ghosts?" Isa inquiries.

"Yes," answered both men.

As Isa opened her mouth to answer, the sound of an explosion erupted inside the building. Bursting out of a shadow in the corner of the room is Haru with widened blackened eyes and neon hair.

"S-s-she's"

"Who?"

"T-t-the"

"Out with it boy!" John shouts at him.

"The Seer Slayer! She's here!" Haru said, coming out of his trance as the whites of his eyes appeared on the surface.

The building shakes once more and screams fill the air. Instinctively, both Seers instructed Haru to take Isa somewhere safe as they called for reinforcements. Alarms were blaring and debris was everywhere while Haru tried to guide Isa out of the meditation room.

Holding the door open, Jack rushed everyone outside and told them to use their portals to get out of there. When he saw Haru and Isa, he had a small moment of relief until another shake snaked underneath their feet. They all slam to the ground and place their hands over their heads.

"We gotta portal out of here," Jack shouts over the alarms.

"You do that, I need to find Vero. Go without me." Haru spouts as he meticulously types on his watch. In that instant, Haru grabs the small cube from his pocket and opens a portal.

"Wait, I don't have my transporter!" Jack shouted right when Haru was already out of sight. He glances over his shoulder to meet Isa's horrified expression.

"What do you mean you don't have your transporter?"

"It's in my room! Quick get away from the win-" another blast hits.

Isa yelps as the cracks widen underneath the heels of her feet. One wrong step and she could slip to her next life.

"Jack!" Her voice grows wary. She scanned for any solid ground, except, there was hardly any.

"Hold on!"

"To wha-"

The center of the building splits into two, widening the cracks until there is nothing to keep them together. All magic that once kept the building bound crumbled underneath whatever strong force was used. Debris was in the air, clouding Isa's vision, leaving every opportunity for her to accidentally fall into her grave (which she did).

The poor girl slid into a three-floor free fall until her hand caught onto a steel metal wire hovering between two sharp cracks in the glass flooring. There was one small opening, and it was to the bottom. In that instant, she felt like she was dangling on a tightrope, and sharp glass was her safety net.

Unlike her, Jack had the leverage of his ability and was thrown in the opposite direction where he was not at risk of being crushed. He caught himself mid-fall and created little stepping air pads beneath his feet.

(It's one of the benefits of being an elemental sorcerer.)

He carefully runs to Isa as there is nothing but air for him to walk on. However, he couldn't go right to her as Isa was caught in between two edges that Jack by no means would be able to fit. There was an opening large enough for her to slip through if she was brave enough to fall.

"Let go and grab on to me,"

He fiercely extended his hands a few feet below her. Shards of glass were stuck to her hair and trickled down to the cuts at her knees. She made one look beneath her shoes and instantly regretted it.

"Ni madres."

Half of the building at this point was ready to collapse and she was well aware of how high up they were. The air was thin enough to choke her.

"You don't have a choice. Please, just trust me this once." he cries as tears cloud his eyes.

"Trust you?" Isa defensively asks herself, thinking back on Dylan. She allowed herself to fall once. It was her biggest mistake.

What makes Jack any different?

"Agh!" Isa flinches, feeling small burns on her knuckles. There were shades of orange and red approaching.

"Jack!"

"You have to let go!"

"No, there has to be another way." She negotiates. The wire was bending, and Jack was trying not to move away from his position. He was close to being impaled by a random spear that must've come from the weapon room. It sliced past him and hit the center of a burnt dart board.

"There is no other way. You have to believe me."

"But-"

"Please, Isa!"

"I can'-"

"He is your teammate. Trust him." A feminine voice inside of her commanded. Isa's fingers twitched and the sensation in her stomach grew. She ignored it once before and paid the price. She had to listen to it.

"You swear you'll catch me?" Isa bites her lower lip as she loosens one hand.

"Yes!" Jack shouts, raising his hands higher for her. "Hurry!"

Swinging from the wire, Isa unravels the thorns of her flower. She swiftly lands into Jack's hold and makes sure to never let go. A final explosion erupts above them sealing the fate of the remaining levels.

Not far from them was the attacker on a high-tech hoverboard throwing electrical bombs. The figure shouted a few things here and there, but none seemed clear against the piercing wails of the structure. The attacker wore all black and had a metal face covering.

"It's the Seer Slayer!" Jack said, far too loudly. Regret washed over him as the Seer Slayer turned their attention to them.

"Oh fae."

'THERE YOU ARE ISA!" The Seer Slayer screeched followed by a strange maniacal laugh.

"JACK RUN!" Followed another voice.

Zooming at the edge of the clouds with a replica of the Seer Slayers hoverboard is Will. From the scratches on his face and the slashes on his body, it looked as though he had been fighting hand-to-hand with the Sleer Slayer.

"Get ready!" He hollered, throwing a small cube past them like a baseball. He ditches his hoverboard and freefalls into the portal with Jack and Isa in front of him. Meeting Isa's gaze he turns his head and spots the Seer Slayer spiraling downward in their direction.

When she nears the opening of the portal, she plummets off her hoverboard and dove further in closer to Isa. Her hands widened with talons on her fingers, excited for her new addition to her collection of captive Seers.

Isa was the one Seer she needed. She was the one who could either help or get in the way of the Seer Slayer's goal.

Horrified, Isa fights her off within the portal as Jack and Will both do their own part. Jack held tightly onto Isa's waist while Will waited for the perfect moment to close the portal.

The Seer Slayer's grip on the other hand was impeccable compared to a hawk as her nails dug deeper into her skin the more Isa tried to fight her off. At some point, Isa needed to unravel Jack's from her waist in order to have more mobility to fight off the Seer Slayer. Doing so, she strikes Jack away from her and uses her legs against the Seer.

Isa then instructs Jack to throw a ball of flame at them. He hesitates at first but does as instructed. He throws one directly at them and maneuvers his body closer to Will.

"I can't keep us in for much longer," Will yells spreading his arms open like a bird as if he was bending the portal open.

Luckily, Isa swayed at the right moment causing the ball of fire to burst open and hit the Seer Slayer in the torso. She flinches in pain, loosening her grip on Isa. With one strike of her metal gauntlets, Isa escapes and kicks the Seer Slayer further away from her. This whole time she had been wearing them after Jack had knocked on her door. It was for precautionary measure.

"Close it now Will!" Jack shouts over his shoulder to Will and shoves Isa closer to the exit. With all his might he pulls out his ax and swings the metal-faced woman away.

With a bang and crash landing in the other realm, Will immediately closed the portal behind him, with only a few seconds to spare.

They lay there inside the dimmed realm that had cushioned their fall. All three were breathing heavily.

"Let me guess, that was the Seer Slayer?" Isa asks, picking herself up.

The floor was incredibly cushioned as it felt as though she was on a trampoline. In the realm they landed in, the sky lacked the sun as it was always night. The golden sand beneath them soothed Isa as if it begged her to take a nap in it.

Around them sounds of rivers and streams played in the background followed by various snores coming from houses near them.

"Yup." Both Jack and Will respond simultaneously.

"Well, isn't she just lovely," Isa yawned stretching her body. She felt a stinging sensation as pieces of sand were slipping under her skin.

"Ouch," Isa flinches spotting the place where her body hurt the most.

There on Isa's arm was an elongated scratch the Seer Slayer left.

Betrayal

14

Betrayal

They were a few miles away from the facility in the Flialight forest after Will portaled them out of the Night Realm.

When Will first opened the portal he thought of dropping them off somewhere that had rocks and boulders, so if the Seer Slayer were to attack them, they would have more of a high ground with Jack's Elemental abilities. Though he would much rather not have them crashing to their death.

So, his best bet was the Night Realm, the origin of the Sand Man's territory. The sand would cushion the fall and if needed, Jack could maneuver the sand around them and like quicksand, consume the Seer Slayer.

It was one of those niche Realms no one minded and often left untouched. Once you sleep in the Night Realm, there is no waking up. It was one of the reasons why travelers and sorcerers do not portal there despite its alluring nature. Any newcomers should be cautious as it was often confused with the Vampiric Realm. Both were dark in the atmosphere but had their fair share of features.

"Well, what do we do now?" Isa asks lifting herself off the ground and dusting herself. The scratch left from the Seer Slayer remained completely present on her skin making it clear Isa is the one she is after. It was aggravated and bled down her arm.

Coming out of the portal, Jack responds, shaking off the sand particles.

"We walk. Doesn't this place seem familiar to you?" He gestured to the world around them.

Underneath their feet were small shards of glass that looked like Isa's previous glasses. Above them was a nice clear sky of hues of blue, pink, and orange intertwined and huge thick trees that towered over them. Beside Isa was a bush filled with orange-looking berries. She pulls one off the bush and eats it, tasting the familiarity of it. It reminded her of an orange soda drink as it disintegrated in her mouth.

"It does." Isa blinks scanning her surroundings. The climate has changed as a breeze caught hold of her hair dragging it behind her.

It is the exact same place Isa had landed on when she first came here and was thrown out of the portal. That must mean that Elder Arthur's house must be close somewhere in the midst of the forest.

"We'll need to patch up your arm first before we head on over," Will says pulling out a first aid kit from his backpack he conveniently had on. He hands it over to Jack who knows how to tend wounds better than anyone. Especially since Jack had always been the one to end up getting hurt during battle practices as his training was physically intensive, like his ability. Most of the skills regarding patching things up were all thanks to Jessie the healer.

It was obvious to everyone that the two had a connection. Yet, something was always in the way preventing them from moving forward.

As the two patched their wounds, sitting there on a log slouching is Will. He didn't bother to fix himself up as if he felt as though he deserved to endure every single injury to his skin.

(Most of this damage done was because of him. Yup, you heard me right.)

After Kate's betrayal, behind everyone's back, he kept in contact with her and fed her all the information he knew would help Kate and her soulmate stay alive as minions of the Seer Slayer. Kate knew exactly what she was doing when she reached out to Will because she knew his heart. She knew that he would never deny her because he was still in love with her despite Kate being long gone from her relationship. She was committed to her soulmate, George.

Will didn't want to help her, in fact, he wanted so badly to stop the Seer Slayer, but the tug in his heart was as strong as the siren's songs to an enchanted fisherman. He was well aware that Kate was his siren, and he is the poor fisherman who is about to crash the ship.

It was one of those elf traits of his to be loyal to those who held his heart. As if their bodies were bound and controlled under an oath of love.

In other words, when elves fall in love, they fall deeply. It's one of the reasons why Will despised being half-elf so much, along with the fact that the other elves saw him as some kind of half-breed mutt.

But that's beside the point.

When Elder Arthur had confided in him and the team of his vision of Isa, Will went ahead and notified Kate, who then notified the Seer Slayer. Will has never met the Seer Slayer but based on what Kate had told him, she was ruthless. If a Seer was deemed insignificant, she would order George to slaughter them, and Kate would watch her soulmate do it right in front of her eyes.

"He's only doing this for something greater. He is protecting me. It's part of the deal with the Seer Slayer. If he kills and does what she says, we both live." Kate would tell Will.

Will was incredibly disgusted but still found himself to be loyal to Kate. That was until his eyes met with Isa's. After Isa had arrived, that's when everything changed for him. He didn't care about Kate anymore. It was as if the siren spell broke *because it did.*

He found his pairing. Similar to how werewolves imprint, elves have their way of finding their mates, but in a less physical manner. All it takes is one look and it all makes sense. He wanted to hug her and see what Isa would look like with a smile on her face. Since her arrival, all Isa did was scowl and frown in her underlying confusion and fear.

(Granted Will, you weren't necessarily giving Isa a happy welcome. What did you expect with that terrible mediocre mean guy act? That she'll give you a cookie? Come on this isn't amateur hour.)

Will did his best to not look her in the eyes and suppress any signs that he would be interested in her. He would hide underneath an angry facade that eventually led to a scolding from Haru.

Prior to meeting her, he made the grave mistake of telling them about Isa's arrival. He knew he had to find a way to at least provide herself some protection, so when they arrived at the Celestial facility, he was ready to make her a weapon to defend herself if Kate and the Seer Slayer were waiting for her there.

(I mean, they kinda were…)

"Who is she?" Kate said looking at her bloodied crimson nails while standing in the middle of his living room after he had just taken a nap. He had hoped if he didn't give her any answers it would buy him some time to warn the others.

"What?"

"Who is she? You don't look at me the same anymore. You found someone." Kate responds still not looking up at him just yet. Instead, she walks towards him and grazes her finger on his face.

He says nothing. Absolutely nothing because she was right. She too had been waiting for the day his elf instincts kicked in and his heart would be under a stronger love spell, the long-lasting kind.

"I'm glad you found someone; I can only hope your heart is strong enough for when she breaks it," she said, slicing him with her glare.

"Like you did with mine?" Will snaps stepping away from her, reaching for his backpack. He knew what was coming, it was only a matter of time.

"Oh, give me a break! While I did care about you, what we had was nothing serious. Now your elf imprint mating thing has kicked in! Let's hope she actually likes you." Kate snaps, pulling her hand away from his face.

"Imprinting is for werewolves; elves establish bonds." He corrects her.

"Whatever. Looks like I will have to tell the boss to blow this place up since you won't tell me where your beloved Seer is. She'll find her regardless. She's desperate."

"She won't. I'll make sure of it." His jaw clenches as his thoughts revisited Isa. "You can too, if you wanted to. You know you're picking the wrong side. I only did because my body was tied to your commands."

"You make it sound too easy."

"Cut your strings, Kate. You're not a puppet and neither am I."

Kate's eyes wavered as though she genuinely considered Will's suggestion.

"But it won't change what we-" She pauses correcting herself. "You did. What will the team think once they find out? That they'll accept you without ridicule. You set a bounty on the girl, Will. Let's not forget that. You might as well finish what you started."

Will grimaces, turning the other cheek. "No."

"It's your funeral." Kate flashes a forced grin, disappearing into her opened portal. "It's been fun Will."

Seconds later, that's when the Seer Slayer attacked the building with her mini bombs. He tried his best to fight her off, but she was quite skillful with her hoverboard. She dodged every object Will threw at her like some type of contortionist. She would retaliate by throwing bombs directly at Will and the small blades he once made for Kate.

Now there he was in the forest slightly listening to Jack and Isa talk about what happened.

Isa thanked Jack for catching her and he gave a sly proud remark about it not being a big deal. The two seemed to establish a new rise of friendship that once was unlikely. As they walked, the two both shared bits of their lives and found the common ground in dealing with heartbreak.

Isa had told him about her cheating ex, and Jack opened up about his dating failures. Jack tried to bring Will to the conversation by mentioning Kate, but that only made Will want to keep his mouth shut even more.

"Is that why you are hesitant about the whole soulmate ritual thing?" Jack gently asked while hopping over a log that was in the way.

"Yeah, but I think I'm ready. Talking about it with you helped. Plus, I doubt it will be long until our next encounter with Miss Slayer."

"Miss Slayer?" Jack chuckles running his hands through his hair and flashing his subtle freckles to the sun.

"Clever, isn't it?" Isa smiles wavering her eyes between him and Will. His mouth sealed like the walls he built around him. Isa assumed the attack did a number on him and let him be.

"I also hope you find your soulmate too, maybe we can have a double date after your soulmate ritual?" Isa laughs at her suggestion.

"I like the idea, foxy. I'll make sure it happens." The corners of Jack's mouth lift ever so quickly as if he could imagine the double date right then and there.

Meanwhile, Will remained silent the entire walk, trying to come up with a way to amend the mess he made. He knew what he needed to do once he spotted Elder Arthur, but it was only a matter of what they would think of him after they found out.

By the time they arrived at Elder Arthur's home, right at the door stood Vero and Haru waiting for them. Both of them seemed to be fine, yet they shared a look of concern as they opened the door to the living room.

"We have a mole." Elder Arthur said, sitting on one of the couches with his eyebrows completely furrowed.

Exposed

"Don't worry Elder Arthur when I get my hands on them, I'll- "

Elder Arthur lifts his palm in the air halting Jack from his excitement as he spots the flames channeling at his fingertips.

"That won't be necessary."

"But- "

"I know who it is." He pensively strokes his mid-length bushy beard, barely sparing a glance at Will. "I have kept them hidden for far too long enough, as we have seen after today's incident."

"I beg your pardon?"

"You kept the mole a secret?" Vero stiffens, tightening her grip around her staff. "Why? You were so quick to sever ties with Kate. What makes this mole any different? Huh?"

"Easy Vero. He might have a reason. Right Elder Arthur?"

Elder Arthur sighs and continues to intensively stroke his beard. Isa approaches him placing her hand on his shoulder, turning his attention to her.

"Who is it, Elder Arthur?' Isa prodded. Her eyebrows knitted together, scrunching above the bridge of her pointed nose.

"It's me," Will confessed, out from behind Jack, centering himself in the middle.

"No way!" Jack loudly gasped pressing the palm of his hand to his heart. "Dude! We trusted you. *I* trusted you."

"I know I'm sorry."

"You're sorry? You got the entire facility blown up. It was our home." Haru motions to Vero. Her expression was convoluted to nothing. It was enough to raise all the hairs on Will's neck and make Jack shiver.

"Vero?" He says softly, wishing she yelled at him. Any reaction than this would give him hope that their friendship had not yet been severed. "Say something."

She takes a deep breath, slowly walking up to him; her steps heavy on the floorboard beneath her. Haru's hair shimmered to a light glow.

Meeting the tips of his shoes, her face hovers over his as her eyes stay at the level of his chin. "Tell me this isn't true." She demands, her voice clear and cold as the river water in the Flora Realm.

The corner of his ears turns bright red underneath his darkened complexion. His lips wavered but his vocal cords remained tamed with regretful silence.

"Tell me!" she shouts at him, her fists clenching at the sides.

"It's true." He whispers to her.

"You knew what she has been doing. The people that those sick maniacs have killed…and you still gave her our intel?" Vero questions him, trying to wrap her head around his intentions.

He gulped, lightly nodding his head, barely touching her forehead.

"Look at me when I'm talking to you!" she shouts at him, flinging her weapon to the ground.

Will doesn't flinch. He stands there unable to look down right at his best friend. His best friend who he once spent late nights talking to whenever the world felt too heavy. His best friend who teased him like an older sister, day and night when he had no one. His best friend was also connected to Kate, as much as anyone in the room.

"Very well." She takes three small steps back away from him. Her jaw was completely clenched together as her body shook in anger. "You knew what was coming."

Right then and there Vero raises her hand, causing Will to lift from the air and hit the wall of the living room. Pieces of the picture frames that were on the wall crash onto the ground along with Will.

Using her telekinetic abilities, she picks up Will's body once again and slams him to the other side of the room, shattering Elder Arthur's beautiful display of artifacts.

Shockingly enough, Elder Arthur doesn't step in. Rather, he stood there in silence, folding his hands together.

"Fight back dammit!" She heaves within the depths of her chest as she lifts her hand in a motion as though it were on Will's neck.

"Never." He wheezes. "I don't want to hurt you, Vero."

"You already did." Her grip sharpens. A single teardrop escapes the corner of her calloused eyes, dripping down to her soft chin.

Will's fangs pricked his lips as he struggled against the wall, impotent to breathe under her telekinetic fury.

Haru gently stops her, hovering his hand over hers.

"I'm angry too, but we need to hear his side of the story," he whispers into her ear.

She retracts her hand and uses the other to summon her dropped staff.

"There better be a good explanation."

This moment reminded Vero of her early childhood, prior to meeting everyone. At the age of five, her parents were the first ones to betray her.

Without any notice, in the middle of the night, while she had been asleep, they sent her away with a supposed family relative where she had been put in situations no child should be in.

She was sent to her "aunt" Nix. Upon arrival at her domain, she set fire to Vero's carriage and set free the horses. Ridding Vero's only way to get out of there. She then jabbed Vero with poison and bound her into a locked shed.

When Vero got herself out, she met more of Nix's antics.

It was only the start.

Nix had once thrown Vero into a lake where it had been known for its rouge waves. She claimed it was training so that Vero could learn how to swim for their next upcoming performance. There had been another occasion where Nix had given her the task of balancing herself on a tightrope without a safety net below. When she fell off the beam, Vero used her telekinetic abilities to float herself in time. That's when the new challenges came in.

She battled with flames, mythical beasts, and whatever trial Nix tried to throw at her, but Vero always had something up her sleeve as she learned to use her ability to see what she couldn't.

In every circus performance, she was seen as either a prodigy as she managed to harness her ability to view the world like no other, or the blind child everyone pitied.

She wanted neither title.

After the performances, Vero's parents came to see her but not out of the kindness of their hearts. They only came to see if she was capable. They didn't want a weak blind daughter in a family line of warriors. If she wasn't alive within the next week, she would've died as a failure to them.

Vero knew this of course, as she was often compared to her siblings on a daily basis. The only thing that kept her going was her perseverance in becoming a better warrior than her entire family combined. She wanted to be the one to put them in their place. They do not get to disown her. Rather, she will be the one to disown them.

Though, Vero's troubles didn't end there as her family knew of her intentions. So, they hired Nix for one final task.

One unfortunate night, Nix attempted to come at Vero with a knife while she was sleeping.

Nix unmistakably chose the wrong tactic to get rid of her because Vero learned her lesson since her deep sleep is what brought her to this mess in the first place. When the time came, with her telekinetic abilities, she was able to stop Nix inches before the blade reached her chest. Right on the spot, Vero pinned Nix to the wall and choked her to death in the same way she was about to do to Will.

She in turn picked up the knife Nix dropped and kept it. Vero was tempted to cut off her bones and feed them to one of Nix's pets, what she called the Chupacabra. She decided against it, as she did not want to deal with Nix's body and the potential bloody mess. Instead, she summoned the others using signal fireworks and perfectly arranged Nix's story.

When the authorities came, she blamed her death on a bottle of poison beside her coffee mug that Nix must've mistakenly drunk. (That same poison was in Vero's whip she used to paralyze others. Too much of the poison could paralyze a person's heart.)

No one suspected Vero and soon after, she was sent to the same boarding school where she met Haru. Of course, she had kept her own little secret to herself.

All she wanted to be is Vero. Just Vero. Not the blind girl, the miracle child, the murderer, or any of that sort. With Haru, that's all she was. They indeed had an interesting relationship as the two had their demons tango with one another. She would hold him when he was having one of his dark episodes, and he would hold her in bed just so she could feel safe while sleeping.

Unlike all her relatives and other exes, Haru never gave her a reason not to trust him.

When she wasn't with Haru, she would trust Kate who was like a sister she wished she had. Kate was the one girl in her classroom who stood up for her when the other girls had spread crude rumors about Vero's dating life. They frequently had late-night conversations and at one point were roommates. They would hunt together and do any classic best friend activity such as doing each other's hair (mostly Kate did Vero's) and plan outings for their forest hunt.

When they arrived at the Celestial Facility, Vero befriended Will during their training and then introduced him to Kate.

Everything worked so well when the group was together. It felt like Vero had finally made a family of her own with the people she surrounded herself with.

She never expected that all of it would fall apart so quickly.

"As I said, there is no explanation. It's all my fault." Will quavers, taking full accountability.

"You don't even have an explanation to give us?" Vero snarls as Haru holds her aside.

"No."

"Say it," Isa speaks up, taking their focus, Elder Arthur's included.

"Say what?"

"Your explanation."

"I said I don't have-"

"Bullsh-" Isa spats.

"Language," Jack mutters over her.

"There's always an explanation. Whether it's good or bad, there's always something a cheater-liar has to explain. In fact, I can provide one."

His eyes widen. "And that is?"

"Why you were nice all of a sudden. I thought it was too odd and out of line." Isa scoffs. "Men like you only do that sort of thing before they do something bad. And you did! YOU. You of all people went ahead and put a bounty on me. I am all she wants. " Isa growled as the stirring feeling inside her stomach escalated within her, deepening her emotions. It was liberating yet unnerving as she didn't know how to control it. It just kept growing.

"I should've known the second you accused me of being suspicious at the dinner table. It was so obvious. But yet…"

Just like when she confronted her ex, Dylan, she looked Will in the eyes, and with one hand she grabbed his shirt and pulled him up closer to his face while his knees were touching the floor. In her other hand was an arrow that she had stored in her medieval metal thigh-high boots she found in her closet. They had a perfect pocket to store one arrow on each.

"What I don't understand is why on earth did you decide to craft me these?"

Pointing the sharp tip at his throat, Isa bounces at the tip of her toes. "You have another ulterior motive! Tell me why! I deserve to know. Stop turning your neck and say something."

His lips kept closed and his head drooped downward. Strangely enough, all he could concentrate on was *her*. Her cinnamon scent brushed his nose —— oh how the curls of her hair moved with her body drove him insane. One look at her eyes and he would crumble.

"I said speak!" Isa kicks his side and riles him to the wall breathing heavily. Her temper getting the best of her. "You told me the next time I held a blade to your neck you'll make me pay. Go on. I dare you. Take the arrow from my hands."

"Oh, here we go again," Jack comments under his breath, somewhat covering his eyes.

Planted between her knees, Isa still couldn't get him to meet her glare. She felt ignored. Unseen. Unheard. All the ways Dylan made her feel when she confronted him. It gave her every reason to release the latch to the Pandora's box of animosity she kept buried. It was never-ending. The fact that she was still thinking about him now made her even angrier.

Before she knew it, the arrow had pierced the first layer of skin on his neck. Her brown eyes faded swiftly replacing them with a tint of a darkened red. Vero felt the change in her energy. It was what first drew her to Isa. It was strange. Foreign. Dark. She did not like it.

"Take it from me! Do it!" Isa shouts, her face inches from his.

"Enough!" Jack steps in grabbing her shoulder. If she dug any more than she did, his blood would flood the room and, well you know the rest…

Isa snaps back to her normal state, blinking vigorously as if she had never let herself get this far. Her fingertips began to tremble and the dark matter in her stomach silenced itself.

What's happening to me? Isa unnervingly asked herself as everyone in the room was staring at her. They expected a strong reaction from Vero, but not from Isa. It felt as though her body had been swept from underneath her and taken over by another persona deep inside herself.

She releases him and reinserts the blood-stained red metal arrow in the pocket of her boot. Part of her expected Will to make some sort of comeback, but he had gone silent.

"You will repay the team by giving us all the details you know. The only reason you're still on the team is because I have read your thoughts and knew this was coming. I hope you can keep yourself in line now that you and Kate are done." Elder Arthur says conclusively.

From that point on, the team sat in the living room hearing every single detail Will was able to provide. He told them about the Seers the Seer Slayer has killed so far and how many relics the Seer Slayer has collected. There were only two pieces left, the handle and the bottom stand of the lamp. The key detail Will left out was what was happening with the half-elf part of himself. Knowing that Elder Arthur was able to read his thoughts, he must know about the elf bond between him and Isa.

The entire time Isa was glaring at him like how he glared at her when they first met. She hated him. No. She *despised* him for putting her life at risk.

"Okay, well since Will is no longer tied to Kate as his elf loyalty has been broken, he will remain on this team until we have the two relics. I do not want to hear any more complaints. Until the Celestial Facility is reconstructed, I will be monitoring Will and Isa under my roof. Is that clear?" Elder Arthur said finally.

"But I don't-" Isa began to protest.

"Will has nowhere else to go. Like your teammates, the Celestial Facility is his home. The room you now occupy was his previous room. He has the same reason to stay here as much as you do. I'm going to ask you again, is that clear?" Elder Arthur snaps.

"Yes, Elder Arthur." They mumble under their breath in unison.

"Good, in the meantime, I want you all to get groceries for me at the marketplace. I will have a chat with Will. Isa, you will need to stay here in the living room."

"But-"

"While the Seer Slayer is still out there, you must remain here and train." Elder Arthur snaps once more, swaying his beard over to his shoulder.

Leaving Elder Arthur's cottage, it was clear that they all had their conflict with Will.

In the eyes of Haru, Vero, and Jack, they somewhat had some sympathy for Will as they understood how elves were known for their compassion. They lived in harmony as they mostly led with their hearts rather than their minds. Yet, despite their compassionate nature, it is also the reason why they were cold to everyone else who wasn't their kind. All it takes is one sudden heartbreak from their bond mate or someone they're close with, and they die.

While they slowly became understanding as they spent the day getting groceries from the local shops, Isa was fuming in the living room.

She was surprised she didn't hear any shouting or noise from Elder Arthur's room as Will was in definite need of a good scolding. Filled with curiosity, Isa attempted to put her ear to the door. When she did, it opened right in front of her.

"Couldn't hear anything huh? With some of this, all private matters stay private matters." Elder Arthur said holding up some sort of jar with pink salt with one hand and sprinkling more at his doorway with the other.

"You two will train in the backyard while I call my fellow elders. Before you do, Isa, I do have a matter to ask of you. Will you go outside and set up." He said, turning to Will and then to Isa.

Isa angrily stumbles into the dark room and sits down on a fluffy chair, or at least what she thought was a chair. Next to her is the glowing mushroom she spotted in her previous time coming into his room. For some reason, she couldn't keep her eyes away from it.

"I know you're not happy about this but I'm going to need you to work with me. I also want to discuss the soulmate ritual. Today, Seer John and Jamil will be coming to give you your Seer cloak. They will also be bringing the rose quartz so that you have a soulmate mark to strengthen your Seer abilities. With the events at the facility today, I'm afraid they won't give you the option anymore. In return, I'll give you this as an apology for all that you will be going through."

Elder Arthur then goes on his knees and makes a small bow on the floor right in front of Isa. Soon after, he whispers something in his hand and gives it to Isa. It was a small black teleportation cube with a bunch of runes. Immediately Isa lets out a gasp and returns a bow to Elder Arthur.

"With this, you can go to your realm and swiftly come back, as we do need you, Isa. You don't want me to have Vero hunting you down, do you?" The corner of his lips rises giving a small chuckle.

"Thank you, Elder Arthur. Don't worry, I'll be back as soon as I can." She responds returning a chuckle.

16

Red

The first training lesson, as Elder Arthur promised, is to learn how to use the cube. Standing on the lawn of Elder Arthur's home was Will waiting for Isa underneath the trees connecting to the forest. Perched on his shoulders was a small phoenix. It swung and extended its feathers with glee whenever Will scratched her favorite spot. When it sensed Isa, the bird lifted its elongated bright wings and flew past her cawing in the air with glee.

Isa's mouth widened in awe, placing her hand over her brow as the sun's rays caressed her skin. Her hair brightened like a flame and swayed with the cooling breeze passing through the forest.

Waiving to the bird as it flew further away from the cottage, Isa returned her attention to Will. The sides of her cheeks fell, and her eyebrows reallocated pensively.

"I didn't know you could do that."

"Do what?"

"Smile."

"Don't patronize me."

Isa shoots him with a disdainful expression and fidgets with the cube in her hand as she walks over to him.

On Will's neck was a smudge of green regeneration salve Elder Arthur gave him. As much as he tried to play it cool after the whole confrontation, he was nervous.

Thankfully, Isa could not tell for when she stood in front of him, she avoided giving him a second glance. She couldn't stand how on earth she would be able to tolerate someone who would stoop to his level and put someone's life at risk, especially when he had pinned her for being suspicious.

If he was going to attempt to gain Isa's trust, it was going to require more than a couple of training lessons.

Holding out the galactic black cube in the palm of her hands, Will understood what she wanted.

"How does this cube work?"

"First off, it's called a transporter." He corrects her. "The way it works is that you think of the realm you want to go to. Then you toss it where you want the portal to appear. It's easy, any magic and non-magic *Hue* can do it."

Isa intensifies her glare at the mention of Hues and does as he says.

Watching her carefully, Will couldn't help but gaze at how her hair became that of a sunset at the touch of the sunlight. He liked the way her eyes furrowed, creating a small crease on her forehead as she concentrated on the transporter in her hands.

Additionally, he fought the urge to boop her nose whenever she scrunched her face when she wanted to raise the frames of her new glasses without touching them. The glasses he had made for *her*.

As she held the cube, he couldn't help but notice the roughness of her fingertips. Isa had the habit of frequently picking her hands whenever she seemed tense. She did it when she walked into the portal after Haru had given her the plushie Will made.

If they weren't so distant from one another, Will would most be happy to have her play with his hand for comfort.

"It didn't work, qué porquería." Isa scowls, throwing the cube on the ground frustrated at the ten attempts she made.

"Language."

"Porquería isn't a bad word."

"It sounded like one."

"Isn't there anyone else to teach me?"

'Well, the others are currently out and after this, I will be teaching you archery."

"I can wait. Maybe Vero can teach me."

"Do you really want to waste time? I thought you wanted to go home as soon as possible. If Vero taught you archery, your arrows would never leave the bow. Jack would probably get you hurt by lighting the arrows on fire, and Haru would be too nice, and he often fails to shoot his own arrows properly. I'm your best shot Red."

"Enough with the nicknames!"

Isa frowns gaping her mouth as Will walks closer to her.

"I have a theory," Will says, picking up the transporter thrown next to him, and tossing it back to Isa. "We're gonna try another realm. Think of a place filled with clouds, gold, wine, and a bunch of gods. Just imagine it."

Isa looks at him skeptically weighing the cube at her fingertips.

"What do you get to lose?" She asks herself, taking a few steps back.

She stares directly into the forest, envisioning the realm Will had described. The cube starts to vibrate in her hand, shimmering colors of a rainbow.

"Throw it now!" Will shouts.

Isa tosses the transporter in the middle of the air opening the swirly and colorful portal in all its glory. She dives right into the portal and is greeted by the blinding sight of the Godly Realm. A firm breeze kisses her cheek, causing her to shiver.

In front of her was a Roman temple and a line of people waiting to enter to meet Juno. The clouds underneath her feet felt like she was walking on balls of cotton.

Far up above was the gradual change from a clear blue to a dark black that held constellations. In the night sky area, she saw a small piece of land floating which Isa guessed had been Olympus. Coming out of the Greek structure were somewhat audible sounds of dance music blaring and colorful disco lights. On the clouded area that Isa was standing on were other temples and small shops representing the specific religion they are associated with.

"Let's go before Artemis tries to adopt you like she almost did with Vero or Loki tries to trick you into selling your soul," Will whispers right behind her and gestures to the portal. Isa punches his gut, threatening him to keep his distance. He however was not phased.

"There are so many people."

"Not really." He turns around eyeing their surroundings. In his perspective, there was possibly a handful of demigods or people from other realms traveling to carry on their tasks.

Isa blinks gesturing to the entrance to one of the temples with her arms. "Here."

"I hate to break it to you Red but, there's no one there." He responds as a figure passes through him.

"He can't see us child," The spirit says. "And you shouldn't either."

Oh dwarves.

Biting the side of her mouth with regret, Isa playfully pretended not to notice the spirit as it inched close to her face, trying to provoke her. She doesn't answer it and remains frozen bidding it no mind.

"Oh! So now you can't see me huh?"

Offended, the ghost slaps Isa in the face with its cold hand passing right through her. Isa shivers and maintains her focus on Will who repeatedly calls her name.

Isa presses her new eyewear closer to the bridge of her nose as if she were snapping out of a daydream. (Or, at least trying to pretend she is.)

"Ha! You fell for it!" Isa produces a forceful laugh, playing it off as a prank. "Gosh, you're so gullible." She lightly shoves Will's shoulder in a playful manner, catching him completely off guard. He looked at Isa as if she had lost her mind.

"It's a human joke in my realm," she adds. The palms of her hands dripped with her sweat like the rest of her body. "You wouldn't know."

"I see." He dusts off the shoulder her hand touched. "Let's get going before I change my mind and leave you here."

Isa nods, turning her head as the spirit angrily stomps away giving a not-so-friendly gesture to Isa. In retaliation, Isa sneakily returns the favor and enters the portal throwing some of the pink salt Elder Arthur had given her over her shoulder. The spirit hissed and vanished from sight.

When they reached the end of the portal, Isa had never felt happier.

"I DID IT!" Isa cheers and jumps from the balls of her feet throwing her hands in the air.

"Great, now close the portal." Will replies watching her attentively while crossing his arms together. The corners of his lips lift ever so subtly showing his amusement. With her glasses, Isa could see small fangs poking out.

"You see, I would, but I don't know how."

"Use your head and imagine it closing. Duh! Someone is lacking in the intelligence department."

"So were you when you betrayed the team, you pend-." She snapped, almost cursing at him in Spanish.

"Language." He cuts her off.

"I thought you didn't know Spanish."

"I don't. I just knew you were going to swear."

Just like Will instructed, Isa closes the portal and throws the cube next to him once again.

"You missed, Red." He says picking up the transporter off the ground, tossing it to Isa who was scowling at him.

"I was hoping the portal would open right next to you and swallow you. Why won't it open to my realm?" She sighs, moving a strand of her hair away from her face.

"I hate to break the news to you, but like Haru with the Vampiric Realm, the Hue Realm won't open for you. Is there something holding you back or a reason why part of you might not want you to open the portal?" Will questions Isa this time focusing on her facial expression. He wasn't sure what was going on in her mind, but it was evident that something was bothering her.

"No." She quickly denies.

Will's eyebrow lifts and his mouth shifts to the side speculating Isa.

"I mean yes. Ugh! I do not want to have this conversation with you." Isa spouts defensively. Next to her was a tree she took upon to punch while her gauntlets were still on her hands. The tree itself stood strong, though the squirrels living inside the tree were not so keen about it.

They swarmed out of their hiding holes chattering their teeth. Will quickly moves in front of Isa, stepping in between her and the angry family of flesh-eating squirrels. Their little hands had long talons and their teeth extended past their neck.

The head squirrel chattered to Will, gesturing for him to move. Will shakes his head and chatters back at it. It was rather an unusual sight as it reminded Isa of a certain animated princess that could talk to animals. She can see why Vero found his elfish talent to be laughable.

When they finished their conversation, they scurried to a neighboring tree, surveying Isa.

"What did the squirrels say?" Isa asked, half embarrassed of her actions and the other half amused in watching him communicate with the pack of squirrels.

"Well, for starters, they said a handful of words I rather not repeat. They were pretty angry at you for hitting the tree. Consider yourself grateful that they didn't eat your flesh off for dinner. These squirrels aren't like the ones in your realm."

"Oh. Sorry about that…" sighed Isa while subconsciously picking at the gauntlets she was wearing. They shined with their golden flowery designs. Isa could trace the texture of it for hours. The gauntlets gave her a sort of confidence and a sense of security. She would've loved having these as a kid, though, it would've sent her a one-way ticket to prison and a couple of hospitalized classmates.

Seeing Isa's frustration, Will throws his transporter next to her, opening the Human Realm. "You won't be able to enter, but at least you can see your world." He cautioned, facing away from Isa; dusting himself off to make himself appear uninterested.

Standing in front of the portal, Isa tries to walk into it but when she does, there was some sort of transparent wall in the way that prevented her from moving in, as Will mentioned.

Peering from the other side, at the end of the portal, Isa saw her university, specifically the place where she was last. It was nighttime in the Human Realm and from what she understood, she was most likely reported missing by now.

"How long has it been?" Isa asks softly, feeling a bit sentimental.

"Only just a day. Time works weirdly and it's unpredictable. Usually, two weeks here would be one day there, but the magical force of the relics must've disturbed that." Will answers with sincerity before closing the portal.

"What now?" Isa then lies down on the grass below her staring at the sky above her.

Inches from her head landed an arrow sticking out of the grass that Will had purposefully shot.

"We train until the other elders arrive." Will smirks shooting another arrow next to Isa that could've been otherwise lethal had he not been a professional at archery.

"What the heck Will!" Isa shouts, getting up from the ground and grabbing the two arrows of steel that had been shot at her.

Will then tosses something on the ground and sprints into the forest with his blue bow and pack of steel arrows. Following him, Isa retrieves her weapon.

Entering headfirst into the forest, Isa saw targets all around the place. Some were high up in the trees and others were below the ground. Grabbing an arrow and using her rose-colored bow, Isa attempts to shoot at one of the targets.

She failed miserably.

Laughing right behind her was Will emerging out of nowhere. He then grabs her bow and shows her how to properly place her hands on the bow's grip. He then returns the bow to Isa.

It took Isa several and I mean several attempts to get it right, but when she did, she made her first progress of hitting the target. It wasn't exactly the best shot since it hit closer to the outer rim, but it was something.

At one point, Will attempted to help Isa again, only this time the two were much more physically closer as his body towered over her. At the grip of the bow, both of their hands overlapped while Will helped to position Isa's aim towards the center. For a split second, the two had locked eyes when the bottom of the arrow reached Isa's lips.

Being this close, Isa couldn't help but notice the lightness of Will's silver hair and eyes, in contrast to his golden sun-kissed skin. Both had a sort of gray to them that made him look far from anything near human. His face was completely well structured like a model with his sharp jaw and symmetrical features. It didn't help that the shadows coming from the trees above helped to highlight these features as the sun danced across his skin.

His body hovering beside hers, Isa realizes how attractive he was under all the attitude and utter decency. He had a nice physique, not quite as buff as Jack, but Will was toned to an extent. Isa had also noticed the sharpness of his fangs when he lifted the sides of his mouth. There on his neck was a bruise Isa had left when she pointed the arrow at him. The salve he put on became almost translucent as the river they had passed.

Seeing it, made Isa think of the irony of how in the past half hour she wanted to kill this man, and now here she was checking him out. To be fair it's not every day you see a tall man with elf ears and pointed fanged teeth.

"Ready?" Will asks.

"Ready," Isa states bringing her attention to the target.

Right there, releasing the arrow almost effortlessly it had flown straight into the bullseye of the target. Neither was looking at the other but rather they returned to their original place to put some distance from one another. Isa then continued to practice on her own while Will watched from the side.

Feeling sore after a few runs, Isa quickly lowers her body and asks for some water and fruit. The two sat in silence for a while until she started to feel the jitters. She knew it wasn't poison, but she wished it was.

"I can only have so much sugar since in my case, it spikes like crazy," Isa states, picking an orange berry from a nearby bush. She rolls it around her fingertips, painting the surface of her gauntlets. "I hate to ask but can you-"

Without hesitation, Will opens a portal and pulls out a salad bowl he stole from a random grocery store in the Human Realm. Isa laughs and happily accepts the bowl. "Thank you."

"Diabetes I'm assuming?" Will studies her. In the back of his mind, he kept a small department of little details about her.

"Pre-diabetes actually. Though I share some of the symptoms as if I was already diabetic. It's quite terrifying. You wouldn't know unless—wait, is diabetes a thing here as well?" Isa questions.

Usually, in all the fairytales she read, they would always be healthy or never have to deal with the struggles of having a period. It didn't occur to her that beyond the Human Realm, they would share the same medical illnesses or any at all.

"If there's anything you need to know about the different realms, it is that we all experience sickness. Like any realm, we strive to find a cure but sometimes there isn't."

"I see," Isa said finally, taking another sip from a pouch. In it was water he stored from the river they passed.

"You deserve better," Will said abruptly, turning to Isa.

"We all do, no one deserves to be sick."

"No, not that. Well, yes, but augh." His ears turn pink. "I mean after you told me and Jack what happened with your ex. No one deserves to be cheated on or have their heart broken."

"I could say the same. Though, Dylan wasn't always a jerk. Everything went to his head after he became the university's best swimmer. That's when it all fell apart. An ego changes a person." She sighed recollecting the person he once was.

"When I met him, he was such a sweet and kindhearted guy. He would stay up with me at the library studying despite having little to no homework. He made my lunches when I was far too busy to take care of myself. In a sense, he kept me grounded. Too grounded." Isa bitterly added. "After a certain point, he became cocky and controlling. Then came the rest of the downfall."

Will nods his head, as he too thought of Kate the same way. She went from a caring person to the most venomous Will had met. It was much too gradual of a change to where he grew blind to her new demeanor.

As she finishes her salad, a small bug buzzes close to Isa and lands on her leg. She slams the bug hard with her hand and wipes the rest of its body on a nearby leaf. Will flinches and scoots away from her.

"You just killed a pixie."

"Did I?" Isa rips the leaf of the plant she used to wipe off the bug's body. She frantically apologizes and places her hands together as if she were to be praying.

"Oh god! Please forgive me pixie. I thought you were a mosquito."

Will bites a laugh, as he holds his hand up to his mouth.

"Why are you laughing? Is killing pixies normal for you?"

Will's hands fell to his abdomen clutching his shirt as his head tilted back. He guffaws at Isa, falling off the log and landing on his spine.

"Who's the gullible one now." He howls in between breaths.

"Haha how funny." Isa crosses her hands. She picks up an arrow and loads it.

"You know, you're not bad for a beginner." Will continued, staring at the arrow that Isa shot at his feet. He picks it up unbothered, analyzing its sharpness.

"If that's your way of giving a compliment or trying to warm up to me, you pretty much suck," Isa replied, planting herself on the log and taking a bite from Will's half-eaten apple he left.

"I'm assuming you still want to kill me after all of this?" He glanced at her, watching Isa take another bite and lifting himself off the ground to join Isa.

"Absolutely. You made a mockery of me. For that, I shall put your head on a stick." challenged Isa. Behind them was the sun slowly beginning to set and small fireflies started to flicker around them along with a few mushrooms here and there. Perhaps this is where Elder Arthur had gotten the glowing mushroom that was in his room.

"Considering you were raised in a privileged realm where you do not need to fight to survive and given your poor shooting skills," He stops and eyes her up and down. Isa raises an eyebrow and reloads her bow.

"I'd like to see you try to out beat me." He continues. "Though, I must ask, if my head were on a stick, where would you put the rest of me?" Will catches an arrow mid-air from his face that Isa sneakily tried to shoot again.

His face attempted to remain stoic, however, failed at the constant fight of the smile. The smile he had once thought he lost after being with Kate.

"Well… I guess I will have to figure that out, won't I? Meanwhile, I will generously make you an outfit for your funeral, if you'd like. What's your favorite color?" Isa takes another bite as Will raises one eyebrow with pure curiosity watching her.

"You are strange indeed."

"Wouldn't be the first time. Come now, answer the question." She said, lightly plucking off a leave Will neglected to dust off his hair.

Will pauses for a second, taken aback by her subtle kind gesture, listening to the sounds of the creatures that lurk in the very forest. It didn't take long for him to answer but when he did, he stared at the sky so that the two would not meet each other's eyes.

"Red," he said finally.

Soulmate Ceremony

"There you guys are!" Vero said coming from the trees behind the two. Both Will and Isa jump, scooting away from each other. "We've been calling your names an insane amount of times. I had to come and fetch you guys. The two elders are here with the crystal."

While she did speak to the two, it became very clear that Vero did not wish to talk to Will despite his attempts to make small conversations. The only upside Will could have at that point was that she did not paralyze him or attempt to kill him. Haru and Jack, on the other hand, were considerate as they acknowledged Will by giving him a nod.

Waiting there at the cottage with various preparations in the making were the two Seers that had interviewed Isa. In the hands of one of the Elders was an extremely large rose quartz crystal, while the other Elder drew a circle with symbols on the ground using what Isa assumes is salt.

After the crystal is placed, the crystal begins to glow pink and decides to levitate. The mean-looking elder from earlier, named John, handed over the official Seer cloak to Isa. It clung to her body as if the heavy and thick material were to drown her.

Where her heart is supposed to be, is the patch of the Roman numeral three. Isa was deeply concerned about being one number away from getting four. Though, she did like the interior pockets for when if she ever wanted to hide a small dagger.

"Don't worry, you are still a level two Seer, but the ceremony should boost you to level three. Nothing more and nothing less." replied the nicer-looking elder, Jamil. He patted Isa's shoulder in an effort to provide her with some reassurance.

(It didn't. Isa wanted to hurl. She regretted eating the salad Will gave her and the berries she devoured on her way out of the forest.)

The sinking feeling Isa had the morning of her exam returned with a stir in her stomach.

He then gestures for Isa to take a step toward the circle of salt. Isa complies and shuffles her feet to its rim. Elder Jamil attempts to join her but is cut short at the rim of the circle. His comrade John tries to walk in as Jamil did, however, he too is stopped by an invisible force. This must've angered the crystal because soon after, a forceful blast emitted causing everyone, but Isa, to fall to the ground. At the rim of the circle, translucent walls of pink glowed from the ground and towered up to the sky, blocking everyone from entering the circle.

As everyone began to lift themselves up, Isa heard a whisper filling her ears. "Come to me, child. Touch the crystal."

The crystal glows brighter and creates a pathway for Isa to walk on. She couldn't tell if she was supposed to follow it or not. No one behind the fogged walls could tell her what to do or how to shut this whole thing down. Isa thought about running out of the circle, but a voice told her to stay inside.

"Come." The voice whispers once again, this time more forceful.

Not knowing what to do, Isa walks the lit pathway toward the crystal. Stepping onto the light, her legs, like the rest of her body, moved of their own accord under the influence of the pathway. She couldn't turn away, nor stop herself with each step she took. Bit by bit, her body felt warm to the touch as if she had just run a marathon.

"Come." Its voice harsher and louder the closer she was to the crystal.

The rim of the circle grew luminescent as the walls of light completely sealed the others out and reached high to the heavens above. It was Isa and the crystal, all alone. Facing it up close, the enormous rose quarts began to float off the platform to where Isa had stood as if it had gone impatient.

"Touch it." commanded the voice.

Lifting her right hand to the crystal, Isa felt a burning sensation as if she had touched a freshly made cup of coffee. Her entire body was drenched in sweat and continued to boil under the rays of the light that surrounded her. The closer her hand approached the hotter it became.

It wasn't until her finger touched the crystal, that she felt her entire body incinerate from the inside out as if she had gone into flames. Isa screamed in agony and watched the tattoo burn into her skin covering her forearm with a design she couldn't see. No matter how hard Isa tried to loosen her grip or pull away from the crystal, it remained glued to her hand completely unfazed.

Something is wrong. This is not the feeling Haru explained.

In the outskirts of the circle, Isa heard noises of someone screaming in the background along with banging on the walls of light that surrounded her. When the crystal had been finished with Isa's tattoo, her hand was released from its grip causing her to fall from the floor. Facing her head to the skies, Isa saw loose strands of white lights exiting and entering her body as if she had been a doll stitched together.

Her whole body kept its burning sensation, especially the new symbol that had laid there in the interior of her forearm. Taking deep breaths, Isa tried to feed air into her lungs. Shadows above her started to cover her body, yet she couldn't make out any for the lights had shut off around her.

Isa wasn't sure if she was alive or merely dead to the world inside her head.

Up above had been the constellations keeping Isa company as they watched her weakly walk over to her door. Grabbing the knob, Isa slowly turns it until a figure pulls her shoulder causing her to spin.

There in all her greatness was abuela with her white hair elongated in a long braid and in an outfit that she always wore, an embroidered flowery top and a long thick skirt, both she picked out when she had returned from her trip to Mexico during the summer.

"Abuela, qué haces aquí?" Isa questions.

"I should be asking you the same." She responds in Spanish. "I tried to stop you from this fate, you should've stayed home as I told you to!" she scolds Isa holding up her cane angrily.

"Wait, you had a vision about this and didn't tell me? You lied to me my whole life. You sat there and watched." Isa took a heavy breath and began to shake. Spinning in the heels of her boot, Isa turns her cheek on her grandmother folding her arms.

"You were the one who told my brothers to mess with my alarm. It's no wonder you didn't want me to leave. I failed my exam because of you! I was ashamed of myself because of you! I hated myself because of the decision YOU made." Isa exclaims, frustrated. Surely if she had the same tone at home, her rear would be in a grave by now.

"I did my best to protect you! I did it to protect everyone. Everyone was doing so well, except when you had your abilities. I hoped that they would fade the longer you stayed in the Human Realm, but I was wrong." Abuela shakes her head in disappointment.

"This is you protecting me?" Isa waves her hands in the empty dark space around her. She walks in a circle before returning her attention to her Abuela.

"Yes!" Abuela exclaimed. "I thought that if you'd let it go- "

"You were wrong. You weren't protecting me. You were protecting THEM. Staying in the human realm hurt me! You hurt me. Everyone is hurting me! I don't think I want to go back. *I can't go back*." Tears streamed down Isa's cheeks. She was extremely frustrated and began to realize she had been shouting at her. She didn't want to and would've never dreamed they would have such an encounter.

"You are testing dangerous waters, querida. I don't have time to explain, for it is much too late."

"If you had told me sooner, everything would be different." Isa lifts her head towards the constellations above them, letting the remaining tears fall off her face.

Abuela made a sad smile brushing a strand of Isa's hair away from her face.

"I don't think so. You're quite stubborn like your grandfather. This was bound to happen. Visions don't change. Cielos, I tried to change it!"

Isa stayed quiet watching Abuela's puzzled expression. Her eyes flicked between them, and the creases of her wrinkles deepened.

"You must be careful when you open that door. You may think you cannot be touched, but if another being senses you there, you will be attacked." she cautioned, staring at the handle that Isa's hand was on.

"Abuela-"

The voice of one of Isa's brothers came out echoing in the dark, calling abuela's name.

"I have to go soon. I have one last thing I need to tell you before I go. You must not tell anyone about this encounter, and how you can see spirits beyond the grave. They will execute you if you do. Trust no one but Arthur. You must learn to block your mind, Isabel." Abuela concluded. Her body slowly began to fade away in the darkness of Isa's mind.

At the mention of spirits, Isa had recalled the question Elder Jamil had asked her when discussing her rank.

"Ghosts? Does that mean I'm a level four? How do I block them out of my mind? Abuela please don't go." Isa pleaded, reaching for her abuela but she was halfway gone at the palm of her hands.

"Cuídate." Was the last thing she heard.

Keeping what abuela said in mind, Isa opens the door and enters. Inside the room, was a prison full of Seers of all ranks. They were chained up and starved to the bone. Blood covered the floor and walls along with the smell of feces filling the air. The light entering the dark dungeon had come from the torches flickering on the stairwell when the door opened.

Inside the prison entered a girl whom Isa did not recognize. She had a plate of food that she quickly slipped into the prison before leaving. A few of the Seers muttered insults along the lines of calling her a sick traitor and mentioning her name. It was Kate.

Trailing behind her was another woman wearing complete black and the same metal face covering she wore when she took down the Celestial Facility.

"I'm going to ask again, where are the last two relics?"

Everyone stays silent except for a small boy with dark hair. "I had a vision. I know where it is."

"And where is it, little one?" She said kneeling to his eye level and lifting his chin with the tip of her sharp nail.

"If I tell you, will you release me and my mother? She is sick." The boy said, turning to his mother who was lying on the ground barely breathing.

"Of course, you have my word, dear boy." The Seer Slayer said opening the prison, carrying the mother with one hand and holding the boy with the other.

None of the other Seers attempt to move when she enters the cell. They all remained upright with blank soulless eyes as if she had them in a trance. When she relocked the cell, they all resumed to their normal state, scanning the prison to see who was missing. When they realized the child and the mother were gone, they wept crying out for them, begging the Seer Slayer to not hurt the child.

Isa then follows the two up a stairwell and into a much neater room with a clean bed for the mother to lie on. Following behind them is Kate with a plate of food and a herb that she made into tea. She gives it to the mother and soon enough, color returns to her face.

"The next relic is in a cave where there is water everywhere." The boy explains while sitting on the lap of the Seer Slayer as they watch the mother on the bed.

The scene then begins to fade away and shows the vision the little boy had witnessed, with the exception, that it was just Isa inside a dark cave. Voices of her teammates echoed all around her almost as if they were in some sort of danger. In front of Isa was the relic, the handle of the lamp. It was within the grasp of Isa, yet she knew not to touch it. Behind her was a massive shadow of some kind of beast.

Seeing this, Isa swims away as it chases her. She wasn't sure how she was able to hold her breath underwater this long. Hearing the roars behind her, she swam with great vigor until she saw the white door. It was her exit out of here.

The beast grabs her foot and slams Isa on the floor. She scraped her arm on some part of the cave walls causing a bit of blood to escape her wrist.

Quickly, Isa grabs an arrow from her boot and with her bow, she shoots right into the dark abyss.

The beast screeches and releases Isa's leg allowing her to grab the nob once again.

Opening the door, Isa wakes up gasping for air. There beside her, was Will holding her hand with the same tattoo symbol she had on her forearm. Right underneath it is the scrape she received from her venture into the cave.

18

Aquatic Realm

Bewildered, Isa moves her hands away from Will and attempts to lift herself out of the bed. As much as she wanted to talk to Will about their predicament, right now they needed to work fast if they wanted to get the relic before the Seer Slayer did.

"What is it that you need? I'll get it for you." He lifts himself out of his seat and blocks the door to prevent Isa from pushing forward. Rolling her eyes, Isa attempts to shove him away.

"Move." Isa threatens inches away from his face moving her hand subtly to the doorknob. Her other hand slowly inched towards the pocket of her boot where the arrow had been stored.

"What. Do. You. Need?" He responds, keeping his stance at the door, giving a fight. He knew very well what Isa planned to do and luckily grabbed the arrow out of her hand before she could threaten him.

Isa curses in Spanish and glances at her scratched wrist, tucking it behind her.

"That won't work again this time. You need to find new ways to attack me, it's getting boring." He yawned.

Feeling this close to Will, knowing they were soulmates, made Isa's heart explode into a thousand pieces. She did not like this, and the playful banter did not help her with staying stoic.

Annoyed, Isa steps away from him and the door. "I had a vision. A very important vision."

Noticing the shift in Isa's voice, he opens the door and slips into the hallway announcing all of Isa's awakening.

He comes back and gestures to Isa to walk down the hallway into the living room where everyone had sat staring at her as if she had risen from the dead. It didn't surprise Isa, considering that's how she felt waking up.

"Foxy!" Jack smiles running up to Isa, giving her a hug. He was careful not to squeeze her lungs out. (It happened one time to a poor gremlin.)

"I'msogladyourokayidontknowwhatiwoulddoifyouhaddi edpleasetellmeyourokay."

"I'm fine, now get off of me Jack." She pats his back pulling away from his hug. "Your muscles are squishing me."

Vero chuckles and grabs Isa by the hand squeezing it a little. Vero guides her to a seat on the couch next to her and Haru. Haru mouths "Are you okay?" to Isa, out of simple reassurance.

"I'm okay." She mouths to him bobbing her head up and down. Haru gives Isa a small smile, letting her speak.

"I know where the next relic is," Isa takes a deep breath, her throat a little raspy.

The room went silent.

Isa proceeded, telling them what she had seen in the prison and the cave, avoiding slipping any details of her encounter with abuela. She quickly shifts the balls of her eyes to

Elder Arthur who had walked into the room with pastries he freshly baked. On his hands were mittens of sleeping dragons.

"Well, I suggest you all should start packing and get a move on to the Aquatic Realm." Elder Arthur advised, handing a croissant covered in strawberry jam to Isa.

They all nod their heads and jump onto their portals beside them. Isa took the time to practice a few more rounds of shooting in the forest until the others had returned. They each carried a personal leather bag. Most likely filled with weapons and magical objects they have gathered in their previous quests among the other realms.

Will comes out of his, handing each of them a neon orange wetsuit.

"Did you have to pick the ugliest color?" Jack complained.

"Do you want to get lost in a dark cave?"

"No."

"Then deal with it."

"At least you guys can see each other," muttered Vero as she took a wet suit. Isa followed behind her with a personal bag Will designed for her.

Inside the personal bag that Isa assumed was waterproof were her red bow and a handful of steel arrows. It seemed like he upgraded the bow as there had been a few changes made to it. Luckily Isa's glasses were still able to fit on the bow creating a scope for far targets. A few other items in the bag consisted of three small daggers, one of which Isa stored on in her Seer cloak, her gauntlets, and a speargun she might need to battle the monster that lurked in the cave.

As Isa puts the items back in her bag, Vero emerges out of the bathroom in the same orange wetsuit except she cut the legs to make it short so that she can feel around with her feet.

"Well?" Vero folds her arms.

"I don't think the color suits me."

"No not that. How do you feel? Are you going to talk to Will?" she questions further. Although Vero could barely see anyone's expression, she could sense the weight of everyone's heart. It was one of those telekinetic traits she learned. The weight she felt from Isa was one of which prevented Isa from moving forward. Vero couldn't tell what it was, but she knew it was not good.

"I don't know Vero. It's all too complicated. I've been here for two days and all of a sudden, I'm the soulmate to the most insufferable, lying, scheming man whom I do not know. The last man I was with hurt me badly, Vero. I built myself up and I'm not going to let another man tear me down the same way." Isa huffs out, trying not to raise her voice as she was getting to her limit.

"Tell me, how could you forgive him so easily? Last time I checked, you almost murdered him before all of this." Isa states raising an eyebrow at Vero.

"So did you." Vero points out. "It's been three days since you've been out, Isa. We all sat down and talked."

Isa shakes her head and walks into the bathroom to wash her face, avoiding the mirror. Isa had enough issues to deal with, her self-esteem and insecurities weren't going to be another one.

"Unless I get the ability as a level three Seer to know the truth, I think I should keep the way things are."

Behind her, Vero follows.

"If it helps, I've known Will for years, so we can start there. Besides, the three days you've been unconscious he took care of you and wouldn't leave your side, that must mean something. I know what he did is possibly the most unforgivable thing, but you should let yourself be happy, Isa. I would know, I've been in twenty-seven relationships before Haru. You and Will are meant to be, I can feel it."

"Twenty-seven? Wow! Tell me every detail."

"Isa."

"What?"

"You're changing the subject."

"But,"

"He won't hurt you, Isa. He's not like that. Please believe me when I say this. I don't often sing praises, especially about a traitor, but Will means well." Vero explains, placing a hand on Isa's shoulder.

"I'll think about it…" Isa sighed, putting on her emerald Seer cloak back on, moving herself away from Vero. It was awfully warm to the touch like it was taken out of a dryer.

"I know this is hard for you. I won't press anymore. If you need a friend, that is who I will be instead of a matchmaker." She smiled, handing Isa her design journal that had been on the floor.

"Thank you." Isa gently takes the journal from Vero's hands as the two leave the room.

Changed and packed, Isa was ready to meet the others outside to enter the Aquatic Realm.

Vero, out of everyone, seemed apprehensive about entering the portal. Her telekinetic abilities could do only so much to help her adjust to the world around her. In the other realms, she could do perfectly fine for there was energy around her to feel around to see who was there, but in the Aquatic Realm, there is energy in surges that followed the patterns of the waves under the water. It completely throws off and disorientates Vero. Having Haru as a second pair of eyes is what kept Vero calm so that the portal wouldn't block her out.

Haru knew this of course, for they two had talked about healthy coping mechanisms and tactics to fight away their demons.

He held her hand and whispered comforting words to Vero like he would in any mission that needed the Aquatic Realm. He knew the struggle as the Vampiric Realm had been his realm of troubles. As long as the two were there by each other's side, they knew it was going to be okay.

"Your darkness is my darkness." Haru reminded Vero holding her closer, giving a small lighthearted peck on the lips before entering the portal.

"Why did Haru open the portal? Wouldn't it be easier if I did that? I would be able to open it to where the relic is."

"Yes and no," Jack replied. "The relics have a barrier that prevents you from Portaling directly to them. Like most magic, there's no other way to explain it. It just is what it is."

"That makes sense. Kind of."

"Also opening a portal and entering the Aquatic Realm is a tad bit different than going to any realm."

'How so?"

"Your body is going to change. Not in that way! But um," Jack turns to Will for additional help.

"You'll grow fins and gills." Will bluntly asserts. "Our bodies adapt and change to the different realms such as how the Human Realm dulls any magical folk into normal beings after being there for an extensive amount of time. The portal changes you accordingly."

"You also understand and naturally speak the language of that realm," Jack adds.

"Too bad I had to learn how to speak idiot, and not by choice," Vero remarks in the background from the other side of the portal playfully flipping Jack off.

Like a child, Jack sticks his tongue at her and returns the gesture.

"That also means in your realm, if you cuss at me in Spanish I'll understand."

Isa gives a slight snort at Will's remark. She then gives both of them a nod, avoiding Will's eyes and checking her backpack for all her items.

"Hey, um. Just because we're soulmates doesn't mean I'll go completely soft on you. After all, you're the one who wants to put my head on a stick, remember?" Will teases.

Lifting the corners of Isa's lips, she replies "And I still do. That pretty head of yours would look so nice to display."

"So, you think I'm pretty?" Will smirks crossing his arms and arching his neck.

"Pretty annoying and insufferable? Yes."

"I could say the same."

This engagement brought Isa some comfort as she preferred there to be some normalcy between them. After seeing the same tattoo on Will's forearm, matching hers, Isa didn't know how to react toward Will until now.

Yes, he is attractive. Yes, his new gentle demeanor was growing on her but still. Regardless of how much Isa wanted to throw herself at him, she couldn't.

Jack, wanting to overcome any awkward tension, kept an eye out on Isa and stood in between them to bring them some ease. He would make jokes to Isa which she took lightly despite her internal withdrawal. He hoped that his optimism was just enough to hold everyone together through the mission.

The three proceeded to walk into the portal, and as they had explained, Isa began to grow gills and webbing on her hands and feet. It wasn't painful but rather gave the sensation of a peel-off face mask in reverse order where the peel grew in between her fingers.

On her neck, gills rose and fell at the rhythm of her chest when she would usually breathe air.

Coming out of the portal, everyone had been transformed into merpeople. They all kept their original features they came with, topping it all off with gills and webbing.

"You know, I'm surprised we didn't get tails like mermaids," Isa commented viewing her hands and legs.

"First of all, only sirens have tails. Second, there's no such thing as what you hues call mermaids, here people of the Aquatic Realm are called merpeople." Haru corrects, leading everyone over to a small city labeled Atlantis.

Pieces of jewelry scattered the ground reflecting its lights on the marble towers of the city. Sea creatures of all kinds built their homes in the city's ecosystem completely unbothered by the merpeople of all colors and sizes swimming past them. There had been stores, gift shops, a questionable sushi bar, and homes that were minuscule in comparison to the grand castle poking out of all the buildings.

"That's where Poseidon and King Triton make deals. One of them includes sending a piece of Atlantis to the Human Realm to prank the hues and in return, Poseidon will manage the waters." Jack said in complete awe, staring at it.

On the pillars of buildings, they passed through, were a series of wanted posters. One poster in particular caught Isa's attention. She ripped it off the wall and examined it. The number four was heavily overlined in red.

"Level fours wanted" Isa quietly reads to herself. Over her shoulder was Will. She did not notice him and jumped at the sound of his voice.

"Don't worry," He comments, taking the poster and discarding it into a trash bin. "They won't come after you."

"And if they did?" she asks, poorly hiding her apprehensiveness. Her Abuela's warning crept to the back of her mind. *"You're testing dangerous waters querida."*

"I'd kill them." He quickly replies, tightening his grip on his dagger at his waistbelt. "I've watched their executions at the Plytha Square. Heaven forbids I ever witness that happen to you or someone I care about."

"Oh." She flushed, thinking back on all those fantasy romance novels where she countlessly wished someone had said that to her. It's one thing to be delusional but another for your delusions to come to life.

"I um-mean. Not that I don't care about you or that you don't count as someone I care about. I'm saying I would kill for anyone on the team-" His pointed ears flushed.

"I understand." She raises her hand, biting back a chuckle. "If you can keep your word, and I mean IF you can, perhaps, there is hope for you and your head. That is if I keep mine."

"Certainly." The side of his cheek rises pulling the side of his lips. The rest of the team members call their names to a secluded coral reef they found to settle on.

"What did the outside of the cave look like Isa?" Vero questions with haste.

"That's the problem, I don't know what the outside looks like. I only know what the inside looks like, it was a normal cave, and at the center of it was the handle of the lamp on top of a rock."

"Don't worry I got this." Jack swims to one of the mermen he spotted petting a stingray. The mermen frowned when he recognized who it was and ushered the stingray away from them.

After a few exchanges of words back and forth, Jack swims to the group and tells them to follow the man. Vero slouched at the news and tightened her grip on Haru's hand.

After swimming past the city, the water began to grow much darker and murkier the farther they swam down into an opening inside the ground of the sea floor. The merman then leads them to a great shark whom he calls Toby. The mermen then asks, "Do any of you speak shark?"

Vero's expression goes up like a lighthouse saying Will's name loudly. Begrudgingly, Will talks to Toby the shark. Everyone watched Will's expression change in intensity as the two exchanged a few words. Whenever the shark had spoken, its mouth would move up and down and pause when it was Will's turn to talk.

For everyone else, no sound came out of either Will's or the shark's mouth, which confused Isa. It must've been a mental communication of some sort. She made note of the changes in his facial expressions during their exchange and imagined herself in his perspective.

I wish you and your friend well on your journey, Will," spoke Toby the shark in a musky deep voice, as though he were a regular person.

Isa must've lost her mind because she too could understand the shark. It could've been because she focused too much on their conversation or went inside Will's brain, but she got that one sentence out of them. Perhaps, she should keep it to herself if it was a level four trait.

"We need to go quickly. Toby spotted Kate and the Seer Slayer entering the cave not too long ago." Will presses his hand to his head before leading the rest of the group to the cave.

Behind them, Jack gave a quick thank you and winked at his merman friend.

Swimming deeper into the abyss of the sea glowed lights of the fish with bulbs on their heads. "Why is everything so dark?" Isa complains, making out where everyone is using what little light the fish provide.

"YOU WANT TO TALK ABOUT DARK?" Vero exclaims as if the comment had set her off.

"Sorry." Isa quickly apologized, feeling extremely guilty.

"It's fine, I'm just not in the right headspace and neither is Haru," Vero responds by feeling the grasp of Haru's hand against hers. This time he was the one slowly losing himself. All that he could do to keep himself grounded was the thought of the light that was left by the fish.

"I'm okay." Haru weakly smiles. Vero shakes her head and the two continue to swim.

Seeing Haru struggling, Jack controls the water and traps a fish with a bulb in a bubble, keeping some light as they head deeper into the dark waters.

At some point when the team reached a certain level, the water glowed a nice blue bringing everyone into clarity. Swimming in the cave, there were three openings to enter. One of them had to be the one with the lamp.

Passing through the caves was the sound of the Seer Slayer s' voice against the roar of a monster.

"We need to split up," Jack declares as he impulsively storms into one of the three hollow entries, specifically the one with the sounds of the beast.

"JACK!" Vero shouts, reaching as if she were to claw him. Her gesture was much too delayed as he had already gone into the depths of the tunnel.

"I'll go into this one." Isa gestures to the third opening.

"I'll go with you." Will intervenes, swimming next to her.

"In my vision, I heard yelling, and I was fine on my own. If anything, you should go to check on Jack. I'll go alone, Vero you stick with Haru."

"With this cave, I won't be releasing Haru anytime soon," Vero replies, half-joking and half-serious.

Haru nodded his head slowly regaining his consciousness under the light source of the cave. The gleam in his hair flickered on and off. He did his best to shut out the little voice and inner beast that wanted to unravel in his head. A part of him wanted to slip and slide into the shadows to quickly obtain the relic, but he was afraid if he did, he would be too far in the dark to come to his senses. He needed to suppress those bad thoughts a bit longer.

"Okay but take this." Will snatches a piece of seaweed and a stone off the ground, somehow creating two whistles. One for Isa and another for Vero and Haru to use. "Blow this if you're in danger."

They all agree and split into the three different tunnels of the cave.

19

Cthulhu

Isa was officially alone.

Swimming in the cave, she thought about what Vero told her. She needed to learn how to be happy beyond all the healing she had done the past few months. She mustn't let her past traumas hinder her to something pleasant.

It wasn't the question of whether she was ready to move on, rather, it was merely Isa's fear of attachment that scared her. She didn't know if she was brave enough to come to terms with her own emotions. Granted, she didn't think she was brave enough for these missions, yet here she was underwater in a dark dreary cave looking for a missing relic.

Glancing at her forearm under the minimal light coming from the particles of the cave walls, Isa analyzed her tattoo. Burned into her skin are two small arrows crossing over each other and wrapped around in vines on her wrist with a small crown under the two arrows crossing.

In a way, much like the vines, she was protective of herself. She's always has been.

Perhaps, she needed this. She needed to remove her docile nature, as most of those in her realm taught Isa to be far more scared than she needed to be.

She needed to be daring. To not be afraid of change. To not let others set her limits. Here thus far, she has had the liberty to be as reckless and daring as her teammates.

It was up to Isa to take the reins as she should've once before. If she had been just a little more lenient with herself, she would've had the courage to leave her relationship and venture off to New York.

It was time for her to take the reins.

Determined, Isa swam faster inside the cave, putting aside her claustrophobia when the walls began to emerge together. She ducked and twisted deep in her path, heeding her intuition. Reaching another segment, Isa went on her knees and set about crawling on the ground floor, gliding her webbed fins past sand bugs and insectoids.

Swimming rigorously, Isa manages to shove her way past the enclosed walls and out to the open space of the lamp handle lying on top of the rock. She dusted off the creatures out of her hair inching to grab it.

Right when her finger stroked its surface, Isa felt someone, or rather something, wrap itself around her ankle. Down there on her ankle, a massive tentacle emerged from the crevice Isa had recently come out of.

Behind Isa in one of the cave openings, the Seer Slayer whose leg too was grabbed by the tentacle, emerged.

The Seer Slayer grabs a weapon from one of the pockets of her wetsuit and slices the tentacle off. The monster roared and rejuvenated its tentacle grabbing the Seer Slayer by the waist and dragging her back to the tunnel she came out of.

Sounds of her robotic scream along with two other ones surrounding it, filled Isa's ears. Holding her hands together, Isa hummed a song to keep her at bay.

"Now it's not the time to panic." She told herself.

Out of nowhere, another tentacle comes in and slams Isa to the ground. A roar echoes along with the voice of Vero shouting Haru's name. With the little time Isa has, she promptly snatches the relic and makes a run to Vero's voice.

"Vero!" Isa screams repetitively in the dark tunnel.

She picks up the pace, stretching out her fins until a fist sucker punches Isa's stomach causing her to fall to the ground. In front of her was a man with bulging eyes.

"Agh!"

As the man pants himself on top of her, Isa swiftly retrieves an arrow from her boot and stabs the man in the thigh. He lets out a howl and snatches Isa by the neck, pinning her to the wall. Refusing to yield to him, Isa hauls out a dagger from the pocket of her cloak and punctures the man on the side slashing left and right, and with her other hand, claws out his eyes.

Cursing and screaming, the man drops to his knees releasing Isa from his grasp. As he falls, Isa kicks him with her metal boots, sending him against the cave wall. In a scurry, she fastens him in a chokehold and throws his head against another piece of the dark cave causing him to go unconscious. Isa then pulls out her spear gun and makes a run further into the cave as she hears more voices.

When she reached another crevice, from the other side was Vero held upside down by an enormous Cthulhu. On the other tentacle had been the Seer Slayer struggling to get out of its grasp.

"Do something you worthless son of a b-" The Seer Slayer curses as the monster slams her to the edge of the cave with a firm grip. Rubble and sharp corners of the cave fall down and crash to the ground. One jagged edge almost impaled Isa as it fell down in from the ceiling right next to her.

Kate runs past the struggling Seer Slayer and calls out a name hopelessly. Behind her followed Will and Jack completely smothered with slashes on their skin.

"Haru please come back!" Vero cries out with her hands bound behind her and her backpack opened on the floor with her whip on the ground.

Floating parallel to the Cthulhu was Haru with black eyes as if his soul had left his body. His hair is a vibrant neon blue.

"Don't look at the Cthulhu's eyes, you'll go insane," shouts Jack from the other side jumping over a tentacle under his feet.

Like a puppet master, Haru raises his hand and so does the monster. With a swift quick motion, the monster uses its wings in the water to push everyone away.

Isa lifts her speargun, hovering her finger over the trigger.

"Don't-" Will yells, putting his heart in front of the tip of the weapon.

"If you shoot and kill it while Haru is controlling it, he too will die." He breathes heavily staring into Isa's eyes. Lowering the weapon, Isa spots Jack attempting to use his fire ability to create light in the room. He then pulls out his ax from his backpack to slice one of the tentacles.

"Who said I was aiming at Haru?" Isa replies among the roar.

The corner of Wills lifts slightly but returns to a frown as a tentacle comes at them. Will grabs Isa by the shoulder, and both fall to the ground. Successfully dodging the tentacle, Isa looks back at Haru from her field of vision.

"Now is not the time to flirt guys!" Jack yells as he attempts to make the monster release Vero.

'Right!" Isa flushes. "Um, Haru is controlling it, is that correct?"

"Yes, he must've used its shadow after he went insane by looking at the Cthulhu's eyes as he was controlling it away from Vero."

"So, it's all mental in a sort of way?"

"Technically, yes."

"Perfect, I need you and Jack to distract it," Isa said, sprinting over to Haru. In the process, Isa gets hit by the wings of the monster.

"Jack!'

"I'm on it!"

Jack makes small movements with his body, spinning on his waist with outstretched arms. Doing so, in the cave, he slowly builds a whirlpool small enough to keep the Cthulhu occupied. As Jack maintains the ways of the water, Will cuts Vero free and catches her inches before she hits the ground.

Swimming towards Haru, Isa comes up with a plan of her own. All she needed to do was focus on entering Haru's mind and hopefully, find him somewhere in there. Reaching for his body, Kate tugs Isa's hair from behind and slams her headfirst to the ground. "You hurt my soulmate." she hisses.

"Who?"

"GRAH!" Kate growls, shoving Isa to the ground.

Isa was not sure if Kate made eye contact with the Cthulhu or if she was insane by her crazed demeanor. Lifting herself, Isa pulls out her gauntlets and strikes at Kate. Though, with years of training under her belt, Kate dodged every single attempt.

Kate then retrieves a sharp fan from her pocket, flashing a malicious smug curve on her lips. Her eyes lit up the same way Vero's would when she devoured the unicorn dinner.

Kate's fan was her prized possession as it could cut anyone with a single slice. She had once sliced a man in half with a simple stroke. The blades were personally sharpened by her as she knew how to make them adaptable and flexible to her diagonal maneuvers.

"Oh, come on!" Isa groaned, falling victim each time Kate slashed her skin open in the water. Her gauntlets were an impediment as its metal exterior slowed her motions and did nothing to deflect Kate's blades.

"For someone, everyone talks about, you're a disappointing fighter." Kate kicks Isa from under her and slashes her cheek. Red filled her vision like ribbons as they swirled into her eyes.

"I could say the same." replies a deep feminine voice.

"Thank goodness." Isa smiles at the recognition of her lifesaver.

Without a blink to spare, Vero wraps her whip around Kate's leg releasing the purple liquid of the poison. On her other hand, she tosses a disk to Isa that grazed Kate's shoulder.

It was Haru's convertible Scythe.

"Go get Haru back. I'll deal with her."

She gestures to Isa to run as she lands a punch on Kate's jaw and in retaliation, the fan slashes Vero's leg.

"But-"

"Go!"

Kate hisses and watches her opponent flee the battle. She tosses one of her fans, missing Isa by a single inch. With her remaining fan, she points it towards the person she once called a friend.

Breathe

"Stay out of this Vero," Kate warns, slowly losing momentum from the poison in her body. With a simple stroke, Kate flicks her fan toward Vero's lower half of her body. Vero bites back a yelp swaying her weight to the other leg. "We don't have to do this."

"I could say the same," Vero concludes, moving her whip with the water and blindly letting the tip feel for Kate's body. Kate crashes onto the ground crouching to the sting on her dorsal. She could feel her soulmate, growing weaker.

"You and your cheap moves." Kate spats, the venom entering her gills as though she drank the poison. Putting her fan on the ground, Kate calls to Vero in a whisper falling to her knees mid-battle. Clutching her heart, Kate told Vero that she gave up.

At first, Vero thought it had been an attempt to let her guard down, but after a long pause of no attack, she started to make her way, shifting her whip into her staff.

Taking small shaky breaths Kate slowly watched her vision become foggier. She let out another groan calling for

Vero's name in agony. Cautiously, Vero approaches Kate's body with the tip of her staff ready in hand. After reaching Kate, that's when Vero understood what was happening.

"Can you put me next to George?" Kate shudders, taking another few breaths. Upon close proximity, Vero felt her pulse weakening. It was that of an ill child.

She carries Kate in her arms, lifting her carefully. She felt Kate's hand raise toward her face as her thumb brushed her cheek.

"Thank you," Kate said, as her mouth wavered.

Vero's expression softened as the curves of her lips shifted away from the edges of a scowl.

This was her friend. The Kate she knew.

"Of course," Vero whispered to Kate as guilt washed over her. There was a familiarity inside of Kate that Vero was accustomed to.

"No really. *Thank you.*" Kate emphasized as if it meant more words she could express. "I've seen this happen thousands of times in visions, yet each time I saw you here with me in the end. In my end. I didn't believe what I saw. I thought you'd hate me enough to kill me."

"Don't say that. I couldn't— I wouldn't — Kate, I don't hate you and it's not the end." Vero comments, taking hold of her with a tight grip. A grip of compassion as their fingers intertwined.

"Not for you, V." Kate faintly smiles. "Not for you."

Vero doesn't reply, instead, she listens to Kate's final words as the two flee from the battlefield and to George's body. There he lay as Isa left him. Vero gasped in horror wondering what on earth did Isa do. She may not be able to see him in the dark, but his scattered corpse was more than enough of an explanation.

"Isa, hurry up!" Jack yells over the monstrous cries heaving from the beast. His fire was continuously dying as he and Will dodged attack after attack without lifting their heads past the shoulders of the beast. With every dark second, they lost track of where Isa and Vero had gone.

At one point Will had to retrieve Jack's weapon off the ground from when the monster's wing wacked it out of Jack's hands, landing right into the center of the cave. Will swipes it off the ground and tosses the malleable weapon to Jack.

"Thanks." Jack grins. "You're on my last nerve Mr. Tentacles."

Bending the weapon, Jack shifts it into a Kusarigama. He swings the blades and bends the water into two small whirlpools, wrapping the Cthulhu's wings tightly in chains.

"Got you." He says, having the Cthulhu wrapped around tightly in his hands. His fire dies out, and the two stay in the darkness, waiting for Isa to get to Haru.

Standing in front of him, Isa grabs his hands and closes her eyes concentrating on his mind. Within seconds, she opens them revealing a room filled with black goo, and a young-looking Haru drowning beneath her. His wetsuit beamed brightly enough for Isa to locate his body. Diving headfirst into the black slimy liquid, Isa hauls Haru out to the surface, drenched in the goo. It took a moment for the two to get the slimy blackness out of their system.

"Isa?" said the young Haru fixing his glasses. His eyes widened with terror.

"Yes, it's me!" Isa nods and reaches for Haru's hand once again. He flinches backing away from her and the goo grows beneath them. With his blackened goo-covered arm, he crosses it over to his chest and tightly grips his orange wetsuit.

"So sorry! I won't touch you. Sometimes when I'm overwhelmed, I don't like to be touched either. I'll stand over here." Isa shimmies her way to the opposite wall. The goo stops growing and the two remain still.

Carefully, analyzing her next motive, Isa reflects back to the Seer room in which she found Haru meditating.

"Haru, I'm going to need you to take a deep breath, okay? Can you do that for me?" Isa advised, doing an example of a breathing exercise.

He observed Isa taking a few breaths in a certain pattern and nodded his head repeating after her.

After a few breaths, the goo beneath them slowly leaves the room, meeting their waist. She then instructed him to do it a few times until enough color filled his pale face.

"You're doing great." She reassures him. She allowed him to do it for a few more times until she felt he was ready to talk.

"Listen Haru, I want you to know that whatever is going on, everyone is here for you, and we need you to come back."

"Come back?" He blinks.

"Yes."

As though he is realizing where they are, Haru's eyes widen. "H-H-How do I do that? What happened? Where's

Vero? One minute it got her. And and those eyes! God, I was so angry!" He frantically spins around, causing the goo to rise.

"Woah, woah, woah. Haru please calm down. Everything is okay. I promise. Vero is okay."

"Are you sure?"

"Yes. I am sure. Vero is waiting for you. We all are. I just need you to breathe."

"Breathe?"

"Yes. Just like how I taught you."

"Are you sure?"

"Yes."

"Vero is okay?"

"She is okay. You'll see her as soon as we get out of here. But I'll need you to be calm, alright?"

He stares at the goo around him, blinking a few more times, getting the tears out of his eyes. "Alright." He sighs shakily.

"Thank you. If it helps think of happy thoughts. Think of Vero. I'll do it with you." Isa carefully demonstrates, allowing Haru to concentrate on what she is doing.

At the thought of Vero, he closes his eyes and takes a heavy breath. His hair flickers on and off as he is claiming back a steady headspace. When he opens them, he examines the goo. It lowers to the floor.

Meeting her gaze, Haru sighs and sits on the black sludge cross-legged. He then pats Isa to join him, not saying a word.

"I'll give you a minute to collect yourself. Grab my hand when you're ready." Isa reminds him, monitoring the goo underneath them.

After a few minutes of silence and sitting next to him humming a song, most of the goo had gone away. The room was mostly white and had picture frames of him and Vero. There were occasionally ones with him among the team, including when Kate was with them.

"Your darkness is my darkness." Isa hears him mumble under his breath, opening his black eyes back to hers.

"I'm ready," Haru states, shifting to his modern self. Uncrossing his legs, Haru stands and gives Isa a helping hand. Cheeks lifted, she takes it and the two leave the room.

Opening their eyes, Haru's hair began to glow to its normal blue, providing firelight to the torches in the cave. With a head tilt, Haru crashes the monster against a wall causing it to go unconscious, squishing the Seer Slayer beneath it. A collective sign runs through the cave and together they gather.

"Glad to have you back buddy." Will pats Haru while Jack gives him a bear hug.

"Glad to be back. "Where's Vero?" Haru questions searching around the cave.

"Down here." She sobs, holding Kate's hand right beside the corpse of her and her lover.

Swimming to her, Isa lets out a gasp, recognizing the man she killed. Analyzing her hands, was his vermillion blood staining them; intertwining with her exposed scars, the ones Kate created. She had thought the blood was hers when Kate attacked her. It trailed down to her elbow and covered the tattoo on Isa's forearm as if she had slaughtered a pig.

"What have I done?" Isa whispers, her hands trembling.

Turning her head back to the man's body, clear as day on his side is the dagger she used to slash him, and his eyes bled from all the scratches she gave him. Piercing through his skull is the sharp tip of the cave in which Isa unknowingly impaled him with. His head was severed from his body.

Right behind them, all three men had gone speechless. None of them dared to spare a glance at Isa.

"Are they both?" Wills asks, unable to say the word dead.

Vero slowly nods her head, allowing her hair to hide her face.

Acting quickly, Jack grabs their bodies and opens the portal back to the Celestial Realm. In the background grunted the Seer Slayer out of frustration trying to get from under the Cthulhu. When she did, everyone had already entered the portal.

On the other side, Isa spotted the Seer Slayer with her metal mask facing directly at her. She lifts a finger, pointing at Isa.

"Who's the monster now," cackled the Seer Slayer, as her voice traveled through the closed portal.

Level Four

Returning to Elder Arthur's home, his eyes lowered at the sight of the bodies. That same day, they held a funeral for both George and Kate and had Jessie come over to heal everyone. Jessie slightly lifted everyone's spirits as she picked on Jack by scolding him for not taking better care of himself. She reminded him to moisturize his skin and gave everyone remedies, including a bottle of a lotion of some kind for Isa's scar.

At the funeral, Isa couldn't keep her eyes off the man she had killed. He was tall and had dark hair. Isa remembered seeing his dark eyes when he had attempted to choke her. Now those same eyes were sealed with her scratches.

The same could be said about Kate. She was pale as Isa and had short pink hair. The scar on Isa's cheek was a reminder of the lives she killed. The Seer Slayer had been right, she was a monster.

During the funeral, lanterns were lit in remembrance of the light that shined in the eyes of the deceased. On the side, they held a bonfire to burn their belongings so that they could receive them in the afterlife. George's family had plenty to offer, while Kate had less than a handful of items her parents bothered to bring. Vero contributed a flower crown she made for Kate and Will sent over a piece of paper with a note on it.

Aside from Kate's mother and George's family, Will remained at their grave for the longest time. It wasn't until Vero resurfaced to place flowers that she suggested to him that it was time to leave. Will nodded his head and listened to Vero.

Both shared mutual feelings about Kate for they were the closest people to her. They struggled to comprehend their emotions as there were waves of anger, sadness, and frustration. The Kate they knew prior to all of this was sweet and, like Jack, made everyone laugh. She was the popular girl at their academy who brought attention to herself at her command. When the Seer Slayer came into the picture, Kate lost it all.

(Here's the thing, contrary to Will's and Vero's impression, Kate was nowhere near perfect.)

Her home life was a complete wreck as she covered up all the bruises on her body. The girl everyone saw at school was a complete fake. She learned all the words and actions from Vero and made them her own.

Just like Jack, all Kate wanted was love. After the soulmate ceremony, right there and then she dropped all her balls into one basket. She was willing to trade all she had built for George. The sad part is, she would do it all again, for George too had been the same as Kate. He knew the traumas of abuse and what it was like to be someone other than himself.

If the Seer Slayer had not threatened his life and forced him and Kate as her loyal servants, the two would have lived in some house in the Human Realm with a beautiful family and possibly a pet cat named Vero.

Vero was the one person Kate did not need to hide from, yet she betrayed her and Will. She betrayed her team and her family.

(Tragic, am I right?)

After the funeral, each member individually dealt with their contemplations in their own fashion. Starting with Isa, she had ripped her skin apart. She washed her hands vigorously until the dermis of her skin peeled away. No matter how many showers she took, the memory stung her body. She tried to keep her mind busy by focusing on the sounds of Will's tossing and turning in the living room. Like Isa, he had no other home besides the wrecked Celestial Facility.

There on the couch, Will grabs a pillow and rests his head. He thought of all the encounters he had with Kate, the good and the bad. He sighed at the notion of which he felt there was something he could've done differently, either in the cave or perhaps when they first met.

Jack too, blamed himself for the turn of events. When he fought Kate in the cave, the two exchanged words that Jack regretted saying. By the time Will came to the rescue, he stopped the Seer Slayer from attacking Jack from behind. In the midst of their fight, the intensity spiked when the Cthulhu's tentacles emerged out of nowhere and grabbed everyone by the legs.

Back at Vero's and Haru's cottage, the two wept into each other's arms sharing the guilt around them. Haru apologized over and over about the Cthulhu incident, and in return, Vero stroked his head and whispered reassuring words. Despite the reassurance, Haru faced a deep level of regret and self-hatred. Soon after, he spent several hours meditating in hopes of managing his demons.

As the night sky kept her company, soon enough Isa was swept into a dream. She was back at the cemetery grimacing at their graves with flowers in her hand. She kneeled down, patting the surface of where they lay with her finger.

"Don't feel guilty, I would've killed you if you hadn't stabbed me," said George as a ghost next to her, staring at his own grave. He was wearing a black suit and tie.

Isa stands still, not responding to the ghost. She places a flower on each grave and turns around. Right in front of her was Kate inches from her face. Like George, she was barely translucent to the human eye. She wore a white dress, and the flower crown Vero made her.

"I know you can see me." Kate crosses her arms.

Isa purses her lips attempting to maneuver herself away from Kate.

"Stop avoiding me. I know a level four Seer when I see one." She says, blocking Isa.

"How-"

"Much like you, I was a level four Seer." Kate cuts off Isa. "Like many of our kind, I used mind manipulation to modify my rank."

"Mind manipulation? Many of our kind? There's more of us?" Isa asks slightly hopeful of her odds.

"Yes, mind manipulation." Kate nods.

"Most of us use it to flee our fate," George comments. "But it isn't always guaranteed."

Isa thinks back to her grandfather.

"You too will someday need to use it to conceal yourself. You'll have to learn on your own."

Kate's eyes roam up and down examining Isa from head to toe. She then squints down to Isa's exposed tattoo on the wrist, giving a smile. "So, you're the lucky girl." She mutters to herself.

"If you're a level four Seer, I need you to answer me something." Isa asserts, moving a strand of hair out of her face.

"Shoot." Kate smiles amusingly.

"What can level four Seers do?"

"Well, we can do everything the other levels do and more. We can see the dead, as you can tell. With enough concentration, we can manipulate minds and borrow abilities for a limited amount of time." Kate answers and shifts her gaze to her tomb. "With that much power, it can be dangerous if used wrongly or *handled*, that's why many of us were killed years ago."

"Oh god." Isa shivers. "Please tell me it doesn't get worse."

"It does. For those of us who can't handle our ability. *It* becomes corrupt, like..."

"Like who?"

"The Seer Slayer."

"No!" Isa throws her hands at her sides. "She can't be!"

"Yes. The Seer Slayer is a level four Seer. That's how she got into our heads and twisted them to stay with her. The only way to stop it is if you block her out of your mind." George adds, shivering.

"This is the worst! Why are you telling me this now?"

"Because we can. We're free Isa, and we're here to warn you. We may have not been able to fight her, but you can. We don't know much but, what we do know is that she is from another dimension. Somehow, she came here undetected." Kate shakes her head with intense eyes urging Isa to listen.

"What? None of this makes sense. If she came from another dimension, that must mean she's trying to get home, right?"

"That's what we thought too, but she wants something more."

"More?" Isa thinks, not understanding what they are hinting at.

If she is not trying to go back home and has the ability of a level four Seer, what more could she want?

"Everything," Kate says finally.

Slowly the world around her begins to spin and both George and Kate look afraid.

"We've said too much. We must leave." George's eyebrows furrow and the two fade into dust.

"Wait! No! What does that mean? How do I block her? What's happening?"

Flashes of screams surround Isa as there is red blood in her hands once again. Looking down is Jack's body giving Isa a sad smile. Specks of snow covered his hair.

"Help!" Isa shrieks at the void surrounding her. In the palm of her hands is the whistle Will gave her in the cave. She blows it hoping it will call someone.

Behind comes in wide-eyed Jessie with a first aid kit telling Isa to find the rest. Isa nods her head and calls out her teammates' names. She kneels on the floor gasping at the slice on his waist.

Isa lets out another cry as she holds him. Feeling her body burn from the inside out, Isa woke up out of her bed. In the dark, hovering above her is her soulmate.

Cobalt

"Are you okay?" The breath of his words touches the lips of Isa. She could smell the sweet scent of honey from a pastry he had eaten not long ago. His hands were firmly grasping hers as if she needed to be restricted.

"Um." was all that could escape Isa's mouth as there was an attractive tall and shirtless elf inches away from her face. She moved her hand slightly, feeling the surprisingly warm and soft pair of hands, on top of hers.

"Oh shoot. My bad!" His eyes widen, releasing Isa's hands.

From the moonlight pouring out of the window, Isa saw his ears turning pink as he moved away from her. "I heard you screaming, and you were thrashing everywhere," he explains placing his hand on the back of his neck.

"Never mind, I'll explain in the morning," He sighs closing the door behind him. On his back were scars of the floggings he received in early childhood.

With a crevice in the door left to spare, Isa half whispers "Wait."

Opening the door, a little further, Will's head pops out, full of concern. Isa gestures for him to enter the room.

"You can close the door."

He takes a seat on a chair next to Isa's bed. "I had a vision," she says finally.

"Do you want to talk about it?" Will asks, his eyes meeting hers.

Shaking her head, Isa sinks her back into the pillow and lets out a sigh. "I will, probably in the morning, but right now I don't want to be alone," she murmurs.

Hearing the words coming out of her mouth, Isa became embarrassed. She was never like this. As a child, when the storms scared her, she never asked anyone to be by her side. She grew up with a 'tough it out' mentality no thanks to her family.

"Gosh, this is stupid. Never mind you can leave. I'm a grown woman for goodness' sake!"

"It's not stupid."

"It is."

"It's not." He places his hand on top of hers. "As much as you hate it, we're in this together. I'm your soulmate, and I am here for you."

"Soulmate." She heartily whispers.

"Yes." He confirms.

Isa stays silent, her heart racing. His hold grew tighter against hers. Fighting away flashbacks of her past relationship, Isa takes a heavy breath and reluctantly slides her hand away from his.

"I'm sorry." Isa moves her hair from her face. "I'm just..."

"Scared?"

"Hurt. I'm a mess. It's all new, and I don't know what to do with myself." Isa began to babble, spewing words incoherently. "Ugh, I'm always the problem. What is wrong with me? I feel like I'm messing everything up- "

"Hey, hey. It's okay. There's nothing wrong with you." He reassures her, lightly brushing the tip of her finger with his. "It's new for me too. I also got out of a long-term relationship, remember? Let's just take baby steps."

Isa's heart fluttered as she took a deep breath. "Right. Baby steps."

"Exactly. At the end of the day, when you wish, you can always say the unmatching vow if you ever choose to want to be away from me or find another."

"Why would I ever do that?"

"You don't want to?" His heart stops.

"Do you?" Isa asks, her eyes pouring into his.

"No."

"Neither do I."

Unable to process their interaction, the two locked eyes frozen in place. Sounds of the forest among other potential beings squawked, purred, and buzzed outside of the cottage.

"What do we do now?" she asks him, flickering her attention to the window.

"Well…since you won't be able to sleep, and neither can I," he continues after a pause. "I know a place to keep our mind off things for a while, but it's going to require a bit of a walk." The corner of his lips lifts playfully revealing the small fangs Isa liked.

"Sounds perfect," Isa replies. "I can go for a small nondeadly adventure."

Getting up from the bed and biting the bottom of her lip, Isa puts on her Seer cloak and metal boots. The two gleefully leave the cottage with Elder Arthur sleepily mumbling "You two better save your energy for tomorrow's training." before falling back to sleep.

Side by side underneath the night sky like in any cliche moment in a fantasy romance book, the two began to make small talk as they made their way up a hill deep in the forest. They slowly get to know each other as they reveal parts of themselves.

"Aside from taking girls into the forest in the dark half-naked, what other hobbies do you have?" she asks him, glimpsing his physique from the corner of her eyes.

"My eyes are up here." He comments grabbing a handful of leaves on the ground and creating a shirt to put on.

"Disappointed?" Will teases, grinning slightly.

"No, not at all." Isa lies, brushing it off. "You were saying?"

"Ah, yes. Well, I don't take just any girl out to the forest at night, Red. I have standards." He responds defending himself against Isa's insult.

"Rude." Isa comments and lets him continue.

"As for hobbies, does training count?"

"I suppose it does." Isa sways her hands at her side, touching the neighboring trees of the forest. With her cloak, she felt like a huntress.

"In that case training."

"That is all?"

"My training is what allows me to be one of the best. It allows me to create what other sorcerers cannot. It's what granted me admission to the Celestial Facility, which you were lucky to enter." He informs, providing details of the rigorous process it took to be admitted.

Essentially it is the equivalent of a magical Harvard or Yale. Few acceptances. It was for the best of the best. Of course, there is the occasional classism in which elites may purchase their entry behind closed doors.

"Wow, Will. That's quite impressive." Isa praises him.

"I can't take all the credit. It's all thanks to Elder Arthur. He adopted me and trained me to be where I am today. In return, I do what I can to help him with every little free time I have. It's not really a hobby, but I would gladly do it. Not all half-breeds like me are lucky where I'm from." He explains, helping Isa over a log that was in the way of their hike.

"Understandable," Isa says as she recalls a chapter in one of the books about magical creatures Haru had given her. Isa skimmed that chapter briefly where she had read that elves prefer pure blood of their own and often disregard the rest of the half-breeds elsewhere. According to research studies, half-breeds were prone to neglect, abuse, and low mortality rates.

(The part Isa ironically did not catch on to was about elf bonds.)

As he told her about his life, Isa couldn't help but think about hers. Much like Will, she too drowned herself in her studies, as he did with his training. That was until she landed in the Celestial Realm.

Despite the world's fate being rested on her shoulders, Isa has never felt freer. It was as if no one and nothing was tying her down from experiencing the world around her. Not once did she ever feel as alone as she was in her realm. Here, she was a Seer. A person with purpose and importance. She was valued.

"I owe you an apology Will," Isa says, lowering the hood of her cloak. The breeze of the forest travels through her hair lifting the curls of her shoulders.

"No, you don't."

"Yes, I do. I attacked you, and later on, I snapped at you when I couldn't go back to my own realm."

"I deserved it."

"While you did, it still wasn't right. I hear you tell me about your life, and I can't help but look back and despise mine. It's the reason why I can't go back."

"Red, my life here isn't all sunshine and rainbows."

"I know that, but at least you can call this realm your home. I cannot do that with mine. Every single day I felt as though the life was being sucked out of me. It's like I'm a ghost to everyone around me as I watch them move on with their lives, while I am barely enjoying mine. I was reprimanded and disrespected at every turn, and because of that, I cannot find the will to go back."

Will slows his pace, staring at Isa while she focuses her attention on the trail and from time to time, the sky. He knew that the Human Realm could be harmful to Dreamers, but he didn't realize what it's like firsthand. As Isa mentioned, he was happy with Elder Arthur, but it meant fleeing the Elf Kingdom.

A small amount of pain for a lifetime of happiness.

"You see, the thing about having a home is that sometimes you have to make one. Luckily enough, all I needed was Elder Arthur for that at the time. You may not be able to go back as of now, but someday, you will be able to find the strength to not let the Human Realm affect you so. Each of us in our group has a realm we struggle with. You're not alone. You have us."

"I do. Don't I?" Isa's expression softens as she picks up a small pebble from the ground and tosses it in the river. The pebble jumps a few times before sinking.

"Yes, you do." He smiles and guides her up a few rocks they had to climb. He opens his hand for her to reach.

"Thank you, Will. Once again, I'm sorry for lashing out at you. I can be a bit hot-tempered."

Seen and understood, Isa lets him pull her up to the next landing of the tall mountain they climbed.

"That you are, but so am I." He comments as the two haul their bodies over to a flat surface.

After a few more hurdles and climbs, Will places his finger to his lips, gesturing to Isa to be quiet. She nods her head and tiptoes behind him as the two emerge out of various vines and bushes.

Underneath a narrow waterfall was a dragon curled up with her nest of eggs in the center.

Sniffing the air flying to them, the mother dragon senses Will and brushes the top of his hand with her head. She was three times the size of them with royal blue scales. Watching the nest behind the waterfall, was a bigger black dragon eying his mate. Spotting Will, the black dragon nods and settles back to sleep.

Like a puppy, the dragon became overwhelmed with excitement as she inhaled the scent of a newcomer. She flaps her wings lifting herself partially in the air.

Isa planted her feet on the ground as the powerful force of the dragon's wings blew chills down her body, dragging her cloak behind her.

"Woah, easy there Cobalt. We don't want to scare her away, don't we?"

The dragon soars horizontally to the clouds twisting and flipping herself in circular motions. She then lands in front of Isa, tilting her head downward.

"Can I?" Isa inquires, moving carefully enough to not to frighten the dragon.

Noticing Will's nod of approval, Isa steps closer to the dragon and raises her hand to pet her.

"This here is Cobalt. Cobalt, this is Isa."

The dragon makes a rumble similar to a cat's purr as Isa strokes her scales lightly.

"She's about 5,000 years old. She still needs a couple of thousand years till she's about the same size as Phantom over here." He refers to the darker dragon.

Cobalt makes a grunt correcting Will. "Fine, she's actually 4,979. Happy?" he rolls his eyes.

"It's very nice to meet you, Cobalt. Might I say, you look absolutely stunning tonight." Isa curtsies, slightly giggling.

Isa felt content. She could imagine her life doing tasks with her team and raising Cobalt's baby dragons with Will. Maybe on the side, she would run a boutique and sell clothes she designed.

No more dealing with Dylan. No more Lyra. No more extra shifts at her local job. No more feeling like an outsider.

At that moment, for just that moment, Isa allowed herself to forget the troubles she had until it was time to return to the cottage. Yawning on the way, Will offered to carry Isa, which she surprisingly did not decline. It started with a simple lean-on and further progressed into a piggyback ride. She drifted away as she slept on Will's shoulders grabbing him close with her arms wrapping around him.

When Elder Arthur shouted for her to wake up, Isa found herself tucked in her bed as if it all were a dream. The only evidence she had of the night was a loose scale she found on the ground tucked inside the pocket of her Seer cloak.

23

Kingdoms

At the breakfast table, Isa informs them of her late-night vision, taking out details of her conversation with Kate and George. She feared that if her team found out about her true rank, she too would meet her end. Isa wasn't ready for that.

Her team asked her a series of questions, most of which Isa could hardly answer. She had no clue where or when the vision would be brought to life. All she could take in were the haunting details of Jack's sliced abdomen and the burning experience as if the top of a stove were to coat her flesh.

"What about the next relic?" Vero asks.

"Nothing. I got nothing. Isa replies, touching the relic piece she retrieved in the cave. She hands it to Will, and he passes it to his other team members.

"This is all we have thus far. Ugh, I feel awful." She groans.

"Don't be. You're doing what you can." Will takes a seat next to her. "Taking on these visions isn't easy."

"Yeah, foxy, most Seers weren't able to see what you have. Heck, I don't think I'd be able to handle being in your position."

"Exactly, we know you're doing what you can. If anything, at the end of the day you can't force yourself to have visions and manage what you see." Haru states, adding to Jack.

"It doesn't feel like I'm doing enough…those poor Seers." Isa mumbles, fidgeting with her fingers, barely touching her food.

Will offers his hand, and Isa gratefully takes it, tracing his matching soulmate symbol on his arm.

"We'll save them." Vero asserts, taking her turn with the relic.

She slowly traces her finger around the small and intricate patterns of the lamp's handle. She memorizes a few details such as the bulk of the jewel planted at the bottom as the handle curved out.

"I hope so." Isa sighs.

"We know so. You need to have faith." Will plants a few berries he found onto her plate.

"We got this!" Vero shouts, handing the relic back over to Isa.

Isa lightly smiles and stows the relic away in her boot, replacing the arrow that was in the pocket.

"You are absolutely correct Vero." Elder Arthur says, emerging from the kitchen with the last batch of muffins he baked.

"As for the Seers, two of them have been saved."

"Two?" Isa questions, dropping an orange berry into her mouth. "Prisoners from the Seer Slayer?"

"Yes," he nods, plopping himself onto a makeshift wooden chair. They all stop eating, focusing their attention on Elder Arthur.

"I wanted to tell you all when you have arrived, but the timing was not right."

He reaches for a cup and Haru lifts from his seat, pouring a blue tea of some sort for him.

According to Elder Arthur, while they were in the Aquatic Realm, a search team of Celestial officers managed to find a small little boy and his mother on the other side of the country they were in.

They were specifically found in Alcania, the Kingdom of the Elves. The kingdom where Will was originally from.

It was the elves who first found their bodies by a river. They took care of them long enough for the search team to arrive.

From one of the pockets of his parcel, Will takes out a map and displays it to Isa, circling the whereabouts Elder Arthur provided.

The forest surrounding them is the Fliaght forest, miles from the Celestial Facility, separated by the Valley of Milway.

Anything beyond their region is divided into various Kingdoms. These Kingdoms are separated and based on common species such as the elf, fae, and werewolf. In the Elf Kingdom, also known as Alcania, goblins, leprechauns, and elves alike create a community to fight any potential attackers.

The fae kingdom, also known as Tylwth, mostly forest, associates their kingdom with cyclops, centaurs, and fauns.

The werewolf kingdom, also known as the Okami, is open to all with the precaution of closing its gates on the night of the full moon. No one can go in or out.

In a simple sense, just like in the Human Realm where we are one big planet consisting of countries, the same applies in every realm, except in this realm, it's mainly divided by magical species.

"We should go there!"

"Woah, hold on there. We don't want to risk an unnecessary attack." Haru cautions, his blue hair wavering in color.

"Do you want to die?" Will questioned.

"I'm sure I'll be okay, it's gonna take twenty centaurs to knock me down," Jack exclaimed happily when deep down he was petrified. He didn't want them to worry about him, especially after they recently dealt with the sudden loss of Kate and George.

"Jack, this is serious. As much as you get on my nerves, I don't want you dead, I don't want any of you dead. You guys are the only family I have that I intend to keep." Vero replies slamming her hand on the table.

"That is the sweetest thing you've ever said to me V!" Jack awes, covering his heart with one hand sentimentally. Jack attempts to hug Vero, but she counters it by grabbing his hand over her shoulder and flipping him to the ground.

"Don't get used to it." Vero scolds, causing Haru and everyone else to laugh.

In a consensus, the team and Isa agreed to inform Jessie about this matter as they might need her for the next destination that is to come. They hope that based on Isa's vision; Jessie might be able to save Jack's life.

The rest of the day consisted of hours of training. Elder Arthur watched them on his recliner as they ran into the forest and back, testing each other's speed.

Isa was the slowest.

It was going to take her hours and days of training to keep her up to shape with everyone else.

"I need to pee." Isa runs into the house to take a bathroom break.

"You good there? Do you need any menstrual products?" Vero checks in waiting outside the door.

"Nope, just my pre-diabetes making me pee a lot. Might have to cut back on Elder Arthur's pastries." Isa frowns, coming out of the restroom. She then grabs the water pouch she refilled when she ran past a stream of water earlier. Drinking it and grabbing a carrot off the table, the two head off back to train some more.

During the combat session, Isa struggled to keep herself on her toes. Without using their abilities, all of her combats would end the same way, with Isa falling on her butt.

The more rounds she had with each member, the more she understood their techniques and fighting style.

For example, Vero's fighting style consisted of acrobatic movements she learned (no thanks to Nix) as she flipped in the air. Like a sheepdog, she rounded up Isa, distracting her until she made her final strike. Holding up her spear to Isa's chest, Vero smirked. In the second round, without her weapon, Vero used a similar technique except she used her ability to harness Isa's energy, targeting all her weak spots. When Isa swung, Vero dodged and punched her in the exposed rib cage. Seeing with energies around her, Vero knew where she needed to put pressure. If she used pins and needles as weapons, Vero would've completely paralyzed Isa using deadly acupuncture.

Jack's technique was much more about force if anything. His strong and muscular physique allows Jack to throw fast and hard kicks and punches around Isa. The metal armor Will had made her along with the gauntlets in her hands slowed Isa down a bit for they added some weight to her. During their combat, Jack would cheat at times by using his ability under Isa's feet by shifting the ground below her, causing Isa to fall to the ground, vulnerable. Of course, Jack being Jack, he would apologize and allow Isa to lay a pitiful punch on him.

With Haru, he studied the way Isa's body moved and worked against it. When Isa would throw a punch, he would swiftly move his body to where he could grab her hand mid-punch and bend her body to the floor. At times he would catch Isa's legs when she attempted to make a kick and flung her over his shoulder.

His attacks weren't necessarily attacks, but rather defensive. Instead of using force, he used the opponent's weaknesses against him. Not once did he attempt to use Isa's shadow, for if he did, it would be a losing game.

Will's attack was much more vocal. He would taunt Isa to throw and punch and when she did, much like Vero, he would strike her in places that pained Isa the most. When he could, he used the environment around him to his advantage by jumping from the trees or hiding in bushes away from Isa's field of vision. That's when he would strike Isa.

Using the little info Isa had, she hoped that if she practiced enough, she could outwit each and every one of them.

"Ouch." Isa flinches landing on the ground for the millionth time. "Let me try that one more time."

"Are you sure?" Jack furrowed.

"Yes. Come on lay one on me." Isa rolls to the side. She puts two fits in the air, one wrapping around Elder Arthur's grip.

"I'm afraid that will be it for today young one."

"Hey!" Isa protests. "I thought you wanted me to train."

"Yeah! Come on Elder Arthur. One more spar."

"While I do enjoy your sudden enthusiasm, the crows are coming and there is no point in being out here when you are as small as a faun reaching rigor mortis."

"Huh?"

"He means there's no point to be out here if we're tired and hungry. Rest up."

"You actually understood that?"

"What can I say, I'm a natural poet."

"Hit the showers." Elder Arthur ushers, grabbing them both by the shoulder.

"Yes, Elder Arthur." They moan.

Inside the cottage, after Isa had finished taking a shower, Isa found more clothes Will had made for her inside her drawers. Half of them were her standardized black jumpsuit with the Seer symbol in the center in red, while the other half were shoes, socks, pieces of metal armor, and pajamas. While her Seer cloak hung outside drying in the backyard, Elder Arthur gave Isa some of his level three Seer cloaks.

While getting ready, Vero and Jessie portaled into her room while the boys stayed outside preparing the table. "Can I ask you both a question?" Isa asks, putting on her cloak.

Shrugging their shoulders, they nod their heads.

"What skincare do you guys use? How is your skin perfect?"

"Potions, elixirs, river water, and whatever Jessie gives me," Vero says.

"Well, if you stay in the Celestial Realm long enough, your skin learns to adapt. Not to mention the other stuff Vero mentioned. After all, have you looked at your skin? Seems like the cream I gave you helped with your scar and smoothened your face." Jessie points out touching her green hair.

Running to the mirror Isa avoided numerous times, she noticed that Jessie had been right. Despite the scar, everything about her face was smoothened and plump to perfection. The curls of her ginger hair seem to look shinier and livelier much like Vero's hair when it's not in a thick black braid. She too acknowledged the way the large cloak Seer cloak sat on her body contrasting her hair and newfound silver armor she possessed.

Chains draped from her shoulder pads and on top of her jumpsuit, she grew accustomed to her metal chest plate and elongated arm piece covering the scratch the Seer Slayer left.

Her new knightly attire was far better and nicer than what she wore in the Human Realm. If Isa came back looking the way she was, everyone would assume she was some sort of cosplayer from a medieval fantasy game. Nothing is wrong with that, but Isa would rather not deal with the stares of others.

"What are these?" Isa parts her hair, examining what is coming out of it. She adjusts the frame of her glasses, blinking back at her reflection.

"Antlers," Vero says.

"I know they're antlers."

"Then why did you ask?"

"Because they weren't there before!" Isa exclaims, touching them lightly with her finger. They were sturdy on her head and well-rounded.

"Your body is adapting to the realm." Jessie approaches Isa, analyzing her head.

"But, my grandmother didn't have antlers."

"Your grandfather did."

"Huh?"

"Isa, remember when we went to the Aquatic Realm, we grew fins?"

"Yes,"

"The same applies here."

"I know that, but why are these horns growing in NOW?"

"Because they have been suppressed for far too long in the Human Realm. Isa, it's the reason why your visions grew weak. It's a common side effect of Dreamers like you. The Human Realm suppressed everything, including your features" Jessie explains.

"In other words, I've always meant to have antlers?"

"If you lived here in the Celestial Realm, yes."

"But Jack and Vero look normal."

"Our ancestors didn't have horns, Isa. If Haru and I had kids, I'm pretty sure their hair would be blue like his. It's completely normal."

"This is normal?"

"Very."

"It's puberty all over again. So, because my grandfather had antlers, I now have them?"

"Yes," Jessie says.

"And my horns might get bigger?"

"Antlers."

"I suppose."

"I need a minute." Isa exits the bathroom and sits down on her bed, crossing her legs into a fetal position.

"It's fine."

"It's not fine. I am growing horns out of my head."

"Antlers." Corrects Vero once again.

"Whatever!"

"This is a good thing! It means you're becoming more like us." Jessie smiles.

More like us. Those words stuck onto Isa. They felt foreign to her. It wasn't something she expected.

All those years she spent trying to fit in her realm were easily traded in the few days she spent in the Celestial Realm. She didn't have to try as hard to fit in or need to prove her worth.

For once, she wasn't so-called crazy or odd. She was ordinary.

Normal.

Perfectly normal.

This was her normal.

Thinking back, Isa never once recalled a moment where her teammates had made fun of her ability. Her designs were not questioned, and she walked around with more grace and confidence. She felt empowered wearing her outfits and slowly learned to embrace her Seer cloak. Rubbing her fingers together, she noticed the scabs on her fingers slowly began to heal as she didn't pick them as often thanks to the gauntlets.

If Isa hadn't peered at the mirror, she wouldn't have spotted the antlers poking out of her head as she could barely feel them on her. It felt as though they were always there. She wondered why no one had said anything.

Perhaps they too, are much too used to these incredible features. After all, when Isa glanced outside the windows of the Celestial Facility, she saw people like her with antlers, horns, and animalistic features. Some walked around with a complexion of a green ogre, and purple like Jessie's eyes.

"Food is ready!" Jack shouts, knocking on Isa's door.

"Come now. Let's get food in you. That will make you feel better."

"Alright," Isa breathes and trails behind them.

At the dinner table, Jack told Jessie about Isa's vision. He explained to her why they needed her on her team, despite not being part of it in the past. For the most part, she nodded her head and flickered her purple eyes to Isa when her name was brought up.

Isa confirms and mentions a few other details Jack might've missed.

"Will you please join our team?" Jack asked, the corners of his mouth lifting.

"We're pretty desperate." Vero mumbles, taking a swig from her chalice. She added a bit of a questionable neon pink elixir from one of the pockets of her belt.

"Well, the universe is technically in our hands, and I don't think I'd want Jack to die, sure. It's not really like I have any other option. Do I?"

"No, but we're thankful you're willing to support us." Elder Arthur harks, pouring nectar into her cup.

Without hesitation, Jessie quaffs the drink and slams the cup upside down when it's empty. "Remember, I'm not so good in combat, I'm a healer, not a fighter. It's why I rejected your initial proposal." She reminds the group turning to Elder Arthur.

"Don't worry Jessie, I'll protect you." Jack flexes proudly. His eyes brightened red as the flames that produced out of his hands.

"Oh yeah, and who's going to protect you, big boy?" She inches close to his face, flashing her purple fae eyes to a malicious fae glow. The type of glow a human would be hypnotized with while they are lured into another trap.

"I, uh, what were we talking about again?"

The glow disappears from her eyes and the glimmer around her fades. Holding out in the palm of her hands is the weapon she stole from him.

This is why you should never look at a fae directly in the eyes.

(Trust me.)
If kissed, the fae may take the creature of their choosing
to be their eternal slave as their glimmer stains the victim's lips.
If they choose to, a less merciful route would be death.

Truth

After dinner, the day was ending, but not for Isa. Isa had two more things, or rather, two more people waiting for her.

"Isa." Elder Arthur and Will say simultaneously.

"Yes?"

"Will, your archery lessons can wait. Isa, come with me." Elder Arthur gestures to her in his room.

"Oh okay!" Isa trails behind him.

"I'll wait for you outside." He shouts past the closed door.

Sitting in the room at their usual spots, Elder Arthur tells Isa to think of an item. Right on the spot, Isa pictures the relic in its final composed form. Still maintaining eye contact, Elder Arthur vocally repeats what he saw in Isa's mind.

"How did you?"

"I'm a level three Seer Isa. You will be able to do the same with enough practice. Now, to prevent this from happening again. I will teach you how to block your mind so that no other Seer can enter it."

"You will." Isa gaps, excitedly.

"Yes." He gruffs, slightly lifting the corner of his mouth, contagious with Isa's enthusiasm. "If we had more time, I would've taught you further down the line, but dangerous times are arising and there is nothing more treacherous than someone accessing what is on your mind. As a Seer, you must be careful with what you share and with whom you share with."

"I see." Isa follows his gaze to the picture frame of her grandfather. He possessed the same expression when Isa mentioned a level four Seer.

'Are you ready?"

Nodding her head, the two begin the session. The way Elder Arthur put it, is that he wanted Isa to envision her mind like an egg. Her brain and all her thoughts were the yolks, and whatever was protecting it, is the shell. Level three Seers can easily break the barriers of the egg as if they cracked it with their hands. All Isa needed to do was to envision a hard metal shell blocking everything and anything from infiltrating them.

Elder Arthur would tell Isa to think of something, and he would repeat what he saw. Isa struggled every time as it became a mental toll whenever he repeated her inner thoughts. At one point, she felt as if something was physically knocking her head.

When Elder Arthur mentioned the word wedding, that's when things took a turn. At the time she thought of Dylan. It was a vulnerable thought, so she blocked him out imagining a mental wall between them.

Grinning, Elder Arthur asks Isa, "Were you thinking about something private?"

Isa inclined, anticipating for Elder Arthur to spew out details of Dylan.

Isa was tired of thinking of him, and it was her fault. It was as if he lived rent-free in the bedroom of her mind. Deep down she knew she loved Dylan, the old Dylan, and wasn't sure what to do now. Soon he'll be wedded into the family and Isa will have to watch them on the sidelines.

Though, it wasn't necessarily him. It was the relationship. The wedding. The love.

She wanted that.

She waited so long for the day she would find everlasting love. But Dylan wasn't the one in the end.

(I guess you could say, Isa, dodged a bullet, for she deserved better.)

"Whatever you were hiding, I didn't see." He grinned. "Go and prepare for your archery lesson."

Isa nods her head and gives him a bow. Rising, a thought occurs to her. "Wait, how can I tell if someone is lying or telling the truth as Elder John did?" She said, stopping at the door.

"My dear one, if you can block me out of your mind, knowing if someone is telling you the truth will be just as simple." he gruffs once again, taking a sip from a bottle next to him.

He indeed was telling the truth; Isa could feel it. She didn't know how, yet when she blocked her mind, it felt as if it developed. It was only a matter of time before she adopted the other level four traits. After all, she did see the dead.

Nodding her head, one final time, Isa leaves the room and walks to the backyard to meet Will.

"Ready?" His heart stops at the sight of Isa. A corner of his mouth lifts, displaying a fang.

"Ready."

Side by side, the two headed off into the forest and trained once again, only this time, Isa was able to hit the targets. In the forest, torches surrounded them filling shadows and lights. In the trees and around the ground, curiously, squirrels and small creatures watched Isa maneuver herself around.

Thanks to Will's mechanical modifications to the bow, all Isa needed to do was aim at the target, pull, and release the arrow. It was ever so effortless as if the wind went against its will, slicing through gravity. Will expected a slight cheer or joy, but instead, Isa remained trapped in her mind occupied with her thoughts. Will could tell something had been bothering her.

"This feels like I'm cheating at archery." Isa aims at Will. Shaking his head at her attempt, she then shifts the bow to a target next to him and releases it.

"It is, but I rather you cheat at archery than die. After all, if you die, I die," he responds, pulling out his own, and shooting his arrow next to hers on the target.

Isa then reloads another arrow, removing her glasses, and shifting it into a scope. She aims at another target in the distance and hits it right in the center, releasing a sigh on her lips.

Eyes furrowed with concern, Will walks over to Isa.

He suggests the two take a break, to which Isa agrees. The two sit in silence staring at the stars above them. Passing by is a shooting star. Isa didn't know exactly what to wish for, since she got what she wanted, so why is she so frustrated?

"Did you make a wish?" He asks Isa as he removes the arrows from the targets.

"No." Isa lowers her shoulders and shrugs.

"I did, I wished for your combat skills to improve." He jokes, putting the arrow into its holder.

The corner of Isa's lifts slightly. "Once I improve, you'll be the one wishing for better combat skills. I might let you off easy if you beg."

Smiling at her threat he jabs her on the side and stands up. In retaliation, Isa lifts herself and begins to fight Will. The first few spars Isa fell on the ground on her back. She felt bruises on top of her bruises. When she had enough, she focused on Will's mind.

Analyzing his technique, she managed to dodge a few attacks here and make a few punches at him. At times, he would catch her hand, and in return, she would use her legs in swift movements to make him fall underneath her. Mid-fall, he would grab her waist and bring Isa down with him. The two would wrestle on the ground until they managed to escape their grip.

"Careful, you might hurt yourself. We wouldn't want that." He would tease, whispering close to her ear and grabbing her right wrist.

"Who is this 'we' you speak of?" She slips underneath him and throws him over her shoulder.

Twisting and turning, their shadows danced against the flames of the torches around them. The more Isa focused on his mind, the easier it was for her to escape his clutches and throw punches.

After a while, when it got to the last round, Will and Isa fought with swords in their hands. The weight of the sword was one that Isa was not familiar with, but it did contribute towards all the metal she had been wearing. Swords in hand, whenever Will used the trees to climb or use the surroundings around her, she would peek into his brain to predict his whereabouts so that she could foil his plans. It worked of course as he began to lose some momentum and started to run full speed at her with the sword. Dodging his strikes, Isa pulls over her sword and swings at him. Countless times Will and Isa clashed swords with their faces inches apart. When they pulled away, they rejoined once again metal against metal.

The battle eventually ended when both had been on the ground, Isa's body on top of Will's. Isa had her sword pointing at his shoulder and he had his pointed at her metal chest plate. Frozen in place, Isa and Will breathe with eyes locked to their faces. Lowering their weapons and moving away from the ground, both agree to call a draw and finish for the day.

"Will, can I ask you a personal question?" Isa moves a strand of her hair from her face and catches a small firefly that landed on her nose. Cupping it in her hands, she watches it glow.

Away from Isa, Will collects the remaining arrows and blows a few torches out.

"Only if I can ask you one back." He returns with the arrows and leans on the other side of the tree Isa was resting on.

"How did you stop loving Kate?" Isa blurts out to the abyss of the forest, waiting for a reply from Will. Not wanting to squish the firefly, she opens her hand watching it fly to Will's side of the tree. She thought about what she hid from Elder Arthur and considered Will's previous relationship.

"I never did." Will sighs, watching the same firefly returning to its group. "I don't know about you Hues, but we elves continue to love someone despite their cruel action. With Kate, while I did love her, it took me a while to realize that the love I felt for her is the type of love I feel for Vero, Jack, and Haru. Besides, the 'romantic' love she had for me wasn't real and I guess I could say the same."

Will didn't hesitate to answer because he was always honest with himself. Unlike Isa, he preferred to deal with his emotions headfirst and act upon them in a secretive manner. Hence the small efforts he makes towards Isa, now that he no longer has to pretend.

Truth. Isa detects naturally, focusing on Will's voice and words.

"Now, if your question is, am I in love with Kate, the answer is no. But, I do love her as a person, not a partner." He responds by climbing on the tree from his side.

Truth.

"I never thought about love that way. I always thought about love as a romantic emotion rather than platonic." She comments, slowly reassessing her emotions.

"Now what is it that you're dying to know about me?" Isa raises an eyebrow and bites the side of her cheek out of underlying nervousness.

Waiting for Will's question, Isa traces the tattoo on her forearm with her finger watching it dance against the light of the torch near her. From above Will hangs himself upside down from a branch like a child. Isa smiles and tells him to come down before he hurts himself.

"Worried about me now, are you?" He teases, lowering his body to another branch. It makes a loud crunch when he puts his body weight on it.

"If you die, I die, remember?" She nags, mimicking his voice.

"I do not sound like that." He falls to the ground right next to Isa. On his head, is a leaf Isa plucks off.

He lifts himself from the ground and stands in front of Isa.

"Are you by chance, still in love with Dylan?" The words flow out of his mouth as a starfish would explore the sea, slow and steady. She had a feeling this question was coming considering she asked a similar one. Now, Isa truly needed to be honest with herself.

Searching his gray eyes for her brown ones, Isa's heart begins to race. She was thankful that his shadow covered the slight pink of her cheeks, or at least she hoped it did.

"You don't have to answer if you don't want to." He steps slightly away creating a larger gap between them.

Closing the gap, Isa responds as if the weight on her shoulders lifted away any mixed feelings she had previously.

"No. I love Dylan, but I'm not in love with him." She replies confidently.

"For months I fumbled asking myself that. Hearing you talk about Kate is how I feel about Dylan. I loved Dylan, and the only reason why I care now is because of Lyra. If anything, I was more jealous of my cousin."

"And so?"

"So, that must mean what I had with Dylan wasn't real. Sure, I love him, but not romantically."

That was it. Isa came to a complete closure seeing Will's reasoning and putting it into her perspective. All the messy thoughts running through her head had ended, once again thanks to Will. He was the clear air in a world so polluted.

"Standing here, I think I know the difference," Isa adds glancing at her tattoo and then at Will who never lost sight of Isa. For once, Isa felt butterflies in her stomach, it was scary and very real.

Although it wasn't necessarily a confession, it was a small step towards something bigger.

For both of them.

Alcania

Like complete idiots, they stood with their eyes locked onto each other, smiling slightly. Almost by instinct, Isa grabs an arrow from his quiver and starts to reload. Enlightened, Will accepts her challenge, and the two shoot targets surrounding each other, until they had no choice but to rejoin Elder Arthur as he called out their names.

Getting ready to sleep, Isa heads over to her room and changes into her pajamas. Underneath Isa's pillow and mattress are daggers she hid. It was out of habit as she could no longer see herself without weapons surrounding her. It made her feel safe.

"Good night!" She hears Elder Arthur yawn and close the door to his room.

"Good night." Will and Isa reply simultaneously.

Positioning herself on the side of the bed, Isa couldn't help but feel a bit anxious. When it came to her visions, Isa didn't like how she didn't know what or who she would see. She knew that if she wanted answers, she would have to close her eyes and allow herself to drift inside her brain for the horrors that awaited her. After all, the previous vision she had wasn't a happy one.

They never are.

"It doesn't matter what I see. I need to do this to save the realms and the Seers. They're counting on me." Isa lets out a breath, tossing and turning for a good half hour.

"Everything okay?" Will whispers behind the door, knocking quietly.

"You can come in," Isa whispers, telling him to close the door so that the hallway light doesn't bother her eyes. "Is it stupid to ask for you to sleep here?" With the words leaving her mouth, she realized Will stood there without his shirt and regretted her request.

"With you on this one bed?"

"I-I mean I can sleep on the floor. Hand me a sleeping bag and I'll be fine. I need you in here just in case I go into another frenzy." Isa explains, her face flushing as she tries to move her eyes away from his body.

Flabbergasted, Will stuttered. "I-I- mean sure. I'll sleep on the floor."

"No need, I can do it. Hand me a sleeping bag and I'll be out in no time."

"Elder Arthur raised me better than that. Besides, this is you we're talking about. Your delicate Hue body doesn't seem so mighty for the cold floor." He smoothly composes himself, grabbing a shirt from his old closet, and putting it on.

"I've slept in worse conditions."

"So have I."

"I like my space."

"I do too."

"We are not going to argue over this all night."

"We could do something else."

"Will!"

"I meant we could both sleep on the floor. Get your mind out of the gutter."

"How about, we split half and half? I'll put pillows." Isa negotiates, running to the living room and grabbing pillows off the couch and bed to put in between them. She was thankful now that he was fully clothed again.

Satisfied with the setup, the two crawl into the bed.

"Try to keep your hands away from me. I know it's tempting for you Red."

"Don't get ahead of yourself. If it wasn't for my visions, you'd be on the couch." Isa grumbles, turning to the other side of the bed.

Despite her antics, it made Isa glad that Will was there in the room to distract her. Listening to the sounds of his breathing worked wonders for Isa. Her mind began to clear on its own and her body relaxed. She found comfort in hearing another person for it was all she could hear at night in the crowded house back in the Human Realm. Eventually, she manages to entice herself into slumber.

Falling asleep, Isa found herself in the dark space of her mind with the stars in the sky. There beside her, the door glowed brighter than usual. Wanting to get over it, she touches the handle and opens it.

This vision was much different from the previous one. In front of her is a massive stone castle coaxed in nature. Vines crept up their way on the side of the castle reaching its stained-glass windows. At the tips of the vines was an abundance of flowers and moss showering the gaps of the stones.

Among the crowd were blue-eyed elves, grumbling packs of leprechauns, and the occasional wide-eyed alien-looking goblin. They all roamed around the gates, avoiding the castle at all costs as if it were a sin to enter.

Running around, are elflings with their crossbows and archery equipment. They shoot at pots and pans that were hung up in shops, receiving a scolding from merchant owners.

Isa ventures through the city until she notices a small elfling crying in the corner of an alley, his hair silver and ears hardly pointed. His grey shirt, made from scraps of socks sewn together, was stained and tattered with crimson on his spine. Next to Isa was a level three Seer consoling the elfling, cleaning his wounds with a damp towel.

Kneeling on the ground with the boy in his arms, the Seer wipes a single fallen tear on the boy's cheek with a gentle stroke of a finger. Wet and vulnerable, the elfling shivered as bumps coaxed his body. In response, the Seer removes his cloak and drapes it over the child.

"Make a shirt out of it if you'd like." The Seer grinned, lightly touching the boy's shoulders, careful enough not to reopen any fresh wounds.

"I can't," he mumbles.

"Are you not a sorcerer of creation?"

The boy doesn't answer the question. Instead, he heeds to a headmistress standing outside of the orphanage glowering at him.

"She'll lash me again. Originality is a curse. My gimmicks they are a sin to the Kingdom despite their uses." He reveals a small mechanical music box cupped in his hands. It looks like it had been previously smashed by a rock.

"They are no sin, and neither are you. With me, you will create your deepest desires, and I will not reprimand you. Dear child, your creations will be enough to capture the attention of gods." The Seer boasts with a passion of thunder, rumbling his throat.

"But, sir-"

"Come now," he tells the child, waving over to something in the depths of the forest. The boy cautiously follows the Seer, trailing its shadow. Patiently waiting by a river is a beast with scales.

"Wait with her. She will protect you as you will someday protect her." The Seer said.

"And what if I cannot?"

"You will. You mustn't doubt yourself before being given the chance. Doubt will only help you sink, not swim."

The beast huffs out steam, coaxing the boy with warmth. He giggles brushing his finger over its scales.

"As of today, you are under my care." the Seer said, patting the child's head, and instructing him to remain with the dragon.

Following the Seer, Isa storms into a spacious ballroom. Sitting in front of him is a woman with a crown of spikes pointed downward into her scalp. Woven in her pearl-colored hair are beads and feathers of all sorts, draping past her waist and reaching the floor. Trailing along her hair is her patterned golden dress.

Recognizing the Seer, her crystal blue eyes widened, and her elongated ears perked.

"Take him far away from me."

"He is your child!"

"He is a half-breed. While I do admit that is my fault, his kind has no room for the court of Alcania." She snaps staring outside of the window, peering at her son with the dragon from a distance.

"And you decided to discard him to the orphanage, rotting with the rest of his kind?"

"He is fine."

"He was flogged. I came to pay a visit to my dearest nephew, and I find him flogged!"

"He used his curse."

"His abilities are no curse. It is you who curses him! He shares my brother's gift!"

At the mention of his father, the Elf Queen rises from her throne.

"No one must know of my affair, nor the half-breed."

"Prince William." Elder Arthur corrects angrily.

"He is no prince in this kingdom, and as of his birth, he is no child of mine. What will the people think- "

She turns away from the window and stands tall in front of the Seer.

"And what will he when he finds out the truth?" He snaps.

"He must never find out. No one must. Elder Arthur, you do know I respect you, as you once helped my kingdom with your visions, but there is a line you cannot cross." She replies, ending the last sentence in a hushed voice. Behind them, sitting on a throne underneath a pair of curtains is the King listening.

"He is my nephew. He shares just as much of my blood as he does yours. Don't you dare forget the sacrifice my brother made to keep you and your son alive." Elder Arthur grumbles. His grey eyes are much more prominent.

Out of anger, Isa steps into the Queen's space, and the scene changes.

In the darkness, Isa returned to her place inside the dungeon. Crowding her figure are several Seers expecting her arrival. They groveled on their knees as they crawled to touch her.

"We're in Alcania. Save us!" A Seer shrieks grasping Isa's arm.

Isa froze in place whirling her head, sparing every detail she could mentally capture. The Seer's grip painfully tightens against Isa's wrist, giving her no choice but to pull away.

"Please!"

"We are dying!"

On her metal boots are stains of blood trickling out of a Seer's mouth.

"I will! I'll notify them!" Isa shouts to them, telling them to release her before the Seer Slayer enters the dungeon.

More hands cover her body and bind her to the ground. Struggling out of their grip, Isa closes her eyes shut, shaking them off her. Images of their faces and shadows flickered whenever she re-opened them.

As she breaks out of her vision, there on top of her is Will twisting her arms. He shouts Isa's name and attempts to disarm the weapon she was holding.

"We have to get to Alcania! The Seers are there! We need to leave!" Isa yells over and over as she breaks away from the sensation of their hands on her. She spots parts of Will's face in them and in the process, drops the blade.

Blinking in and out of her vision, Isa slowly regains control and seals herself out of the dungeon once and for all. When she fully opens her eyes for the final time, she notices the slashes she left on Will.

Gasping in horror, and trembling in her bed, Isa quickly opens the cabinets of her drawers, searching for a salve. Smothering the paste over him, Isa weeps and Will gently drapes her cloak over her.

"I hurt you."

"You didn't mean to." He whispers. "You had no control. If you were to hurt me, I would let you know."

"Did I?" She hiccupped, wiping her nose with her hands. Her hair was completely in disarray as the rest of her. "Tell me the truth. Did I hurt you?"

"No. You did not. The only way you can hurt me is through your words. These cuts are nothing."

Truth.

A small reflective light hits her eyes from the floor. It was the blade she had tucked. At the corner of it, was a light crimson stain.

"I'm a monster," she murmurs, tugging the cloak's hood over her head. Kate's and George's corpses flood Isa's vision. She still couldn't fathom how she was able to disfigure George the way she did.

"You are not."

"But I am. Look at me, Will."

She curls her neck downward, clenching her jaw as she digs her nails on the sides of her wrists.

He lightly brushes the top of her fingers, stopping her. Taking her hand, he unravels her fist and places it on his chest. He takes a deep breath and Isa repeats after him. With his other hand, he curled his finger around her chin and softened his gaze when their noses met.

"Listen to me, you are not a monster. As long as I can feel your heart as you do mine, you are a saint. A saint. A Seer. A dreamer."

"A saint? Look at me! I am far from that. There is blood on my hands Will."

"Because you were defending yourself. Believe it or not Isa, our team has had to make difficult decisions because of the previous tasks we have done. My hands are just as stained if not more."

Isa shakes her head. Despite his reassurance, all she could think about was the Seer Slayer.

Monster.

Monster.

Monster.

"Red?"

Isa blinks, trying to find a way to form her thoughts into words. She always sucked at it.

All she could think of was to continue the metaphor Will had planted. "What if—what if I— hypothetically speaking— fell from the heavens? Huh? What if I slip and fall to the wrong side of things and end up like the Seer Slayer?" The sensation in her whirls. "What if I do something awful? What if I took more lives? Would you still stay? Huh? What then Will?"

"I will fall before you do." He answers. "I will catch you if it means I will need to grovel on my knees. I will seek for you in the depths of hell if I must and endure the price to everso meet your grace." His words linger lightly over the tip of her ears.

"You shouldn't." She sputtered.

"But I want to."

"Why? Why do you care so much about me? Why don't you hate me? Why—"

"Because I love you!" he exclaims, staring directly into the windows of her soul.

"You can't."

"But I do."

"I'm not someone who can be loved."

"You are."

"How do you know that?"

"Because I can feel it." He takes the palm of her hand to his chest. "I feel it right here. Ever since you met my eyes, I felt as if I wanted to be with you all the time. Every chance I see you I get so excited because I want to know more about you. I want to hear your likes. Your dislikes. I've seen how your eyes light up at the simplest details of the fabric of your clothes and how much you poured into that journal of yours. I want it all. I want *you.*"

Isa's eyes widen, allowing a tear to fall from the other side of her cheek. "I know we're taking it slow —which we most certainly still can — but the more I look at you, the more I want to express myself so I can show you what you deserve. You deserve so much, Red, especially when you think you don't. You do." His face inches closer to hers. "I see you, Isabel. I'm not going anywhere. I won't abandon you. Not now ever. No matter how hard you try, I'll fight to be by your side."

She was falling. Falling so hard. And she let him catch her.

"Promise?" Isa hiccups unable to fight his affirmations any longer.

"I promise."

Truth.

He spoke nothing but the inevitable truth.

Unable to control herself, Isa sobs into her hands. She waited to hear those words her entire life and as she was hearing them, she didn't know what to do. She couldn't believe it. She couldn't believe someone could care for her the way Will did. God knows many times she has wished and begged for someone to love her the way she wanted to be loved. Yet here he was, holding her with nothing but concern and compassion.

As much as she wanted to let him completely in, she knew there would always be trouble in paradise. That's what Dylan taught her. Afterall, her visions where never kind.

Knowing what was hidden in Will's lifeline, guilt ate her soul like a bloodthirsty leech.

Mother

Isa's grip woke Elder Arthur out of his slumber as her nails pierced his skin. At first, Elder Arthur thought he was being attacked and so he struck Isa hard in the face with a mighty fist. Isa fell back and slammed onto the wall and then the floor.

Like the eyes of an owl, in the abyssal that is his room, Elder Arthur detects her panic and realizes it was no attacker, but rather his fellow Seer.

Startled and apologetically, the old Seer situates himself out of his bed and attends to Isa's sudden matters, lifting her. The two sit in their usual spaces in his room, giving Isa his full attention. From the start, he revealed little to no reaction as Isa spouted and spewed the secrets he had once held. They were a few of many he kept.

Throughout her excessive ramble, he would validate what she saw and insert personal details her vision lacked. Such as how his brother, Merlin, was in fact Will's father. He was often rumored to have died in a war that occurred between the Elf Kingdom and the Fae Kingdom as a talented general.

But that was far from the truth.

Yes, he was a general in the Great Celestial War. That part was true.

His death was not.

His brother was killed but not in the war. He was poisoned by those whom he once worked alongside with.

Elder knew this as he was the one who found his brother's body in Alcania's soil. Next to him was William in a basket with his name etched on the side. With respect to the fallen general, the King hosted a funeral, and under the Queen's rule, William was sentenced to life in an orphanage despite Elder Arthur's protests.

"Although I vowed to remain silent under the Queen, as the team's Seer it is up to you to reveal what you wish." He carefully advises her, picking at his words.

Isa took notice as she too realized the liberty she possessed. Unlike Elder Arthur, she did not swear under any secrecy. If she wishes so, she could crumble the throne's honor.

In terms of their critical urgency to Alcania, Elder Arthur had to contact the Alcanian Court for their arrival, otherwise, the elves would take any measure to chase or kill them out of their territory. The team was given seventy-two hours to meet with the Queen personally as non-trespassers. To extend their stay, they would need the Queen's or the King's approval.

If Isa was going to inform Will, Elder Arthur suggested she should do so before the grand meeting of the Queen.

That same morning, the team, including Jessie as their healer, teleported to Alcania. As expected, their arrival was met with various unfriendly stares and gestures as they were not elves. Everyone except Will that is.

Two individuals who were half-breeds like Will greeted them with a basket of pastries and fruits. Taking the basket, Jack couldn't help but indulge himself in the lovely delights, which led to a scolding from Jessie.

"We skipped breakfast." He expressed defensively.

"Doesn't mean you should skip your manners." Jessie taunts, snatching the basket from him and dispersing a few to the other members.

In contrast to how he was at the funeral, Haru gave the impression of being in a better state of mind as he happily led Vero around the Kingdom stopping to dance whenever there had been a musical band playing. They spun and twirled light on their feet, slightly levitating as Vero dropped her staff, harnessing her telekinesis in between them. Petals resembling cherry blossoms fell out of her braided hair, decorating the cobblestone streets of Alcania. They received various applause and sounds of awe as locals stopped to watch the two float around the sky intertwined, lost in each other.

A horned goblin cuffed in chains was greatly moved. Displaying gnarly yellowed teeth, he ran around catching the various petals falling down as his warden struggled to pull the goblin back to his laborious duty of shoveling away kelpie muck out of a stream.

Despite everyone having a good time, Isa couldn't help but ponder on the prisoners as she sat and saw the poor miniature goblin forced into the hazardous river with his chains. He stepped on a stable landing, careful not to fall in as he had previously seen what would happen if he did. A fellow prisoner was dragged in by a kelpie when he mistakenly petted the monstrous being.

Sneaking behind Isa, Will offers her a pouch full of her favorite berries. She quickly declines, unable to stomach them, feeling the swirling sensation in her stomach once again. She refused to feed *it*.

Worried, Will attempted to raise her spirits with a snarky remark and a heartfelt gesture of reassurance. Isa would bite back a response and quietly turn to Vero who was equally as concerned. Jack too tried to get a reaction out of her by plopping a flower crown on her head by surprise. To his dismay, Isa kept her hood up, hiding her small antlers, creasing her lips to a decline.

Will didn't enjoy seeing her like this. It was as if something was bothering her. Isa has always been a vocal person until last night. Her silence loomed over him to an unease. He thought of all the possibilities of what he could've done wrong. Had it been for the fear that she might hurt him? Did she need space? What did she see in her vision that caused her to avoid him? Questions piled his head to no end.

By the time they were instructed to enter the castle, right then and there Isa pulled Will to the side.

"Will, there's something you should know before entering that room." Isa grabs his hand, catching his perplexed gaze.

She made her decision.

"The Queen is your mother."

"What?"

"The only reason I know about Alcania is that, in my vision, I saw your past. Not all of it, just the part where Elder Arthur gave you Cobalt and he entered the castle. The Queen is your mother. She put you in the orphanage because…" Will listens intently.

"Because?"

"She had an affair," Isa says finally.

"Come on, you can talk to each other later," Jessie shouts down the hall rushing them into the main trenches of the castle. There, sitting in all her glory in her throned crown filled with crystals is Queen Liva distracted by one of her sons as the two were discussing some matters.

When they entered the room, her eyes widened, and her mouth opened revealing the top fangs on the roof of her mouth. Making a quick recovery, the Queen turns away from Will, changing her strong blue eyes into icy bitter ones.

Grown up to the man he is, the Queen and Will share various facial features, revealing that he, in fact, is her son. Like hers, his nose was curved to a point and their cheekbones enhanced their strong facial structures such as their distinct jawline.

Stepping forward away from the group, Haru greeted the Queen and informed her of their urgency. "We need your land and assistance to find the Seers." he compels the Queen kneeling at her feet.

Out of everyone, Haru was the most composed.

"Interesting. You all are…interesting." She ignores Haru and turns to Vero, eyes moving up and down her body.

"You were such a good performer as a child. It's sad you chose to waste your efforts on this. You were remarkable, might I say. I'm sorry for your loss. Nix, was it?" The Queen stands tall towering over Vero.

Biting her teeth, Vero responds "Yes, your highness." sternly.

"Tell your noble family I said hello. You do talk to them, do you?" The Queen grins meticulously waiting for Vero's reaction.

"No, I do not your highness," Vero replies, keeping her head down. She did not want to give the Queen the satisfaction of peering at her face.

Nodding her head, she turns to Jessie in disgust as though she had smelt something spoiled. "I'm not usually fond of the fae, especially half-breeds. You do understand, don't you? Don't try any tricks and you'll leave here unharmed."

"Yes, your highness," replies Jessie, biting back an insult.

"Where are your wings?"

"They were taken from me, your highness."

"Oh really." The Queen grazes her hand over Jessie's shoulder. "How is it that you are able to walk if you do not have your wings?"

"Hours of physical therapy," Jessie answers.

"It's hours of physical therapy, your highness, to you."

The Queen clasps her hold on the shoulder she grazed and forces Jessie to kneel on the ground. Alarmed, Jack defensively rips the Queen's hand from Jessie's shoulder and recklessly scowls at her.

Acting on personal instinct, it sparked an inferno in him as his hair blazed into flames. Red as the roaring firelight in his eyes.

When she regains her balance, Jessie hauls Jack away from the Queen tugging the back of his shirt fiercely. The royal guards load their arrows and aim at them waiting for the Queen's signal. They all wore matching armor uniforms, resembling each other with their snow-white hair falling past their shoulders, covering the bottom half of their pointed ears.

Unfazed and untouched, the Queen instructs her guards to lower their weapons. "Glamour by her fae, are you?" she asks, gesturing them to rise to their feet.

"I was not glamoured by her fae, your highness. She is simply a remarkable person and healer of our team. I understand that the fae and elves are not in the best alliances, but she is a team member, and is to be treated like one." Jack replies, lifting his head and speaking directly to the Queen. A subtle sign of disrespect but not quite enough to attract the Queen's attention.

"Very well," she replies, walking past Jack.

"Still creating things, I see. Such a pity." The Queen speaks without giving Will another glance to spare.

"Yes, mother." Will replies.

The Queen turns on her heels over to Will. The whole room stops and stares intently.

"It's your highness," she corrects him, her voice lowering in a slight whisper against his face. The King and all three sons are ordered to leave the room.

"Elder Arthur told you, didn't he?" Her expression turns sour as the grin falls from her face into a stern accusatory glower.

"Elder Arthur kept his silence; I am the one who told him," Isa answers right before Will opens his mouth.

"I saw the conversation you had with Elder Arthur. You had an affair with his brother." Isa lowers the hood of her Seer cloak allowing her presence to be well known in the room. The lighting of the windows bounced against the walls perfectly shining the red in the loose curls of her hair despite it having a tint of brown.

Haru shoots Isa a glance as if he is telling her to keep her mouth shut.

"So, you're the Seer everyone is talking about."

"Isa."

"Isa." The Queen scoffs. "Talented, I presume, and to think you were a knight under all the armor you wear, instead you're a coward just like your grandmother. Hiding, fleeing the Celestial Realm to produce a human half-breed. How naive of you to think you can march in and humiliate me without consequence." Queen Liva raises her hand wide open.

Isa catches her midway before the Queen can stain her cheek with her touch. Fuming, the Queen shouts to a soldier to fetch her a royal sword with blue eyes cold as crystalized ice.

"I never mentioned my grandmother," Isa says, releasing the Queen's frail wrist.

"I beg your Pardon?"

"You mentioned my grandmother when I have not. You were well aware of me."

The Queen's anger fades and her facial expression twists into sudden amusement as though they were playing a game of chess.

"And what of it?"

Isa curls her finger gesturing the Queen closer to her. The Queen leans close to Isa, meeting her ear.

"You know why we're here don't you?" Isa whispers. "Know your place, and I'll know mine."

Pulling away from Isa, rather than the expected anger, the Queen's grin widens evilly. One of Queen's soldiers arrives on their knees hoisting the steel sword in the sky for her to retrieve. In the center is a small crystal gem similar to the one she is wearing. The sword's steel was freshly sharpened excited for a beheading as its light details glowed in ecstasy. Its cross guard spiked out as if the thorns of the vines looming on the stained glass windows were taken and placed into its fine detailing.

"I'll allow you and your team to use my land and resources to see your captive Seers but on one condition. You must beat me in a duel," she replies with a sword in hand pointing it at her chest plate.

"I'll take her place," replies Will from behind Isa.

Not leaving Isa's eyes, his mother replies. "I challenged the girl and the girl only. Anyone who meddles, will by default claim me as the winner."

Carrying the weight of the lives of her Seers, Isa nods her head and strikes a deal with the Queen. Shaking her hands, Isa turns to Will for a sword. He pulls out his personal dagger and flicks it into a sword with the first letter of his name engraved at the bottom of the handle.

Right on the spot, Isa removes the metal armor she had been wearing along with her boots. Socks on her feet and wearing a simple white blouse and black pants under her cloak, Isa turns around to the Queen who has finished murmuring something to one of her soldiers.

"What are you doing?" Jack grabs Isa's shoulder impeding her from removing more armor.

Telling Jack to go away with the rest of the team on the sidelines, Isa balances Will's sword measuring its weight.

Next to Will, Haru pats his back. "She's got this."

Fighting to use her telekinetic ability, Vero informs Jessie to narrate the battle for her.

Taking their places on opposing sides of the ballroom, both warriors raise their swords.

"Your highness as you can see, I am no coward. Strike me if so, without my armor." Isa yells across the room waiting for the command.

"Very well, foolish Seer, or should I say, mere half-breed Dreamer."

Taking her sword, the Queen does not hesitate to slice the air toward Isa.

Duel

Jumping on her toes, avoiding her blade, Isa falls to the ground rolling on the surface of her knee, using Will's sword as leverage.

The Queen pounces once again on Isa and wields her sword diagonally in the air. Reaching the blade, a large chunk of Isa's hair falls freely to the ground along with the tip of her right antler.

"Are you serious?" Isa gawked. "Now my horns are uneven!"

"Antlers." Vero remedies Isa's lack of words from the sidelines.

"You know what I mean!" Isa jeers, sternly reinforcing her sword to a defensive turn. She ducked and glided past the Queen's scabbard, maintaining her position in the center of the room.

Putting her abilities to the test, when she invaded the Queen's mind space, it was enough for Isa to figure out her motive.

Figure out her next action.

Her next strike.

At the back of her mind, Queen Liva devised a plan to display her corpse in front of the castle as a reminder to fear and respect those who ran the throne.

In her time spent with the King, she learned intimidation and fear were two components of a unified kingdom. That's how it always was in the castle and behind closed doors.

It inspired her as she wanted to cover the entire blade with Isa's body, preferably in one clean swipe. After all, she needed the corpse to be in perfect condition for display.

She was not one to be messy, certainly after her scandal with William.

She had to set an example.

She is the Queen.

Queen Liva.

Despite her efforts and skills with the sword's proximity, she was not fast with her legs. She hardly orchestrated the timing to catch Isa in time for her blade to brush her body.

The half-breed swept across the shiny floor, using her socks in a mannerism of skating on ice. Perchance, Queen Liva made an error in coaxing the girl to remove her armor for it gave her speed and coordination.

Among the clashes of their swords, nearing the girl, Liva notices something off. She was much more skilled than she led herself to be, or rather, something in her, wielded the sword in Isa's place. The tip of her fingers grew dark, and the girl murmured to herself occasionally.

There was nothing human about the look in her eyes and the motions of her sword. Rather than deflective, her swipes grew vicious and threatening. It took Liva aback as she could not recognize Isa.

Something was off.

The girl vigorously gained momentum and sudden strength to alarm the Queen as she started to break out in a sweat. It was enough to make her relentless with the sword. Instead, she discards the weapon, tossing it to her soldiers and tearing a spear away from a knighted statue.

"I never said you couldn't use other weapons." The Queen's lips lifted. Sprinting to Isa at full force with the weapon.

Reclaiming her sword, Isa carefully swings at the right moment, ushering the spear away from her body. Letting out a yell, Isa presses full force and shoves the Queen away from her. The Queen comes back with a second strike, spinning her spear from the distance and thrusting it directly at Isa, striking her shoulder, and impaling the girl to the wall.

The entity flickers inside of Isa and moves out of her head and back into her stomach, defeated.

Equally out of breath, the Queen smiles sinisterly at the return of the girl's normal state. "Not so hot are you." The Queen digs the spear deeper into her shoulder.

Isa lets out a howl clutching her sword tighter. On the other hand, Isa tries to wriggle herself out of the pushed weapon still in the Queen's hand.

On standby, her teammates shoved against the guards barricading them.

"Out of our way!"

"The duel is not over." a female guard speaks.

"Our Seer is hurt."

"The battle is not over until the Queen says it is." The guard reiterates, calling over more guards to restrain them.

Haru's eyes glow, commanding the guards to not lay a hand on them. The guards back away in a linear fashion and the team huddles together to their original positions inside the throne room. Jessie informs Vero of Isa's current situation; both of their bodies tense. Will remains hostile, clenching his jaw tightly, and planting his fists at his sides. Jack reassures him, clamping his large hand over his shoulder. Silence kills their anticipation, hearing a curse word escape out of Isa's throat.

"Give up?" The Queen inches herself to Isa, hovering the bridge of her nose. She sloshes and twists the spear's point, forcing the girl to submit.

"No!" Isa heaves into a throaty shrill. The entity rises to her chest but does not make it to her mind. Isa fought for her control.

Using the Queen's proximity, Isa releases the grip of her sword and latches onto the Queen's hair smashing her head against the wall various times until she releases the weapon impaling Isa.

Using the open space, screaming in agony, Isa yanks the spear out of her shoulder with one hand, and with the other grabs an arrow from her boot to point at the Queen's throat. Dropping the spear, she draws a dagger she stored in her cloak to the Queen's chest. Instinctively Isa kicks away the spear out of the Queen's reach, securing her victory.

"You never said, I couldn't use other weapons." Isa huffs out, throwing the Queen's own words against her face.

"Go on, make me bleed." The Queen spits with a sly smile, curling her lips upward on one side revealing a single fang in the same fashion Will does. When her eyes glowed, Isa slammed her head once again. The Queen hissed in pain, sucking her teeth.

"I'm not here to kill. That is not what I want." Isa asserts.

"I beat you and played your game. Now lend us your land and assistance, *your highness*." She commands with a deepened rasp to her.

"Very well." The Queen surrenders, and for the first time, admires the human girl or dare she say, the Dreamer.

The guards disperse out of the ballroom, allowing the teammates to console their Seer. The fresh wound pours out of her shoulder, calling Jessie into action.

"Woah there foxy." Jack grabs Isa's waist, holding her up. "I'm supposed to be the one to get hurt remember?" he softly jokes concealing his weariness.

Isa musters a small smile and takes another shaky breath, dropping the weapons in her hands to the ground. The whirling sensation in her stomach diminishes like a fire slowly going out.

Hauling her equipment out of her satchel filled with potions, creams, and other magical materials, Jessie applies it on Isa's shoulder, pressing her arm on top of it all.

Isa felt slight discomfort as her body began to shake from the cooling sensation coming out of Jessie's hand. In the process of the pain, she lets out a wail and clutches a hand by her side. It was Will's.

Dusting herself off, unharmed, the Queen sends Isa, Jessie, and Will to an infirmary to deal with Isa's injury while Jack, Vero, and Haru discuss the details of the search parties with her.

In the infirmary, Isa was coming in and out of consciousness due to her blood loss and the intensive treatment she had undergone. Jessie managed to heal Isa enough for her arm to have some momentum, but it was going to need at least another day or so for her to fully recover.

"Isa, you need rest."

"I need to find the Seers."

"If I go join the search party, will you promise to stay here?"

Isa weighs her options and flinches in pain when she tries to lift herself out of bed. "Fine."

Jessie half-smiles and provides Isa with a sedative to ensure she will stay rested. "Keep an eye on her for me?" She says to Will on the way out as he stands guard at the door.

"Of course."

"You do you know you can watch her from inside."

"I want to give her space."

"Suit yourself," Jessie replies as she briskly takes her leave.

An hour passes as the team makes the most out of their visit when the Queen approaches Will outside of the infirmary. He assumed she was here to visit Isa considering she abandoned him as a child. Why should she care about him now?

To his surprise, she instructs him to follow her outside to a garden. He hesitates at first, casting a look over his shoulder at Isa lying on the bed.

"Don't worry, she will be fine. It will only be for a few minutes."

"Five." Will asserts. "Five minutes."

"That's all I ask." She turns on her heels and gestures to walk beside him. Will blinks, and trails behind her in a linear fashion as a protest.

In the garden, there were no guards and no maidens to surveillance them. They were alone in the luscious bed of flowers to keep them company, listening to them intently.

"She's quite something. Determined to say the least." The Queen would comment, meeting an orchid from under her feet. Her finger hovers over the petal caressing it gracefully.

Will kept silent, eying his supposed mother in a long flowy dress that faded from white to pink. A new crown of thorns hovered on her head, spiraling in gold wiring and steel.

"If I had been any ordinary mother from another realm, I would say I approve." She peered at Will's forearm where the symbol stood out against his skin. His complexion matched hers. Sunkissed and bronze as burnt honey.

It reminded her of the times when she too once bore such a symbol.

Returning her gaze to the orchid, she plucks it.

"What happened to my father?" Will asks.

"It's going to be painful for her. Having a half-breed soulmate. There's a reason why it's forbidden. Especially for Seers. Do you know why?" She questions twisting and turning the flower in her hand.

"Did you even love him?" Will pressed his question further, wanting to change the subject.

"It's because it's far too painful. I can only imagine how the ceremony went. Sometimes, it's best to pull away from our attractions, for they have everlasting consequences." The Queen replies plucking a leaf from the flower.

"I'm a consequence, that's what I am to you."

Watching all the petals she removed fall to the ground, the Queen sighed at the remaining pieces kept on the stem.

"The Seers are in my dungeon. The Seer Slayer threatened to attack my children, so I allowed her access to the dungeon. Your friends should find them soon." The Queen crushes the plant in her hand.

"For someone who despises half-breeds, you sure are a hypocrite. You created your own consequences. If you weren't so stuck on pure breeds-" Will stops himself.

Not missing a beat, he turns the heel of his foot, leaning away from her.

The Queen grasps his shoulder tightly, stopping Will. "I suggest you run to your soulmate. She's the one you should worry about."

The Queen releases him, witnessing her son run away from her as she did to him. He may bear her features as her other children do, but beyond his exterior and underneath the hurt, resides what was left of his father's heart.

Such as shame that the King had poisoned him, just when the Queen herself was about to run off carrying Will.

She did what she could to protect him.

To protect her child.

Her son.

Her prince.

28

Envy

Alone in the infirmary with Jessie and Will gone, Isa found herself slipping in and out of consciousness. She didn't know how to control it. The last thing she could remember before falling into a deep slumber was her urging Jessie to help find the Seers. That was her mistake as an unexpected visitor crept inside.

The Seer Slayer.

Before entering the room, she passed countless guards with little to no issue as she had been sworn in under the King's protection. He was more than happy to lend her a helping hand, as she promised him better cards in return. She entered Isa's chamber with such confidence that the stain-glass beckoned for her to stay away.

"Well, aren't you comfortable," gawked the Seer Slayer as she gazed at Isa across the room. "Now where did you hide it?"

Stepping further into the infirmary, the Seer makes haste with the limited time she has to search for the relic. At first, she tried opening drawers and panels inside of the room where they would likely store the rest of Isa's items. She found her bow, boots, and pieces of her attire; all except the relic.

Isa murmurs a few words in her sleep, captivating the Seer's attention to her emerald cloak. It was strange watching her opponent so vulnerable and so close. At times Isa's eyes would open and close profusely, almost as if she was fighting to stay awake rendering the Seer Slayer to move frantically.

Eventually, she found the handle of the lamp inside one of the many pockets Isa had in her jumpsuit and assembled it with the rest of the other pieces in her possession. It was only a few weeks before the blood moon, and if she wanted to complete the lamp, her time was now.

The Seer Slayer easily could've killed Isa right on the spot, but what's the point in that if she was going to lead her to the next piece? Isa was the Seer Slayer's one-way ticket to fulfilling the lamp.

All she needs now is for Isa to tell her where specifically the next piece is, and the Seer Slayer will have complete and utter power over the dimensions. For a moment, the Seer Slayer observed Isa listening carefully for any other details she had to spare whilst Isa shifted in her consciousness swaying back and forth. She caught a simple word and grinned with satisfaction.

"For once you're not a nuisance." She seethes to Isa. When she first became aware of the girl, the Seer Slayer immediately knew she was going to be a problem, not because she had the visions the Seer Slayer wanted, but because she knew who exactly Isa was.

She envied her for various reasons, reasons that no one would know unless you knew the Seer Slayer personally. With her hand, the Seer Slayer pulls out her dagger and slashes Isa's forearm splitting the middle of her tattoo with blood and opened skin. With the same dagger, she reopens Isa's wound by stabbing her.

Isa shrieks like a banshee, eyes fighting to stay open. For a split second, Isa managed to break out of her frenzy, spotting the Seer Slayer's mask before falling into another flash of visions.

Hearing running down the hall, the Seer Slayer takes out a tracker disguised as a piece of the relic and places it on Isa's Seer cloak knowing she would take it everywhere. If anything, Isa would unknowingly lead her to the next relic. By the time the infirmary door busts open, the Seer Slayer uses a transporter she stole from one of her prisoned Seers and teleports to the next realm, plotting and planning.

Will spots her and sprints over to Isa who begins to tremble vigorously in her bed. Instead of following the Seer Slayer, Will grabs hold of Isa telling her to wake up. When she did, Isa's face flooded with absolute confusion seeing blood surrounding her.

"What happened? Who was in this room?" Isa sits up in absolute pain. "Augh!"

"Isa!"

In the flashes crossing her eyes, she saw a Victorian ballroom filled with people, mostly vampires, an explosion of some sort, and Isa standing there with the Seer Slayer holding the relic in its complete form assembled under the blood moon above them. Isa was covered in blood that she assumed was her's or Jack's based on the previous vision. Glancing around in the storm, Isa makes a mental note that she is in the Vampiric Realm and mistakenly says it out loud, hoping that whoever heard it had been Will or Jessie in the room.

When the Seer Slayer struck her the first time, Isa could feel the pain shoot up her arm as if she had been electrocuted in one spot. At the same time, she saw her family sitting at the dinner table. At the center flickered an image of a poster with her face on it and red words below spelling missing.

"No!" Isa gasped, breaking out of her battle between her mind and body. That's when she spotted the metallic faceplate of the Seer Slayer. Having her this close, Isa saw past the mask and caught her deepened dark brown eyes. Isa blinked and flailed into another vision. The Seer Slayer's past.

There on the floor was a small child with long wavy hair and tall antlers sticking out of her head. She didn't see the child's expression, but it didn't take a wise person to understand that the child was crying in a dark room.

Reaching for her, Isa felt another shooting pain from when the Seer Slayer reopened her wound.

When she woke up, she was troubled by the way Will cupped her face as his expression fell. His sun-kiss skin was as pale as his eyes. He was entirely out of breath.

"Isa, I need you to do me a favor. For once, keep talking." Will holds Isa, putting his hand on the back of her head, holding her tightly, and carrying her out of the room.

"Talking is what I do best."

"Good."

"Can I say a bad word?"

Fixating on her wrist, blood crept out of her and dripped partially to the floor.

"Why am I always getting hurt?" Isa murmurs, attempting to make him laugh.

He of course doesn't and paces down the hall.

"Was your hair always this shiny?" She pets his head, keeping herself distracted. The sedative Jessie used on Isa still had its side effects on Isa as the lighting of the stained-glass windows created a Kaleidoscope.

"Yes?"

"It's soft too."

"Never thought the first compliments you'd give me would be under these circumstances."

"Enjoy it while it lasts."

Will smile slightly surfaces before fading into concern seeing Isa struggling. Bleeding and frigid, she started to slightly shake in his arms.

"Will?"

"Yeah?"

"Promise me that when all this is over. We'll go somewhere nice. Somewhere I won't get attacked?"

"As long as you stay alive."

"Deal." Isa weakly smirks, biting back a grimace.

Shouting for a nurse and typing into his watch, rushing down the hall are her team members in a swarm of Seers in terrible condition.

In that instant, Haru opens a portal and instructs everyone to enter. Weakened by using too much of her ability, Jessie lay there, unconscious in Jack's arms. Surrounding everyone from either side of the hall are soldiers under the King's command.

"We must not let them leave." He yells angrily while the soldiers point their arrows.

No one moved, freezing in places like ice sculptures. Small children of the Seers began to shake. In the corridor of the castle stood the Queen shouting different orders.

"Go." The Queen intervenes lifting her arms in defense and ushering everyone into the portal. "If you shoot them, you shoot me!" She announces to all. She peeks at Will and Isa as they fly past her and enter the portal.

When they were all gone, the Queen was left with an angry King.

29.

Sekhmet

Isa could not believe her eyes when she woke up. Surrounding her is a cotton candy-clouded room from the bed she had been lying on. The room itself was as bright as a lit-up stadium. Next to her smiled a person with a lion's head and on the other side of the hospital is a hippo in a doctor's uniform wearing glasses.

"Did I die?" Isa mumbles, her head exploding.

"No, but you did bleed quite a lot." replied the one with the lion's head. On the name tag read Sekhmet.

"No way! Your Sekhmet!" Isa notices a needle in her arm connected to a bag of what seems to be water. Though, she could be terribly wrong. Sekhmet carefully removes the needle away from Isa's arm placing a cotton ball and medical tape over it.

"The one and only. Your friends were right in your reaction." She giggles. "It's always enjoyable and entertaining watching Dreamers like you."

The heart rate monitor connected to Isa displays elevated vitals.

"There's more of me? Where? Here? Oh, jumping jacks I feel so unworthy right now. I mean I'm just me, and you're a goddess!"

"Well, the rest of the gods are busy, and I enjoy what I do. Not to mention, young lady, you are important and more than worthy. Last time I checked, there was a big buzz about you. You are Isa the Seer, correct?"

Isa nods her head; her mouth is slightly open in awe.

"Well, you are the young lady who will save the realms. Not the Godly Realm of course, since we have some influence over dimensions, but the rest of the realms are in the palm of your hands! As someone familiar with war, I know how messy saving the world can be. If you don't fight for yourself, fight for everyone. Lives are depending on you. They're counting on you, Isa." She fiercely advises Isa and encourages her to lift herself out of bed before she does it herself.

"Woah. That is the nicest and most beautiful thing anyone has ever said to me."

Without complaints, Isa does what she is told and follows Sekhmet to a common lounge where she finds Will sleeping on the couch with a cup of coffee in one hand.

"Your other friends are currently in the cafeteria. Take care, Isa. Don't forget to watch over your blood sugar levels." Sekhmet tells Isa, handing her a small glucose monitor before heading away to her next patient.

Isa sits in the empty chair next to Will and gently puts his head on her shoulder. His expression remained uneased as he kept scowling until he realized whose shoulder he was resting on. Had it been Jack, he would've turned himself in the opposite direction and covered his ears as it was Jack's favorite pastime to play with them while Will rested.

"They're so cute and pointed like a gazelle." Jack would comment.

He doesn't do that anymore, of course. Not since Will punched him in the face for tugging his ears too hard. Jack ended up with a black eye that Jessie refused to heal. After that, they couldn't be roommates anymore.

"I'm glad you're okay." He murmurs, keeping his head against her now healthy shoulders. However, on her forearm remains a scar from when the Seer Slayer sliced her. It was a simple diagonal cut.

"Well, if I die you die remember?" Isa lightly jokes. Humor has always been her remedy. "It's kind of my job to keep you alive now that you think about it. You should be grateful. Head over heels amazed by my epic strength."

Will was a bit mortified but went along with her despite it. "Oh yeah? What about when you're in a coma?"

"It's called hibernating."

"What are you a bear?"

"I wish I was. I could claw you out with a single strike."

"Trying to get your hands on me, are you?"

"Don't flatter yourself."

"So, if I take my shirt off right now your eyes would stay on my face?"

"Would your eyes stay on mine if I took off this gown?"

"Touché." The corner of his lip lifts slightly, fangs pointing out. His eyes darted down to Isa's legs and back up her eyes.

He takes a deep breath.

"You know, you were pretty out of it. You were out for a good two weeks. They wouldn't let us visit you often, including me. Sekhmet threatened me once."

Isa chuckles, imagining Sekhmet scolding and telling Will to go away. Her smile then fades as she recollects the reason she was hospitalized in the first place.

"I know where the next relic is, and Seer Slayer knows it too." Isa taps her foot on the floor, her fingers ready to pick at each other.

"And we'll be ready to cross that bridge when we get there." Will replies, playing with her fingertips, reassuringly. The perfect distraction from her habit. "Let's wait for the team to get back. Don't fret."

"I'll try not to." Isa sighs as she watches Will trace the pattern of her fingerprints.

"Do you want to hold it?"

"Hold what?"

"Do you want to hold my hand?"

"Moving fast, are you?" He comments amusingly and with worry. He debated on whether to call back Sekhmet to check up on her.

"Is that a, no?"

"Only if you are okay with it."

"I am as long as they keep mine warm," Isa replies, slightly shaking from the cold hospital and the very minimal warmth the thin hospital gown had to offer.

Without hesitation, from his bag, Will pulls out Isa's Seer cloak and hands it to her. It was as warm as Will's hands.

Putting it on, Isa searches the pockets for the relic. Analyzing it carefully, she noticed how different it weighed and glistened.

"She took the fake one and swapped it out with another fake one I told you to make," Isa replies analyzing the item closely.

"How long do you think it'll take her to notice it is a dupe?"

"Let's hope long enough." Isa sighs, sinking into her chair.

"Do you want to sleep?"

Isa shakes her head. "I don't think I ever want to sleep. Every time I do, something terrible happens. I much rather change into my clothes."

"I had a feeling you would say that" opening a portal next to them, is a way to Isa's room at Elder Arthur's.

"Do you want me to come with you?"

"And see me change?"

"You know what I mean. Get your mind out of the gutter, Red."

"I'll be fine." She laughs. Mid-step, she felt a slight tug.

"Sorry!" The tips of his hears turn pink. "I just wanted to tell you before you go. If you're ever scared to sleep. You know I'll be there for you, right? I'll help you if you want me to. I'll sing to you despite having zero to no vocals. I'll read you a book. I'll act the voices out– "

Isa spins into a full circle, wrapping her arms around Will. He stiffened until she reassured him that his embrace was welcomed.

"Will."

"Yes?"

"Thank you."

"Of course."

"No really, thank you. For everything. Your patience. Your company. Your affection. You have given me so much."

"I have yet to give you enough," He whispers.

Isa's eyes tearfully soften. She could list all the reasons why he shouldn't, but she knew he'd negate each and every one of those reasons.

"I hope you know that I meant what I said. Back there in Alcania. About us going somewhere nice when this is over."

"That would be lovely."

Isa released him slowly, wanting to take every inch of his scent as she was afraid it would disappear. Out of all the pressure Isa went through and facing near-death experiences, she realized the fragility of life. How it must not be wasted every second as anyone could die any minute.

30

You and I

Stepping into the portal, Isa couldn't help but feel unnerved to be inside her room. There was a sickening silence and an ominous stench that filled her nostrils. Isa gagged a few times as she speedily zipped herself in her jumpsuit and layered significant places of her body with armor.

She never smelt a sent this awful than the time she had to clean up the vomit and liquid feces underneath her brother Alfonso's bed after he had gotten some kind of virus.

Isa weighed her options and thought about alerting the others but decided against it as she wanted to see *who* was inside the dwelling before they escaped.

If it is who she believes it is, Isa wants to face the intruder herself.

(Big mistake on her part, if you ask me.)

As Isa puts on her boots, she hears a shuffle in the house. The intruder could hear her. Isa could sense it by the slight creeks of the wooden floor.

If there's one thing she learned about having strict parents, it was recognizing footsteps. Those were not Elder Arthur's.

"Eugh." Isa recoiled.

The stench grew stronger as she inched herself closer to the door with an arrow perfectly loaded in place.

With her foot, Isa kicks her door open and points the arrow down the hall. She noticed something on the floor, unmoving. As she neared the entity, a gasp escaped her lips. "Elder Arthur."

There he was pinned to the floor with a sword launched directly into his heart.

"Were you going to shoot him with your arrow of love Cupid?"

'Don't call me that." Isa stiffens.

Sitting on the stool by the open door with her legs crossed was the Seer slayer. Poised and unbothered.

"Do you have any idea how long I've waited for you? I was aiming to kill your stupid little boyfriend but then I saw his tattoo. At that point, I definitely couldn't kill him. Oh, dear god no! I couldn't risk killing off my prized Seer." She snickers.

"So, you killed Elder Arthur?" Isa growls, meeting Elder Arthur's eyes despite there not being a single soul behind them. He had been dead for at least two days.

"Not at first. He was kind. Selfless is another word to describe him. He kindly invited me to stay here while Will stayed in the Godly Realm. Such a shame he refused to tell me where you hid the real relic." She picks at her nails not looking at Isa. "We could've been besties by now."

"You-you-you bit-"

"Nuh-uh. Watch your language." She tuts, placing her foot at the front door; her face covered with the ridiculous metal mask. "A pretty gal like you shouldn't use such words."

She closes the door slamming it behind her and grabs a muffin that Elder Arthur must've baked before she killed him.

Eyes stinging at his corpse, Isa shoots an arrow at the Seer Slayer. Miraculously the Seer Slayer raises her hand catching it and exploding the arrow in her arms. "I used to be so innocent, as innocent as you. I'm not entirely the bad guy you make me out to be."

"What do you want?" Isa clenches her jaw shooting another arrow at the Seer Slayer.

"Come on now, you know the answer to that."

The Seer Slayer dodges the arrow by tossing the muffin directly at its tip. The muffin explodes, leaving burnt crumbs everywhere.

"Great. You made me waste a perfectly good muffin." The Seer Slayer grumbles as she chucks a smoke bomb in the center of the living room, clouding Isa's vision. "And you're going to pay for that."

Like one of Haru's shadows, the Seer Slayer attacks Isa from behind, wrapping her forearm around her neck. "Not so hot are you."

Isa turns over her held arrow and stabs it directly at the Seer Slayer. The Seer Slayer flinches, breaking off the arrow from her sides with her hands.

When she is free, Isa throws back her elbows and swings forth with her right fist, punching the Seer Slayer's mask.

It barely leaves a dent.

"What the hell is your mask made of? Titanium?"

"Close. Elkish Steel," remarks Miss Slayer.

"Elkish steel? What the Hades is that?"

Swinging her gauntlets from under her, Isa plants a punch directly at the Seer Slayer's ribs causing her to back up from Isa.

The Seer Slayer catches Isa's second punch and flips Isa over her shoulder like a bean bag.

"That's going to leave a mark," Isa groans, lifting herself back up. Closing her hands in fists and tucking her hand she throws another punch towards the Seer Slayer.

To her disappointment, the Seer Slayer dodges her attempt, leaving a giant hole in the wall in the shape of Isa's gauntlets.

"Are you freaking kidding me!" Isa exclaims. She throws her leg into a high kick, hitting the Slayer to the ground. The Seer Slayer intertwines Isa's other leg with hers and pulls Isa to the floor with her.

Having her in close proximity, Isa unsheathes the dagger she hid in her boot and points it directly at the Seer Slayer's neck.

"Gotcha!" Isa says enthusiastically. The dark sensation whirls inside of her. Greedy.

The Seer Slayer smiles at Isa in approval and disengages the weapon from her hand with a swift hand movement.

"Hey!"

"How disappointing." she flicks the sharp edge underneath Isa's chin. "I'd expected better from you after your duel with the Queen. Nice haircut by the way." She notes from when the Queen's weapon had sliced it.

"Thank you. You can make it shorter if you'd like." Isa leans closer to the blade.

The Seer Slayer quickly drops the weapon and steps away from Isa. "What are you doing?"

"I'd like to ask the same." Isa inches her fingers closer to an arrow on her hip.

"You don't want me dead. Do you? You could've killed me at the infirmary, but you didn't. You know the realm where the last relic is located." Isa states, glaring at the Seer Slayer. "So why keep me alive?"

For a split second, Isa caught the Seer Slayer off guard as she attempted to enter the Seer Slayer's mind to figure out her next move.

However, the Seer Slayer was quick to block her out and slip into Isa's, unraveling an unfortunate memory.

It was nothing like Isa had experienced before.

She went from one battlefield to another.

She was back at Dylan's apartment complex carrying a basket with their favorite Tim Burton film along with a series of snacks they frequently shared. At the time she wore her favorite blue butterfly dress that made her feel beautiful. Special. Confident.

After this, she burned that dress in the back of a shopping mall where she was left alone. Unbothered.

On this specific date, she had planned to make it special as she was excited to tell Dylan that she had decided to stay at the same university as him. That they were going to live together. That she was willing to put her dream school on hold for him.

"No! Get me out of here! Stop it!" Isa screams attempting to snap out of the memory.

But she doesn't.

Past Isa takes a heavy breath as she places her hand on a handle, afraid of what is on the other side. She recalled the vision she had the night before.

"He wouldn't do that to you. It was a silly nightmare." she foolishly whispered to herself as she peered at her engagement ring. It glistened with hope and thousands of lost commitments that had yet to be completed.

Isa turned the handle and heard herself shrill as she watched the love of her life intertwined with her cousin.

Isa forced herself to close her eyes as it was painful to experience it twice. The single drop of her wedding ring was all it took to snap Isa back to the cottage with the Seer Slayer.

Before she knew it, she was slipping, and *it* took over her. Isa launches herself directly at the Seer Slayer's neck pinning her against the wall with her metal gauntlets.

Her eyes burned red as a rose. The sensation grew twice as strong from when she fought the Queen.

"Go ahead kill me, kill as you did in the Aquatic Realm. I know how much you want to do it." The Seer Slayer snickers under Isa's grasp. With gauntlets on, Isa easily could've snapped her neck. She had every chance to do it.

The Seer knew this. Oddly enough she wasn't scared. She was very pleased with Isa, impressed.

"You feel it, don't you? Don't you see? We are far from different. We both have been betrayed by those who we love-"

"Do not say such things!" Isa growls.

"Oh, but it's true! You saw it for yourself! And it's only the start. When your team finds out about your level, they'll drop you as quickly as that man did to you."

Isa tightens her grip. The Seer Slayer wheezes, kicking for air.

"If you work with me and give me your piece of the relic and the next, we can be unstoppable. We can bring on change. Our kind won't be hunted anymore. You won't be abandoned. Not by me. Because you and I are the same." The Seer Slayer croaks, losing her breath.

Following the Seer Slayer's gaze, there in front of them is a broken mirror. The Seer Slayer somehow shifted it so that Isa saw her dead and bloodied.

Horrified at herself. Isa slams the Seer Slayer to the opposite wall. Picture frames fall off, flooding the room with glass shards underneath them.

"You don't know me. Not at all. You're trying to get in my head." Isa reckoned. She can still feel her presence like a snake, twisting, and turning every crevice inside her head to find Isa's weak points.

That's how she managed to persuade the others, how she managed to lure the Seers into the dungeon and convince the King to allow her to seek refuge in the Elf Kingdom.

A level four skill Isa had yet to master; mind manipulation.

Underneath the mask, the corner of the Seer Slayer's lips lifted, eyes entertained by Isa's defiance. "You're an interesting one Isa. I can see why people find someone so quizzical as yourself to be charming. Though, charming can only take you so far. Give me the real relic!" The Seer Slayer orders Isa, growing impatient.

"You'll have to rip it out of my cold hands." Isa reloads her bow and shoots an arrow, this time striking the Seer Slayer's shoulder. Isa considered this as payback for doing the same to her back at Alcania.

"I would rather have you deliver it to me personally. I'm not here to kill you, remember. I'm more than willing to kill your friends instead as an act of a little persuasion." The Seer Slayer takes out the arrow from her shoulder, laughing maniacally.

In comparison to the trials the Seer Slayer had been through, this was child's play.

"I suggest you think about my offer before it is too late, *Isabel.* Otherwise, the next victim will be one of your little friends." Her name naturally rolls off her tongue with a slight Spanish pronunciation.

Isa sneers at the Seer Slayer loading another arrow to her bow.

"Leave them out of this."

Shaking her head, the Seer Slayer replies swiftly "Let me get you a bit of advice, if you want to get things done, you need to remove your heart. It's every person's greatest weakness dear."

"And the best kind of weapon," she murmurs to herself.

The Seer Slayer grabs her transporter and steps right into it. When she does, she closes it immediately so that Isa cannot stop her. Isa recognized the background like no other as she knew the Seer Slayer would be waiting for her in the Vampiric Realm.

Alone with Elder Arthur's body smelling the stench of his corpse and examining the destruction of his cottage, Isa dropped to him. As much as she wanted him to come back, he wouldn't. His soul wasn't in the room, otherwise she would've sensed it.

Popin Peekin

When Isa opens the portal to the hospital, she carries Elder Arthur's corpse to them, the weapon still lodged in his chest. Isa's eyes remained darkened, filled with guilt, almost as if she felt responsible for this death.

She spotted her teammates running down from when she alerted them using the watch Cindy provided her. They received the message and slipped out of the cafeteria.

It looked like they had a food fight while Isa was gone judging by the red sauce on Jack's head. Vero had dunked it on Jack when he tried to take a bite of her loaded unicorn potato French fries. From there when things got ugly.

When they reached Isa, they couldn't believe the position they were in. Will was the most distraught out of all of them.

"No, it can't be, I was with him a few days ago." Will runs his hands over his head.

"Will-" Haru starts.

"No! No! No! Don't touch me!" Will tumbles as he pushes Haru away from him. Isa silently walks towards Will, carefully holding Elder Arthur to him.

Will doesn't recoil at the stench of Elder Arthur's corpse and holds him. His teammates watched as Will desperately attempted to search for any life inside Elder Arthur's body. He waives his hands around his eyes and touches his wrist to feel a pulse.

Will curses loudly when he doesn't receive a heartbeat and takes out the sword of his uncle's body completely disregarding it. The smell of the room intensified under his arms.

"You can't be gone." He mumbles, touching Elder Arthur's face, taking every crevice and detail.

From behind him Jack crouches to the floor and bows down to Elder Arthur's body. The team does the same, Jessie whispering a prayer under her breath.

Checking out the smell, a few patients, some of whom were rescued Seers, spotted Elder Arthur's body in Will's arms. Some kneeled while others in wheelchairs lowered their heads. The room was silent enough to hear the heart monitors of patients in the hospitals along with other machinery.

He takes his uncle's body and places him on the floor bowing him out of pure respect, jaw clenching, eyes gray of clouds on a rainy day.

Behind them stood Elder Arthur's ghost. He was right above Will touching his shoulder. Isa didn't say a word as Elder Arthur placed his index finger on the top of his lips.

He simply stays beside Will whispering a few silent words of affirmation before fading into thin air.

For a while, Will stayed with his uncle, burying his face in his uncle's clothes despite the smell emitting from his body. It got to the point where the officials had to rip Will off his uncle's body so that they could start the preparations for his funeral.

When he did let go, his sensitive elf heart stung enough for him to collapse. This time Isa was quick enough to catch him in time. She stayed by his side and monitored Will while the team members handled the rest such as informing important Elders' and helping with funeral preparations.

"He had a heart attack, but he'll recover with enough time." The nurse informed Isa.

Isa weakly nods and keeps her eyes on him. "I'm so sorry Will."

The funeral itself was similar to Kate and George's. Close to the cottage, they set a roaring fire to send items to Elder Arthur. Will had sent a letter he wrote to Elder Arthur and one of his favorite pastries. Isa had sent him a copy of a picture of all the Seers including Perla and Beau. The rest of the team members sent their own items, each with a personal connection to Elder Arthur.

Though, the funeral was only the start of the day. The team made it a goal to restore Elder Arthur's cottage to a stable condition, or rather, now Will and Isa's cottage.

When Isa first teleported to the Celestial Facility, Elder Arthur stayed back. His reason was to complete his will. It was almost as if he knew what would happen to him.

(Wink. Wink.)

Cleaning up the house, Vero was in charge of helping Haru with the dishes, since she could not stand the stench of Elder Arthur's corpse roaming in the house. Will fixed up any destroyed furniture and did some light cleaning and tending while avoiding Elder Arthur's room. Isa was nervous for Will knowing how close he was to Elder Arthur. She was afraid that the damage she and the Seer Slayer had done would've sent him into a coma.

In her opinion, his actual reaction felt worse. Nothing. He kept a stoic expression as he saw pieces of the picture frames scattered on the floor. Isa opted to clean the hardwood floors to remove the dried-up blood. Will didn't oppose. None of them did.

Jack wanted to comfort Will a few times, but Jessie stepped in and stopped him. "Let him settle first."

Jack frowned and peered at Will once more before heading into the forest with her to search for any reminiscence or signs of the Seer Slayer.

Disappointingly enough, they didn't find anything.

It was getting dark, and hunger was setting in. Subconsciously, the team met together at the dining table outside with the fireflies to keep them company. As their stomachs rumbled, there was a silent realization.

Elder Arthur wasn't there to prepare them dinner anymore.

Will sighs, following his gaze to a singular firefly in the distance. Isa places her hand next to Will's, openly offering it to him. A faint one-sided smile appears on his cheeks. He whispers a silent thank you and tugs her hand closer to him.

"Food anyone?" Jack offers, opening a portal to who knows where. Without thinking twice, the team eagerly hops right in. Together, they come across a tavern with a sign titled Poppin Peekin.

From the outside, it was covered in moss, barely unrecognizable. Any pedestrian could walk past it thinking it was a massive tree lying sideways had it not been for the long line leading to the corner of the small town.

To enter the tavern, you must say a secret code to the bouncer. In their case, it was not necessary. When the bouncer spotted Jack and the team, they were immediately let in. The restaurant was cozy as it had a fireplace in the center of the room along with small lanterns hanging from the top of each table. It was dimly lit enough for anyone to take a nap, which there was a gremlin or two who did.

The bouncer, who by the way is a purple-haired ogre, led them to the tavern hall to a slightly older woman in pirate attire. She leaned in her chair appearing to be asleep and opened her eyes when she heard them enter. Stretching, the pirate lady completely woke from her supposed slumber.

She gladly greeted every one of them and with a hooked hand, she reached out to Isa to shake.

"Isa are ye?" Her eyes glimmered green. She maneuvered in her golden wheelchair equipped with small cannons and swords.

"Yes?" Isa replies, unsure if she should shake her hook. It was sharp enough to puncture the center of her hand.

The pirate harks a peal of laughter and bumps the round area against the knuckles of Isa.

'Allow me t' introduce meself! Name's Carol. I'm thy owner of tis establishment thou see'st!" She smiles revealing a golden tooth in her mouth. "Food is on meh!"

"Are you sure Carol?"

"Mor shure than me ma! You'est a hero. Aren't ye?"

"Well…"

"Ye too humble!" Carol harks. Her golden tooth catches a tinge of orange as the light of the fire reaches her smile.

Vero cackles and Haru slowly tries to move Isa away for her own sake. "We'll if you don't mind Carol we'll go ahead and-"

Shaking her hook in the air, Carol shouts a name and outcomes flying a fae with purple eyes like Jessie. Her wings kept her afloat and, on her name, tag it states Evlyn. Like the other waitresses, she wore a brown apron with a hook.

"She'll be ye severer!" Carol's rough voice glees with a slight growl.

"Thank you, Carol." Isa gives a slight bow showing her respect. Carol harks and allows Evlyn to show them their table.

"Ye a fun'ny one Isa. E'njoy!"

Centaurs, pixies, fae, duendes, and other magical creatures occupying the restaurant eye the group as they pass through them. They all gave a nod of assurance and admiration to Isa and the team.

A small little girl with black curls in her hair runs to Isa and grabs her leg. "My daddy told me how you saved him. Thank you for letting him come home."

A mother with a level one Seer cloak comes and grabs the little girl's hand. "I'm so sorry." She shakes her head, and they go back to the table where the father sits. He smiled at Isa and gave her a small nod. The man had been one of the Seers who grabbed Isa's body when she appeared in the dungeon. His face among others was unforgettable. Isa made sure of that.

Although everyone saw Isa as some sort of Seer hero, she felt the opposite. Like a sort of mark of disaster wherever she went. A fraud.

When they got seated, Isa felt the weight of her presence. She forced herself to keep her hands at her sides to stop them from shaking.

"We can get takeout if you want?" Vero whispers to Isa feeling her anxiety.

Isa shakes her head and peeks at the menu hazy with the descriptions of each dish.

In the corner of the table next to Jack, Jessie's eyes gaze upon the waitress's wings. She once had them before they were cut and taken from her.

For centuries, there has not been a cure to heal or regrow broken wings. When her wings had been cut off by her crazed widowed fae mother, Jessie spent her free time formulating and figuring out a way for her wings to regenerate.

After all, wings were an extension of themselves.

She could still recall all those months she spent in a wheelchair learning how to walk and balance herself without her wings. She took various notes of her progress and contributed them to her studies. It was a bitter miracle she could walk, let alone stand. To this day, Jessie still struggles with phantom pains in her spine and frequent moments of imbalance during her sparing lessons at the Celestial Facility.

She would not give up until she found a solution. It would be groundbreaking for the fae community.

It can be argued that Jessie was the most studious out of everyone because of her personal project.

Many found her to be foolish to consider such a thing, but Jessie didn't care. She wanted to fly. She wanted to feel the wind against her face again.

Her discovery of a regrowth skin serum using various combinations of potions and elixirs is what got her a scholarship to the Celestial Facility in the first place. When Jessie could, she spent late nights conducting experiments here and there.

As a fellow half-breed, Will occasionally helped her for they had been there for each other through their trauma and similar struggles. For years they had been friends and when they had gone to the Celestial Facility, Will was the one to introduce her to Jack. They naturally became friends, and when the teams had been formed for the missions, she then met Haru and Vero. Vero then introduced Kate to everyone.

Out of everyone on the team, when Jack found out about her project, he found it quite amusing. He may not have been the brightest bulb to understand anything, but when he got hurt, (which was pretty often), he allowed himself to act as a lab rat. The two would eventually spend time together as Jessie gave him tutoring lessons to repay him.

In terms of their relationship, Jessie and Jack went back and forth, for she knew someday Jack would find the one, which she knew she wasn't. She knew how much Jack anticipated the day he was able to participate in the soulmate ritual. If she wasn't his soulmate, Jessie had no other choice but to move on. Will had been lucky to be paired with Isa, though at the expense of a deadly ceremony that could've cost both of their lives. So, to prevent the pain, she stopped pursuing Jack, but that did not stop her from loving the senseless goofball.

At the restaurant, Jack noticed her gaze and reached her hand over the table. She playfully flicks his hand away and sips her multi-colored drink.

The remainder of the time, as the food was arriving at the table, Isa kept asking "Will this kill me?" before taking a bite.

It was humorous to the team as her human curiosities reminded them of a little lamb exploring a new field. Granted, they haven't been with a Dreamer this long before. It's not every day that a Dreamer is lucky enough to find their Realm.

It was forbidden for quite some time after several lives were lost when Humans erroneously were guided inside the portal. Something about being a Hue and portals don't mix well, except Dreamers, yet they're not always easy to find.

Will slightly cracked a smile before sipping down his purple fizzy drink as he thought about Elder Arthur and his tumultuous history.

"So… I have to ask, how old are you guys?" Isa partially burps, covering her mouth with one hand. Jack saw it as a challenge and offered a burping contest, which Vero quickly shut down.

"Don't be disgusting Jack."

"What? I could've shown her what a real burp sounds like."

"None of us want to hear that." Jessie groans, smacking the top of her head with her palm.

"Yeah, some of us have manners, Jackson." Haru comments. "As you were saying, Isa."

"Oh. Um, you guys aren't thousands of years old right? Not that is a bad thing but…"

Vero chokes on her drink. "Are you calling us old?"

"No! Not that! Usually in the books I've read, magic folk are like…" The more she tried to explain the stupider she thought she sounded.

"We're not Vampires Isa, we live the same life expectancy as any Hue."

"If I didn't know any better, we're right around the same as you. Early twenties I assume."

"Twenty-two," Isa confirms.

"Wow exactly the same age as us. Except for Will. He's an old man."

"I'm only a year older! Let it go, Jack!"

"Oh, thank god." Isa brushes the tip of her hair with her index finger. The whole 'old man' part almost had her. Though,

Will was pretty fine looking to where Isa wouldn't care too much if he did end up being a century-old half-elf, having him a year older was a relief in its own way.

"What?" His attention is fully on her. The corner of his lips displays a faint smirk.

"Nothing." Isa denies, revisiting her barbeque ribs.

During their meal, she somehow manages to secretly borrow Jack's ability to keep her food warm. Thankfully they were too distracted by the food coming in and out of the kitchen. All she needed to do was to focus on the person and their ability, and she had it for the next few minutes. She didn't need to touch them or anything.

Not saying a word, Vero felt this through her telekinetic abilities. She could tell when a level four Seer was borrowing abilities by the change of wavelengths from one person to another. She made sure to keep Isa's little secret to herself and discuss it with her later. At the start, she thought it had been because of the soulmate ceremony since her energy had grown, but this exchange of energy was nothing Vero had sensed before. It confirmed her assumptions.

As their orders came in, their plates covered the table to the brim. Vero had a few drinks called Side Sea. The drink itself had fog coming out of it and the liquid bubbled to a nice ocean blue. Isa was tempted to order one and decided against it.

She was thankful she did because she was scared she wasn't going to stomach the food and her drinks in her belly as occasional admirers came to the table to see the iconic "Hero" who saved the Seers. Among them were also protestors who shot dirty looks at their table.

One pink-skinned and green-eyed woman surprised Isa as she was disgusted by the mere fact of her status. "Why are we thanking her? She is one step away from a level four. If I were her, I'd turn myself in and die like the rest of- "

Carol overhears the commotion and immediately orders the Bouncer to kick her out.

"Get your hands off me!" Yells the woman. "You should all be terrified of her! She's a Seer. A no-good-diabolical- "

The ogre tosses her out and all eyes are on Isa. She was shaking inside her green cloak, tugging it tightly on her.

Carol quickly rushes over to the table and starts apologizing to Isa. "Me'est sorry. Tho'est shouldn't bear her."

"It's okay Carol." Isa weakly replies. "Thank you for the lovely dinner."

She meant it.

As Isa rises out of her seat and makes her way outside of the tavern a man in a red suit stops her, handing Isa a white envelope.

Isa eyebrows knit together as she gazes at the embellishment at the center of the envelope, "Mortinae" intricately spelled with an anatomical heart in the center.

Isa looks up from the envelope and finds the man gone.

"Isa!" Her teammates call as they run out of the tavern to catch up to her.

She waves her hand and gestures for them to follow her under a dim lamplight.

"What is that?" Haru inquires as Isa hands it to him.

"I don't know."

"Holy Centaur!"

"What does it say?"

"This can't be good."

"That means we'll only have a day."

"A day for what?"

In the invitation, members of the Vampiric Court, Mortinae, invited the team, (specifically Isa), to the masquerade blood ball in the Vampiric Realm. It was the perfect place for the Seer Slayer to hide in plain sight and for all the five relics to come alive. According to the invitation, masks were indeed mandatory to keep everyone's identity a secret. The ball was famously known to the elites and royals of all realms and thus their identities remain hidden.

For a moment, as Haru read the invitation Isa's field of vision showed her in a ballroom, there in the center is the relic. It was being auctioned.

"This is bad," Isa murmured to herself.

They needed to devise a plan. A quick one, as they were running out of time.

Last Goodbye

When Isa and Will came home, they agreed to check Elder Arthur's room before heading to bed. They made sure to save the room last as Will wanted to build the strength to enter it. Additionally, he felt comfortable having Isa beside him.

"Do you want to enter alone?" Isa asks Will, holding his hand. He had yet to shed a tear the entire day. Isa knew he was about to break at some point in time. She too had once been the same way in her realm. She held all her pain and stress in until she got home and broke down in her room, only to wipe it all away within minutes and drive to her work as if nothing ever happened.

Will shakes his head and insists they enter together. When they did, the room smelt like an old library and pastries, the same smell as Elder Arthur. Knowing how dark the room was, Isa kept a lantern with them as they searched and organized his room. There on his desk next to the glowing mushroom is a letter he left them; his writing is similar to Will's.

By the time you find this, I'll be long gone. Do not be alarmed as I knew the stars would align to this moment. During your time at the facility, I had a vision of the Seer Slayer coming here. If I had been found dead with a sword on my chest, that must have meant I had met my demise. Do not blame the Seer Slayer. Like any of you, she is a hurt person in dire need of healing.

Will scoffs underneath cursing a foul word known and used in Alcania. A word that Isa couldn't pronounce without butchering it.

I took my life because she would've searched my brain to find the relic I had hidden. Isa if you are reading this, which I hope you are, the relic I hid is inside the mushroom. I know how much you like to look at it. I kept it safe as you wanted.

Isa, feel free to keep my closet, I don't need those damn out of fashion worn out cloaks. Think of it as a gift. In my closet, there is a shoebox of mine, there you will find more photos of Perla and Beau I have saved all these years.

Stay strong Isa. You will need to for what lies ahead of you. Don't let the Seer Slayer taint you.

If it is not Isa, to the person reading this, please allow Will to read the rest.

On the next page is an entire letter addressed to Will. Isa hands it to him and proceeds to leave the room to give him privacy. Grabbing her hand gently, he tells her to stay and to read it to him for his elf heart can only handle so much.

Nodding her head, Isa reads the rest.

My dearest nephew,
You have grown into a mighty gentleman. I can recall every moment of the days we spent in the forest teaching you to use a sword like no other. In so many ways you remind me of your father. Victor

would be so proud of you. I'll be with him in the afterlife recalling every tale, though he must already know for he is most likely watching over you.

You deserve to know more about him. He was a general and head of weapon management as a sorcerer of creation in Alcania. The Queen is indeed your mother and the only living parent. Your father passed not long after you were born. I sadly do not know all the details other than his death had been the cause of poisoning.

In the rest of his letter, Elder Arthur wrote about Will's father such as his likes, dislikes, and childhood memories that characterized his father as witty, patient, and loving. He briefly mentioned Cobalt, as she had been the family dragon, along with her ancestors before her. He urges Will to tell Cobalt his goodbye for he could no longer do so.

Near the end of the letter, he finishes it off with a few last words of sentiment or so.

Remember when I told you that I would take care of you? I meant it. The house is yours my boy, and if you desire to share it, Isa's as well. Keep it for it is my way of sheltering you.

Although I am not the best with words, I will say this.

I love you, my dear nephew. Always. Don't blame yourself for what happened to me.

-Elder Arthur

Putting the paper down, Isa uses the light of the lantern to make out Will's expression. She saw tears pouring out of his gray eyes as if they had been dark clouds and the tears were the rain.

His arm gripping his chest to console himself. He didn't expect Isa to comfort him, but she did without hesitation. Isa lightly wraps his arms around him as he melts into them. She hopes to never see him again in such a way. Isa would rather duel with the Queen once again.

"Will, I know how much Elder Arthur means to you. I'm so sorry." Isa whispers to his ears, her hand lightly touching his soft white short elf hair.

He doesn't say anything but nods. He didn't like the fact that she saw him this way. He wanted to be the one to hold her. To comfort her in her struggles and protect Isa from all dangers. It hurt him to see her defeated numerous times.

He sought to protect Elder Arthur too but failed. He failed him.

"Don't blame yourself, Will." He could almost hear him through the letter. It stung like a thousand wasps. One after another.

Reflecting on the last dinner they had together, Will regretted not paying better attention. Elder Arthur was completely calm, too calm for his own good. He suspiciously made Will's favorite dish growing up and gave him the recipe. Will thought it was his usual kind gesture or rather his means of support coming back from Alcania. His suspicions had been awfully right.

Will was thankful that the two had a heart-to-heart conversation and for all the years Elder Arthur had kept him under his wing. Yet, he wished he had more time with him.

He was Will's anchor. His stability. His only parental figure. His family.

Taking a shaky breath, Will turns his back facing away from Isa filled with shame. Her grip stayed on his waist, and she rested her head on his shoulder blade.

"You have us, all right. You have me, Haru, Vero, Jessie, and Jack. We're your family. Nothing is ever going to change that. You're my soulmate, Will." Isa confessed.

As the words ran out of her heart and into her tongue, she slowly became aware of herself how it was her first time saying it out loud. How she was calling her his.

Taking in each other, the two stood in the dark room with the light of the mushroom on the desk and the lantern. Isa didn't know it, but she too had tears in her eyes.

"Do you remember when I said my favorite color is red?" His gray eyes meet hers; a tinge of orange appears from the flame of the lantern. He raises his hand and gently brushes a tear on her cheek where Kate slashed open.

Isa nods, not saying a word. She was falling. Falling hard. She wanted to protect this man. She wanted to heal him. To treasure him as he would to her. She felt it.

"It's because of you. You're my red, Isa." He passionately whispers. The tip of his finger touches Isa's chin, his thumb resting on her cheek.

Truth.

Isa takes a deep breath. Her face and body are warm, only this is a good type of warmth. She could hear her heart pounding to come out of her chest cavity.

"May I?" He whispers, eyes flickering to Isa's lips and returning to hers.

Isa takes in his scent of cinnamon and the forest outside of the cottage on him.

"Yes," Isa responds, moving forward, pressing her lips against his moving together softly and swiftly. Her other hand free from his, held the back of his neck. His other hand trails to her waist pulling her body closer to him.

Hearing the sounds of crickets and owls in the distance and being completely breathless, the two pulled away. They didn't want to, rather they had to. They were wasting time.

They both knew they needed sleep for the nightmares waiting for tomorrow. They dreaded it.

Their war was getting started.

Sleeping on the same bed, Isa allowed herself to doze off from the sounds of Will's sleepy breaths as his chest rose and fell. She found a sense of relief from it. Maybe, because she had gotten used to the notion of death, she saw any signs of livelihood to be assuring. Thinking back on the horrors of the lives lost, she held him close, and he held her closer.

If she wanted to keep this moment forever, she was going to fight like hell tomorrow.

33

Preparation

It was the day of the ball. To Isa's surprise, her slumber had not been infiltrated by any visions or spiritual encounters. Rather, she had a dream, she dreamt about her family, it was a calm and uneventful movie night. They made freshly cooked palomitas with some Tapatío in it. Isa always had to make a separate batch because she hated the texture and wasn't a fan of sharing germs.

"Wake up Red." a voice murmurs softly.

Isa grumbled, digging her face deeper into the pillow.

"Come on. It's time." Will rose from his side of the bed and lightly poked her cheek numerous times before kissing it.

"I hate mornings," Isa muttered, her cheeks turning a light pink.

"I did too."

"How'd you get over it?" Isa stretches her arms and feels around her head. She hated how her antlers were uneven.

"Seeing your face. Are you usually this colorful in the morning?" He pinches her cheek. Isa waves his hand away from her face and shoots him a glare.

"No. Are you this bothersome in the morning?"

"Always."

"Ugh. I want to insult you, but I already said you looked pretty."

"You also said you wanted my head and called my hair nice."

"I was delirious."

Hungry and very much awake, everyone reviewed the plan at the breakfast table clarifying any type issues or flaws within the bites of pastries Jack brought.

There were backups upon backups to ensure the best outcome. Their overall goal is to have the relic in any of their hands before the Seer Slayer can use it.

If the object is assembled and the Seer Slayer has it underneath the formation of the full-blood moon, it will be over for everyone. At this point, the main goal would be to break apart the relic before a wish is made.

Once the blood moon is no longer at its peak, all will be permanent.

Using Isa's designs from her journal as inspiration for the ball, Will crafted outfits for everyone.

"How do you always manage to get sizes right?" Isa asks while watching him craft Haru's dark blue suit. Will simply grabs a pile of clothes and presses it into his hands. His hands create a glow and are replaced with a suit.

"When you make clothes as long as I have and are assigned classes specifically for sorcerers of creation, you learn a thing or two."

Like college courses to specific majors, kids at academies, aside from basic classes, provide specific courses for different sorcerers to put their ability into effect. Will took up various courses, excelling in them to reach the top of his class.

He did so to build himself a future away from his elf counterpart and to prove his potential. He was often underestimated until it was his turn to show off to the class. Sorcerers envied him, aside from Jessie, who was glad someone in their academy had the same drive as her.

Both bonded over the idea of beating the odds and creating their own paths. They were platonic best friends until Kate came in and ruined everything.

She did not like Kate whatsoever. As a half-fae, Jessie could quickly pinpoint when someone had been authentic. She knew Kate was hiding something and was right to be suspicious.

She kept her distance and decided to keep quiet as she resumed her studies. Jack too took into account but kept the peace among the group as Kate had been Vero's and Will's closest friends.

"Wow Will, you really outdid yourself," Jessie comments behind Isa, also watching him make their clothes.

"Don't give me all the credit, Red over here designed these." Will motions to Isa's tilting his head while concentrating on the outfit.

Jessie cringed at the nickname and gave a nod. "Mind if I see what other things you've designed?"

"That would be great!" Isa smiles, proudly handing over her journal.

While they kept themselves busy, Vero had been changing into her dress, and Haru was outside meditating, preparing himself to enter the Vampiric Realm. During meditation, he hears the footsteps of Jack on the grass near him, opening a portal to leave.

At his cottage, Jack started to hyperventilate.

He had been deeply scared. Petrified. Restless.

Sitting on the living room floor, Jack began to shake. He was having a panic attack. Thoughts raced through his mind of Isa's vision thinking about the possibility of obtaining a serious life-threatening injury.

"What's wrong with me." He said out loud. Usually, he could keep his cool and manage to overcome any type of battle tossed at him, but now things were different.

He didn't want to die.

He wanted to live. He wanted to have a life. Have a soulmate and kids.

He could picture his future vanishing from his grip as if it had all been placed into a photo and caught by fire. What could he do?

He's never been in such circumstances, in fact, he always laughed at death. Multiple times, he encountered dangerous tasks as he effortlessly could shield himself with the physique he had built. Day and night he worked various hours at the gym to shape his body to his liking. His strength and ability to succeed in combat was the one thing he was ever good at. He feared nothing.

Until now.

His bravery is what got him admitted to the Celestial Facility in the first place. In his village, nothing but his strength kept him alive. His family couldn't afford his education, so he spent most of his adolescence sailing the seas and taking on dangerous tasks to pay the bills. He considered going to school various times, but life had other plans. He envied the kids who could afford to attend Celestial academies.

It was almost by a miracle, Elder Arthur stumbled upon Jack in one of his missions. Right on the spot, Elder Arthur offered Jack a second chance at life with an entrance to the Celestial Facility.

It was his golden ticket for a better life.

Elder Arthur knew Jack's abilities were far from normal from the way he yielded himself in combat and mastered his abilities over the years he did not go to school. Jack could swallow anyone in the ground by opening it, drown a person in the sea, take their breath away, and most of all, burn them with his flames if he ever needed to.

That all meant nothing considering the blood moon disarmed any and all abilities. Leaving only his weapon and physical strength.

He indeed had been big and brawny, but right now, he felt small and frail.

His life was at stake. He needed to brace himself if he were to die today.

Fighting against his dark thoughts, he grabbed a quill and a piece of paper and began to write a will. He hoped he didn't need to, but he couldn't let fear eat him any longer. Jack accepted the slight chance of dying.

Midway through, the third quill in his hands snapped as he heard a knock at the door. Peeking at the peephole, he saw Haru. He glanced at his inked hands and decided not to open it.

"Everything okay Jack?" Haru loudly shouts.

"Yeah, everything is groovy." Jack musters out trying to sound happy enough. He grabbed a nearby rag and began to wipe his hands.

"You don't sound too groovy," Haru replies through the door.

"I'm okay, Haru." He asserts, frustrated at the stains of the ink that wouldn't come off.

Giving up, Jack leaned against the door and slid down to the floor in a fetal position. His hands ran through his head waiting for Haru's reply in the silent pause.

"I'll take your word for it."

"What?" Jack arched his neck further into the door, listening closer expecting some kind of scolding or for Haru to question him further.

"I'll take your word for it. I'll leave you be and meet you at Elder Arthur's." His voice lowered at Elder Arthur's name as it was technically no longer his cottage.

Jack blinked back a tear that was threatening to eat the edge of his iris and sunk further into his position at Elder Arthur's name.

"Though Jack before I go, let me give you a bit of advice. That's all I will do, and I won't bother you anymore. Okay?"

Haru waits for Jack to reply.

He doesn't.

Haru tosses his head back and closes his eyes as though he is imagining Jack in front of him.

"Take it from me as someone who is a sorcerer of shadows, it's not always best to hold everything in. Eventually, it will start to consume you alive until you can't hold it in any longer."

Jack slowly loosens his grip around his arms and truly listens to Haru.

"In a way, it's like you're a bucket holding water from under a leaky pipe. At first, it doesn't seem like much but over time, it gets overwhelming and everything spills right out of you, creating a giant mess. If it's not talking, you can always write, or journal to yourself. You don't need to deal with things alone. You don't have to explain anything to me either. I just want to be there for you. That is all."

Waiting for a reply, Haru continues filling the slight pause "I'll be meditating if you need me. Feel free to join. It's okay if you don't and want some alone time. I get it."

Turning away from the door, Haru hears it open from behind him. Standing there is a distraught and nerve-wrecked Jack. His palms were bleeding slightly from the shards of the pens he accidentally broke.

"Can I meditate with you?"

Haru nods his head smiling. "You can always meditate with me if you need to. You don't have to talk. We can just meditate. Of course, as long as you don't try to hit on me or check me out. Vero wouldn't like that."

A corner of his mouth lifts. "You do have a fine butt."

Haru punches Jack's arm and opens the portal.

"I'll see you at Elder Arthur's to meditate."

"Good. I'll be waiting." Haru takes a step in the portal.

"Okay." Jack nods his head.

"Oh, and Haru?"

"Hm?"

"Thanks for checking up on me," Jack's chest sinks and bounces back up.

"Of course." Haru adjusts his glasses closer to his eyes, leaving Jack alone with a shadowed smile.

When he finished putting himself together, he returned to the cottage and meditated with Haru who was eagerly waiting for Jack despite not showing it.

When Will finishes making his last dress, he hands it over to Isa. Not saying a word, he goes outside and takes a nap on a hammock close to where Jack and Haru had been meditating.

Isa let him be and brightened at the dress she had been holding.

It was red with a hint of golden details such as the loose golden chains that draped on her waist and around her body. It connected to the skirt of the dress which loosely draped across her legs and down to her ankles. Hints of glitter and shine were sprinkled across the mesh of the skirt to give the illusion of a crimson waterfall.

It was light enough to give Isa mobility and allure potential vampires for a taste.

The top half was cut downward in a V-shape followed by pleated metal armor on her shoulders. Her forearms possessed metal cuffs covered in more transparent fabric and her metal boots were barely visible under the dress's length. Underneath, she wore shorts for when she desired to take off the overskirt.

While she could wear armor, visible weapons were not allowed, thus she had to disregard her gauntlets.

On top of the dress, Isa placed one of Elder Arthur's cloaks, wearing it proudly. It draped behind her in its velvetiness. Around her neck, is a simple necklace with their soulmate symbol engraved.

Happily putting it on, Isa enters her room checking in on Jessie and Vero.

Vero's green dress, out of preference, had a slit on the side and hugged her body like a dream. On her arms are elongated puffy sleeves that stop at her bare shoulders. The corset boning had mesh, revealing more skin, and was lined with golden stitching patterns. Since Vero loved having texture on her clothing, scattered throughout the dress are intricate beading work and lace.

On her neck, she wore a golden choker that had secretly been a weapon. Once she took it off, her opponent would be the one choking. Speaking of weapons, most she hid had been in her hair, all laced with poison. If she needed to paralyze anyone, all she needed to do was take out a sharp pin from her hair and stab them in lethal points. She also hid a blade in the place her body wasn't entirely exposed, her spine. No one would suspect a thing.

Vero also helped Isa and Jessie conceal a few hairpins by putting their hair in an undo and topping it off with all three wearing flower crowns embezzled with red gems and golden flakes.

On their faces were masks reflecting the style of their dress. Vero's had gold wiring; one side of her face covered more than the other as if part of the mask had intentionally been missing. It was sleek and simple, for she did not like having too much in her face, especially around her eyes.

Isa's mask completely covered the top half of her face with the animalistic features of a fox. The ears extended at the top of her head. Sliding down to the tip of her nose is the sharp snout of the animal. Red, white, and gold detailing filled the mask to the brim putting pressure on Isa's face.

When Jessie went into the bathroom to change into her wardrobe, Vero pulled Isa aside to warn her of the Vampiric Realm.

"Isa, I need you to listen to me carefully. You need to be *careful*." Vero whispers, holding Isa's hand.

"So do you."

"No, Isa I mean *really* careful with whom you talk to." Vero's hands tighten.

Isa tilts her attention away from their hands and gazes at Vero pensively. "Whom I talk to? Vero you're speaking in riddles. What do you mean?"

"The Vampiric Realm is crawling with spirits and the dead. If someone catches you speaking to them,"

"How did you-"

"My ability. Unlike other telekinetic sorcerers, I have more perception. I felt the shift of energy towards you during dinner."

"Oh." Isa rubs the back of her neck.

"Isa, if the word gets out about you, who knows what they'll do to you. I need you to promise me you won't use your ability."

"What if I need it?"

"Promise me, Isa." Vero prompts, snapping.

"I promise." She sighs.

"Good. I can't lose any more people. I'm already worried about Jack; I don't need more people to give me a headache."

"How do I look?" Jessie walks out of the bathroom.

"I think she's asking you, Isa." Vero jokes, her voice no longer stern.

"The outfit looks great Jessie. Rocking it." Isa gestures two positive thumbs up in the air.

"I better be." Jessie poses confidently.

Dressed in the living room, the guys and Jessie wore suits made for royal guards, allowing them more leverage to hide their weapons. Haru and Will wore matching colors of their partners while Jack's was all white and Jessie's was a lavender purple, contrasting her dark purple eyes.

Will made a special touch by adding small, winged features such as detailing wings on the cuffs of her wrists and attaching a green silk cape trailing behind her. Her mask was also winged on the sides and covered in flower decorations. Somehow a piece of it extended upward past her head creating antlers.

Acknowledging these details, her neon hair glimmered and brightened sparking her Fae abilities. On her hands, she wore gloves that acted as an ice pack when she took them off.

"How do I look?" Isa asked Will spinning her body.

"Stunning," Will responds breathlessly.

Isa smiles and replies with a sort of sarcastic remark. Will chuckles and adjusts his mask.

"Okay, we get it, we all look hot," Jack says, one of his hands in flames. He flexes in front of a mirror and right next to him, Jessie tells him to move.

"Hey Narcissus, mind sharing the spotlight."

"Only if you can find me a four-leaf clover." He retaliates.

Ready in their clothes and masks, the team enters the portal to the Vampiric realm, their clothes and the weight of the world on their shoulders. They all peer at their watches monitoring the time change as they exit the portal.

"Remember, once the red moon comes out, our powers no longer work. Blow your whistle if you need help or send out the signal." Will reminds the team.

They all nod, taking a heavy breath, and approach the castle, Isa holding the invitation in her hand. After all, she's the one the Vampire King wanted to see.

Meeting the Vampire King

The Vampiric Realm is a dark place.

It's a fact known by any misguided mortal infatuated with Death.

Vampires lurked in every shadow of the night searching for a willing or unwilling victim to prey upon. While it wasn't necessary to drink their blood to survive, it gave Vampires a surge of adrenaline.

One vampire in particular hid in the corner of a a house and bit a tall white-haired woman, depriving her of life. His mouth was wrapped around her neck like a python and loosened when she had stopped fighting. Drops of her silver blood drenched the pavement, leaving little to the imagination. When she regained consciousness, she smiled at her fellow vampire and kissed him.

"Okay, team. Remember to stay calm. Does everyone have their whistles?"

"Yes, for the millionth time Will." Vero groans.

"Are we lost?" Isa eyes the path they are on. The team walked through a snow-covered graveyard. There were bodies halfway buried in dirt, open for rats and woodland skin eaters to take their liberties.

Isa had to turn away when she spotted a two-headed hairless creature feasting on an innocent corpse that had yet to be buried. It resembled Elder Arthur to an extent.

"The Vampiric Realm isn't the most attractive realm. There are graveyards in every other town. This one happens to lead us to the castle, and arguably is the nicest one."

"You're kidding." Isa shifts her attention to the naked trees and withered flowers hanging over her by a thread. At her feet were patches of snow doing the bare minimum to cover any bloodstains.

The only beauty the Vampiric Realm may offer is the night sky as the stars glistened at the team with a shard of hope. The red moon has yet to make an appearance, but soon enough when it's least expected, it will.

"I wish I was," Haru muttered under his breath. After the Aquatic Realm, he had done tremendous work with himself as he didn't want to slip away again. He meditated constantly and did exercises with Vero. He was surprised the portal let him through.

"We're here." Jack gulps as they reach the end of their path. A few clouds began to close in, and the wind slid through the fabric of their clothes, earning a chill from the team.

"I'm starting to re-think this whole saving the world mission."

"You and me both sister," Jessie whispers to Isa.

At the tall, blackened gates, Isa handed her invitation to the sullen guard resting against the brick walls. On his name tag, it spells Jose. The bags under his eyes indicated he never had a day of rest in his life.

"Invitation." He yawns, reaching out his hand.

Jessie pulls it out from the pocket of her vest and hands it to him.

He rolls his eyes and adjusts himself when he recognizes a small stamp on the invitation. "Ah yes." He peers at them. "Right this way."

Jose lifts his back away from the wall and escorts the team to another guard who had been expecting their arrival.

This guard, like the one in the front, had darkened sunset eyes. She happily moved them away from the general direction of the crowd and snuck them into a hidden entrance to the dreary castle.

In comparison to the vampire at the gate, she was much livelier and sociable. She made a few cheesy vampire jokes, none of which members laughed at.

"For someone who is living, you guys are pretty much dead. Where's your sense of humor?" The guard remarks.

"Probably where your soul is," muttered Vero under her breath.

"Vero!"

"I'm only speaking the truth." She asserts defensively. Haru couldn't help but chuckle into his hand.

The guard hisses at Vero revealing a pair of large, pointed fangs.

Vero retaliates by hissing back at her.

Aside from Isa, none of the team members had a fondness for vampires. In every mission, the vampires would try to persuade each member to trade their blood and soul, in exchange for eternal life. None of the team members fell for this, for they saw the ramifications.

(A vampiric life isn't one to take lightly, dear reader.)

Jack personally dealt with enough vampires to learn his lesson to turn away from their offer. He once came close but luckily Vero stepped in before the vampire could pierce the vein on his neck. She stabbed him in the heart with a steel pin that had been wrapped around her hair.

"Which one do you think it is in?"

"Hard to tell." Will whispers to Jack.

The vampire guides the team through the castle, passing a series of rooms, many of which are locked to the public behind decorative steel doors.

To Isa's amusement, the castle did not smell anywhere close to the graveyard. It was pleasant, peaceful, and soothing. She used the scent all the time for her humidifier. Lavender.

The scent carried itself through the waxy bundle of candles and blazing torches that lit their pathway from the sides of the dimmed castle. As they flickered and hissed, Isa couldn't help but compare its atmosphere to the cave of the Aquatic Realm.

"Isa?" Will hollered in front of her as he caught Isa staring at another narrow entry of the castle. The group had made it to the end of the hall by the time they realized she was missing.

"Hmm?"

"This way." Will turned the nook of his neck gesturing to the guard who was slowly losing her patience.

"Chop Chop. The King will not be happy if we are late."

"Sorry." Isa sheepishly replies, catching up with Will. The guard continued to lead the group, earning a few more snarky remarks and dreadfully not-so-funny dead jokes.

"Hey. Are you okay Red?" Will lightly touches her shoulder, turning her to him.

"Yeah. I just um, I keep thinking of…"

"The Seer Slayer, or Miss Slayer as Jack calls her."

"Yes." The corner of Isa's lips pricks upward and collapses into its place. "Her. Ugh."

"We'll stop her."

"Will…"

"We will stop her."

"And what if we don't?"

"Why do you think we won't?"

"Because of this freaking huge castle. It's so damn dark I could fall asleep."

"Language," Vero shouts from the front, purposefully giving the vampire guard an earful.

"Damn is not a bad word!"

"Yes, it is!" Vero chimes. Jack and Jessie grinned and jabbed at each other playfully.

"Anyways!" Isa continues. "As I was saying, remember when we were in the Aquatic Realm, and we had to split up?"

Will's jawline tightens. "Yes." (How could anyone forget?)

"When I was down there and about to get the relic, that psycho came out of the shadows and attacked me. Luckily the Kraken got her leg and stopped her."

"It was a Cthulhu." Will corrects.

"Whatever." Isa narrows her eyes to him. "Because of that encounter with Miss Slayer, I can't help but think of where she is hiding. Like I said, the castle is dark, and she thrives in darkness."

Isa exaggeratively tosses her hands in the air accidentally knocking over a candle. Luckily Will puts it out, saving them from burning the castle down.

(If I may add, this has happened in the past in one of the team's missions. It is also why they are banned from stepping foot in Glaciaver, Kingdom of Ice.)

"What if that happens again? I get close to the relic and she's there. I don't have night vision or a Kraken-"

"Cthulhu,"

"Whatever. I don't have a *Cthulhu* to stop her this time. Not to mention the whole thing with her stupid metal mask! Don't get me started on that! Because of the dang thing, she could be hiding in plain sight! That wench has the upper hand."

"Did someone say wench?" Jack announces further down the hall standing in between two gargoyle statues.

The guard instructs the team to step aside as she caresses the head of the gargoyle on the left. Bringing them to life, their eyes blaze green. The brick walls in between them slide open, unlocking a secret passageway to the Vampire King's private chambers.

"Woah!" Isa gasps breathlessly. She steps forward into the passageway willingly following the guard, captivated like a snake in a trance. Something about the entrance lured her insides.

"Isa!" The team shouts one after another.

"Hey! Calm down your human!" The guard hisses as she tries to match Isa's speed. (Keep in mind Dear reader, Vampires are quite fast.)

"She's a Dreamer!" They shout in unison, chasing after Isa down a staircase as she glides it like butter.

"Why is she like this?"

"Was she always this fast?"

"No!"

"She like a Gatner on catnip." Jack quickens his pace thinking back on a large feline animal with wings and red fur like Isa's hair color.

The dark entity in Isa's stomach swayed with anticipation. Thriving like a parasite. It was enticed with curiosity. One that Isa could not deny.

Bursting through another pair of doors, Isa comes to an immediate stop when she is met with two tall figures sitting on their velvet thrones cross-legged.

The Vampire King and his kin.

She stood there frozen in place as the King smelt the air, capturing her scent. His dark red pupils widen and revert to their normal state.

"Isa what has gotten into you- Your Majesty!" Haru straightens his shoulders after hunching over like an elderly man to catch his breath.

The Vampire guard stumbles into the throne room shooting a disdainful glare at Isa while forcing a smile at her beloved ruler. "Pardon my tardiness, Your Majesty. As you see, your *special* guests have arrived."

Straightening himself, the King jumps out of his seat with high anticipation. Like the prince, he kept his red eyes latched on Isa.

"Thank you for escorting them, Quandra." The King regards his guard, dismissing her from the room. The guard tilts her body into a ninety-degree angle and obediently waits outside with the doors closed behind her.

Jack gulps, tensing as the Vampire King towered over the team like the Celestial Facility. Jessie gently strokes her pinkie with his. Her reaction was that of a statue as she would not falter under another ruler as she did with the Queen of Alcania.

"My goodness, have we been waiting for you!" The Vampire King roars, raising his hands. The translucent cape on his shoulder blades trails down his spine and spreads open at his wrists. For someone who could be thousands of years old, the Vampire King was quite attractive.

He eagerly struts to Isa smiling, the prince behind him smiling greater. His eyes lifted and lowered examining Isa like a starved hyena. Isa had not noticed as she wanted to maintain her attention on the King. Will on the other hand fought himself from making an unfavorable gesture to the prince.

"I smelt your Dreamer blood from a mile away. It's as magnificent as having you close. I see you decided to bring your team with you."

"Yes, I did your highness." Isa awkwardly courtesies, tucking one foot behind the other. She made a mental note to take a royal etiquette class or two after this.

"Bahhh! I do not need such a gesture. In my Kingdom, we are less formal. Address me as King Anton."

"Anton?" Isa blinks, raising one eyebrow higher than the other underneath her mask. "Respectively, I thought the Vampire King would be Dracula?"

"Did she ask what I think she asked?"

"Tragically," Vero whispers to Jack, placing her palm on her forehead in disappointment.

Haru and Will stood there eyeing her with their mouths open wide enough for a fly to choke them. The question was as disrespectful as comparing a criminal to a clown. Surely Hues would know better. Right?

(Wrong. They do not.)

"I beg your pardon?" The Vampire King inquires.

"Is he not..." Isa quickly murmurs realizing her mistake.

The King and his kin share a silent glance, speaking at each other with the shift of their eyelids.

Overwhelmed with embarrassment Isa excuses herself to the rules. "OhmygoshIdidnotmeantodisrespectyou-"

The Vampire King and the Prince cut her off by howling into an outrageous burst of hysterics as they clenched at their chest and threw their heads back. "Oh please, you Dreamers delight me! Has no one educated your human half, child?" The King rumbled.

"No," Isa replies, trying to stop the blood from rushing to her face. If she wasn't committed to taking an etiquette class then, she most definitely will now.

"Oh, you poor thing. You have so much to learn. The vamp you call Dracula is a fraud. He is simply another vampire who managed to escape the Vampiric Realm. A Rouge, we call them." replies the prince reaching his hand out for Isa.

Isa glances at Will for reassurance as she does not know how to feel about shaking his hand. It felt wrong in many ways as the prince's intentions were written all over him.

Will forces a half smile, encouraging Isa to bite the bullet and make physical contact with the prince. She slowly hovers over his hand, and he impatiently grasps hers. Unsurprisingly, like any vampire, his touch lacked any warmth.

When he bent down to kiss her hand, Isa felt her shivers of bed bugs crawling down her spine.

"Pardon me, *Isabel.* I didn't get the pleasure of introducing myself. I am Prince Alister. But *you*, ma cherie, can address me as Alister." He winks at Isa as he releases her.

"My! You look just like Perla. I can almost smell her scent on you."

"You've met my grandmother? Did you know her?" Isa inquires, thinking back on the frame. If they were truly friends, he would surely be in it.

"We were…acquaintances, you may say. Like her, I too was a Seer until I decided to choose eternal life."

The Vampire King clears his throat, stopping Prince Alister from sharing any potential secrets held in the past. Alister obediently yields to his King and does not speak of Perla for the remainder of their conversation.

"A Seer? If that is the case, is Prince Alister not your son? Are you too not a Seer?" Isa clarifies turning her focus back to the Vampire King.

"Heavens no! Vampires cannot reproduce. I merely took in Alister as my own. The poor lad was a level four and came to me to escape his persecution. He granted me his life, and in return, I provided him with a new one. It's quite rare to drink a level four Seer's blood, you know." King Anton explains, swiftly peering at the two bite marks on Prince Alister's neck. Alister stands firm in his position, pretending to be unbothered by the markings.

Isa subconsciously reaches for her neck. "I see,". Her heart rate quickened, and her energy started to shift. One that alarmed Vero.

"Unlike me," Vero abruptly comments. "To an extent of course."

Everyone shifts their attention to Vero, the guys not knowing whether to laugh or to re-avert the conversation elsewhere.

"Seriously Vero." Jessie scolds her.

"What! It's the truth." Vero exclaims, grinning as Vampire King leans away from Isa. It worked like a charm, as stupid as it was. "Right, Isa?"

Isa moves her hand to touch the back of her head as if she were to fix her hair. "Oh right." She takes a deep breath and tries to calm the beating of her heart.

"You have very funny teammates, Isa." King Anton recenters her into his focus. Yet, the Prince never once lost his on her.

"That's Vero for you. Usually, she and Jack are the ones with the jokes." Isa points towards Jack. He straightens himself and nods his head vigorously.

"Arguably, mine are better," Jack smirks, as the flames on his fingers burst in excitement.

The King thunders into another chuckle. As Jack entertains the Vampire King, Alister sneakily takes the privilege of breaking his silence. He draws his glistening bloody eyes at Isa, without showing any regard to her soulmate.

"If I recall, your invitation obligates you to present yourself to our guests on the dance floor later this evening. I'm assuming you don't have a partner. I am quite an excellent dancer." The side of his hand gently caresses Isa's shoulder.

With a single touch, his teeth were yearning to slip around Isa's neck as her smell intoxicated him. Most of the time it was vampires who charmed the mortals, but in this case, he had been charmed by Isa, mainly because she reminded him of Perla.

"She does." Will clears his throat as he steps closer to Isa, wrapping his arm around her waist.

Overhearing Will, Jack and the Vampire King stop mid-conversation. Haru's eyes widened in shock and Jessie held a smirk replicating that of Vero's.

Alister's smile remained on his lips, unbothered and untouched. His pupils, on the other hand, whispered a challenge.

He scans Will's physique taking in every potential flaw he could outwit. When his irises reach Will's ears, he scoffs and resumes his conversation with Isa. "Very well. Should you choose to switch partners, I would gladly take his place. Maybe our dance could convince you to join me in the Vampiric Realm."

Behind them, the King harks, tossing his head back, allowing every opportunity for his colossal fangs to display themselves. "Quite the playboy you are Alister. Come now, we must announce your arrival so that you may do your dance performance."

"Before we head off, may I ask you something?"

"Certainly, what is your inquiry, Dreamer?"

"When is the auction?"

"Midnight of course," King Anton dusts himself and adjusts his cape to his liking.

"Oh." Isa chews the side of her mouth.

"Plan on attending? I hope you are! You'll be able to see my collection by my throne."

"By your throne?"

"Well of course. Where else would it be?" The King rumbles, shaking small vitals lingering in the room.

"Right." Isa weakly chuckles as the guard opens the door behind them, informing them of the time.

"Exciting, isn't it?" The Vampire King carries on as the remainder of the team members lurk behind them.

Overcome with a change of plans Jack curses under his breath. Jessie speedily reaches his pace and glides into his.

Vero had once asked him how it felt holding hands with Jessie as she assumed it was painful given that they were opposites. She was taken aback when Jack explained it to her as

"Like a kiss of winter. The touch of the first snowfall." with such fondness.

Jessie squeezes his fingers until his flames disappear, murmuring to him "We got this."

As they approached another set of doors, the moon crept over the towers of the castle. Mirrors among the walls of their path glisten on its pearly white exterior reminding Isa and the team of what is to come.

"We can't wait," Isa forces the words in between her teeth as she marches with the Vampire King and his kin into the ballroom.

35

Dance

Isa had never visited such an unorthodox ballroom. She's read of them and seen pictures of them. But never once experienced them. Shades of cement gray and moonlight black covered the glossy marble floors. There were small details of the castle's age as there were cracks upon cracks on the stone walls. She gazed at the room in awe until she felt Will's shoulder.

"Will?" Her eyebrows knit together as she follows his gaze overlooking the crowd from the stairwell.

Undeniably, his stare led directly at his mother and her family. They were part of the few with luminescent white hair and crystalized masks complimenting their icy blue eyes. She too recognizes him as if she predicted he would attend.

Past them were more guests wearing masks that gave hints of their realms and possible kingdoms. Those of the Fae Kingdom wore masks made of an oak tree and glimmered with sparkly residue coming from their wings and hands. Few known gods lingered under human-like disguises and kept their attires simple yet fashionable to their background.

Folks from other kingdoms of the different realms blessed the ballroom floor with their over-the-top gowns, jewels, masks, and headpieces. Those of royalty, which were most if not all guest, had worn their crowns displaying their status loud and clear as if they were competing against one another. They all surrounded the ballroom keeping the red carpet clear for the Vampire King and Prince. The same could be said with their thrones as they remained untouched and heavily guarded.

Above the thrones on the opposite end of the room is a clear window displaying the moon in all its glory. Only an hour and a half remained before it displayed like a ruby.

Crystalized tinted windows covered the ceilings, revealing scattered stars. On the sides of the room are more windows exploring the dreary forest past the castle onto who knows where.

Away from the royal thrones is a fireplace providing warmth and most of the light to the ballroom aside from the chandeliers hanging from the ceiling. Notably, the space where low-level vampires avoided as they intermingled with their high-end guests.

Smoke slowly filled the room from a pair of large steel doors which King Anton and Prince Alister stepped out of. King Anton graciously struts down the stairwell while Prince Alister brazenly waves hands and blows kisses to the girls flailing at his feet. They all ushered him, proudly displaying their necks for him to bite, removing their sheer scarves and priceless jewelry.

"Sorry ladies, I only have my fangs for one special person tonight," he says, flickering his eyes behind him toward Isa. Next to her, Will gawked with detestation.

With the King, the two walk on a red carpet leading to two thrones on the other side of the ballroom. Surrounding them on the sides are various guards and the auction objects lined up with their podiums topped off with a glass protector. All team members latched their eyes searching for the relic.

When they spotted it, their faces fell in disappointment seeing its podium nestled in between the King and Prince. They were aware this would happen as Isa predicted, and so they moved onto one of their plans. They typed in their watches vigorously giving everyone roles and procedures as they rehearsed.

With great rigor, Isa types and sends a final message. The team, aside from Vero, views the message with scornful expressions.

"What's the message?" Vero asks Haru.

After he whispers the message into her ear, Vero's molars clenched tightly at the sides of her mouth. Next to them Jessie and Jack gasp at the message and frown, nodding their heads with reluctance.

"Are you sure?" Will frowns and creases his eyebrows together like a puppy. He'd be a husky if anything.

"I have to be sure," Isa composes her shaky posture and camouflages it under pure imaginary confidence.

Will shudders as he peers over his shoulder to Prince Alister "Hades, I hate this plan."

Isa holds his hand squeezing it tightly. "I do too."

He understands and lightly plants a soft and simple kiss on her cheek. Her fingertips longingly touched her cheek as though she treasured his touch. She gives him a solemn smile and whispers a sincere apology before turning her attention to the ballroom.

Standing on their throne, the King announces Isa and her team to step down the stairs. Vero and Haru are the first ones.

During her walk, Vero's telekinetic abilities gradually began to fade. She could barely make out the energies in the room along with detecting her surroundings.

Close to the bottom of the staircase, Vero slipped and reached her hand out. Thankfully, Haru wrapped his arm around her waist in time and guided her to the crowd providing details of the room and placement of the relic. A family relative wearing body armor with a family crest approached Vero.

Vero had to hold Haru back. He did not like her family, knowing what they did to her.

"Veronica?" Her brother gasped. He had a scar similar to Isa's except it was on his chin and it stretched down to his chest. Her name seemed almost foreign against his mouth. The last time she saw him was at the circus. She remembered her experience with him very clearly.

He threw food at her like a caged animal and almost made Vero fall off a beam she was juggling on. At that point in time, her telekinetic abilities were hardly helpful as they were barely developing. She hoped his arrival meant he was taking her home. Instead, it was another evaluation from her family.

"Do better! I did this easily when I was five. Your eyes are no excuse." He would shout from the benches while stomping his feet. As she did a handstand, he threw a double-ended blade at her causing Vero to lose her balance on the beam and fall into a pile of waste from one of Nix's mythical monsters.

Displeased, Nix later that night threw a plate at her head for failing at her tasks in front of a Reliz. "They'll never take you back now!" she cursed at Vero.

Behind the striped curtains, she could almost hear her brother laugh. When it was over, he bid her and Nix a crude farewell. He rode off in one of his luxurious carriages a royal must've rewarded him with.

"It's me. Dominic."

"I know." Vero blows a strand of hair touching her glossed lips. She shoves past his shoulder, slicing a part of it off with a concealed sharpened pin. The metal family crest falls off his armor and ricochets across the floor. Haru sassily turns the other cheek and proudly follows after Vero.

She knew they'd be at the ball considering they always went to these types of events to flaunt their greatness and family crest. It was only a matter of time until she encountered one of them. It must be a smack in the face to them as they never took Vero to one of these events as she was the runt of the litter.

Her family was well known after all. They were one of the best warriors across realms. Oh no! They couldn't afford to bring embarrassment to the family.

She could almost hear her mother's stern voice in the background judging her entrance. She would've had a fit if Vero had tripped while wearing her family's crest. She would never hear the end of it.

It didn't matter. She wasn't a Relìz anymore. Veronica Relìz. That's who she used to be. A nobody. A pushover. A disgrace.

She wasn't that anymore.

She's Vero. Just Vero.

A prodigy. A mastermind who killed Nix.

Vero.

The tamer of beasts.

Vero.

The one with the poisoned whip.

They only wanted to give her the time of day because she had finally made it without them. Her team was well known and her status across realms became heightened. Vero's name would be remembered. She will be remembered as a great warrior and team member who saved the realms.

"Ready?" Will turned to Isa as it was their turn to walk down the staircase while Jack and Jessie stayed at the top to monitor the crowd.

"No. But we have to be." Isa sighed. "I'm definitely not the right person for this."

Isa's name was officially announced, and the crowd cheered. She caught their attention and the spotlight shined on her as she and Will made it to the dance floor by the King's orders. For a dark and dreary castle, the spotlight was fairly strong to blind Isa. She held onto Will tighter, taking a deep breath in her dress knowing the eyes on her.

The dark redness of her dress was a calling to the vampires. Her mask of a fox elucidates her tactical shrewdness that once beat the Elf Queen.

Will and Isa caught a glimpse passing by her on the carpet. The Elf King is not so fond of their presence.

"Do you know how to dance?" Will whispers to Isa as they make their way to the center of the ballroom. He attempts to distract himself away from his mother.

"I've done a few ballroom dances and attended some lessons. Mostly because of a quinceañera and a couple of fantasy events. My skills are mediocre at best." Isa explains positioning herself. When the spotlight moves away from her eyes, she immediately notices Will's attention lingering towards his mother. The Queen's gaze matches Will's, surveying their every move.

To draw Will in, Isa lifts the palm of her hand lightly to his cheek, her thumb touching his cheekbone. Wavered by her touch, frozen in place, he disregards his mother and takes a shaky breath. His jaw tightened and his eyes created a storm of what is to come.

"It's just you and me." She whispers to him tugging him closer.

Isa moves her hand to his chest pressing lightly. She takes a breath, and he repeats. She then steps away and lightly curtsies towards him.

Nodding their heads, the two begin to dance to the music of the orchestra playing in the background. The spotlight moves away from them, causing the room to dim. Candles surrounded them, catching glimpses of their facial expression and clothing. Her dress glazed the floor, and the lightness of the fabric allowed it to move like water. It was as if he was the land, and she was the sea.

Her arms moved around the air and behind them followed Will's weaving in between them.

"Hold me closer," Isa whispers, leaning close to his face as he dips her. She is thankful the mask could cover the blush on her cheeks.

Not thinking twice, Will obeys and tightens his grip on her waistline tugging her closer to his body before separating from each other as Isa spins across the room. When Isa joins him in complete equilibrium, their chests press against each other as they rise and fall out of breath. Around them, they can hear the people clapping, and whistling.

In his seat, the prince rolled his eyes at the close nature of their dance and impatiently waited for it to end. He occasionally shifted in his seat and disregarded the royal maidens near the throne. Irritated, one of his eyes began to twitch as he fought back a hiss.

Holding Isa, Will sways her, making a last-minute suggestion. His hands move higher up her back hinting at his motive.

"Do you trust me?"

"Forever and always." Isa teases

Will's eyes widened in amusement and a smirk planted on his lips. Isa snickers under her mask and positions herself on the dance floor.

"Saying our vows now, are we?"

She laughs and touches his shoulders. His hands slide down her waist accentuating the tightness of the corset. He lifts her in the air, her arms spreading open, the cape behind her opening behind her like wings. Her eyes glistened with delight as she watched the world around them disappear.

Isa felt free as ever. She never thought it possible to do such a dance or better yet attend a ball of this grandeur. Being spun around she could barely feel her hair and make out figures in the crowd. She kept a smile and allowed her body to relax under Will's grasps.

Under the little light of the candles provided in the room, the two might've been lucky enough to make a few mistakes but the crowd was too charmed. They watched their faces, and the slight glimmer of their clothes capturing the flames of the torches around them. Their shadows on the floor were its own narrative for those who could not see.

Had the world not been at stake, the two would have lost everyone but themselves on the dance floor. Time could be limitless. They could be limitless.

Not long ago they had been strangers, yet now, they felt far from it. Will felt as if he had finished searching for centuries to find Isa. Isa couldn't imagine another life without Will. Within seconds of yesterday's kiss, she planned every single moment after this.

Anyone sane would question their sudden relationship, but to Isa and Will, more than ever, it had felt natural. Isa finally understood why characters in the books were so quick to fall in love. How could they not after feeling the way she felt?

When her feet had hit the ground, the room around them thundered in applause concluding their performance. Will bowed to Isa and escorted her to the throne, having her hand hooked to his side. He noticed the way Prince Allister had glinted at her, almost as if she was the last piece of meat left in all the realms combined. He wanted to punch the living daylights out of the shabby vampire but instead, he was forced to maintain his composure.

"Isa."

"Yeah?"

"Promise me that no matter what happens today, you'll think of me. Let me live in your heart as you do mine."

"As long as you keep our first promise. Don't think I forgot about our trip. We have much to talk about, more importantly, about us." Isa turns to him. Her words concise and full of sincerity.

"You got yourself a deal, Red." His small fangs poke out from the corners of his mouth as he grins.

"Charming he is indeed," Isa tells herself.

At the arrival of the throne, Isa's eyes flickered to the prince, the corner of her lips falling from the smile she had on. Will too frowned, giving a small discourteous glare to Prince Alister.

Prince Alister pretended not to notice and played it off by straightening himself in his seat.

After they finished bowing to them, as they planned, Will slipped away into the crowd leaving Isa with the company of the King and his kin.

36

Offer of a Lifetime

When Will reunited with Haru and Vero, they applauded and congratulated him on their performance. Vero tugs him into a small hug and lightly punches his shoulder. Haru laughs and turns his head toward the balcony for any signal from Jack and Jessie. Up there the two were having a slow dance of their own. They stopped mid-step when they saw Haru's hair glow. They pulled away slightly embarrassed and continued to scan the ballroom.

"Haru says you got some moves you were hiding." Vero smirks.

During the dance, the shoes at her feet had been taken off to feel the vibrations around her. Haru portaled her shoes to the cottage and made sure no person steps on her toes. She could tell they were very close to the blood moon as her abilities slipped away. She kept it to herself as she did not want things to escalate any further than they already were. She was happy enough that the moon's arrival suppressed the dark sorcery of Haru's ability since he was finally able to enjoy himself in the Vampiric Realm.

"Oh please! Teasing me already?" Will rolls his eyes with a slight smile. The tip of his ears is slightly red.

The smile fades hearing the crowd murmur as he sees Isa tugged on the dancefloor with Alister.

"Oh, shiitake mushrooms!"

"What?" Vero whirls herself around to Haru.

"Isa is with her new dance partner."

Vero clutches her palms, shaking her head.

Will grumbles and glances over to the balcony where Jess and Jack are overlooking. Jack gives them a nod and the operation begins.

Let's get this over with." He growls, running his fisted hand over his white hair.

At the end of the red carpet, Isa initiates her plan as she approaches the Vampiric Rulers. She charitably strokes her neck and speaks to the king, "If I may, King Anton, have your permission to steal your beloved Prince to the dance floor. One dance is all I ask."

The King's colossal fangs appear as he takes another swig of a chalice full of thick purple liquid. He stops when the golden cup reaches his lips. "You have my fullest approval, Dreamer. Alister? Would you please escort this debutante to the floor?"

"It would be my pleasure." Alister flawlessly lifts himself out of his throne, as if he anticipated the offer.

"Likewise, Prince-" Isa gasps wholeheartedly when he latches his shadowed hands onto her waist. "Alister."

"Pardon my excitement. You look lovely in red." He smiles making his fangs more prominent. Eager to sink into Isa's neck.

"I bet the eyes of a Vampire would bring out your hair." He moves a strand away from Isa's mask.

"I plan to dye it," Isa remarks putting some distance between them.

He scoffs and lifts the curvature of his cupid's bow to its peak. He closes the space Isa had put and motions his hand further down her waist. Taken aback, Isa grabs hold of his hand and plays it off with a subtle dance move. Their hands spread like wings and come down reconnecting.

"You surprise me, Seer."

Isa breaks from him as he circles her like a boa. "How come Prince Alister?" Isa questions.

"Call me Alister." He kneels, touching his gloved fingertips on her chin.

"Very well, Alister." She feeds into his game.

(Bad idea. Extremely terrible idea!)

As he steps into his next move, his lips near Isa's. With the best possible timing anyone could have, she turns her head, and he plants a kiss on her cheek.

Repulsed, Isa purposefully steps on one of the prince's toes with the tip of her heel. He merely brushes it off and continues to sway her side by side.

"I can never predict your next move. It's hard to guess. Everyone always seems to have a different opinion of you. The Fae despise you, the gods tolerate you, and the rest absolutely adore you. They worship you, Isa.

He then forcibly spins Isa causing the room to turn on its axis. She takes a deep breath when her vision realigns. Prince Alister chuckles and dips her.

"I too could worship you." He whispers.

"If I bite you now, you can rule with me. Say the word and I will grant it."

Neck completely exposed, Alister takes a whiff before licking her skin. His fangs lightly caress her dermis.

To Isa, it felt like a rough cold cat tongue. She shivers and maneuvers herself upward close to the prince like a marionette. He seductively caresses his hand where he licked her.

(Personally, lovely Dreamer, I would've stabbed him on site, but that's just me.)

"With all due respect Prince Alister, I think there are more suitable maidens than me for you." Isa twists his arm when he tries to spin her.

"Humble you are." His red eyes glimmered. "Especially for a level four."

"How did you-"

"You made a grave mistake letting me lick you. That three on your cloak could've tricked me. Level fours taste different."

Isa wanted to flee from the prince, but her plans would be foiled if she did. She was thankful for Jack and Jessie as they proceeded with the next step of their plan. Behind them, Jack and Jessie swoop in with a jaw-dropping performance to distract the King while Vero, Haru, and Will retrieve the relic. They began turning the dancefloor into their stage as Jack shifted the tiles, which Jessie flipped over.

"I didn't know she could do that?" Haru whispers to Will.

One by one guards were ordered to abandon their post to contain the rowdy crowd Jessie and Jack brought to life. A Fae with crystalized blue wings iced the chandeliers frozen and swung above them. A batch full of sneaky gremlins barged through an underground entrance and ran around, searching for savory sweets. One sorcerer re-arranged the orchestra with electric guitars and drums. Too many magical folks loosened their restraints and roamed the floor without fear of losing their rank. After all, who is to stop them when all order is lost?

"Let's move somewhere more private, shall we?" Prince Alister murmurs into Isa's ear and gestures to a hidden pathway.

Isa daringly follows, trickling one of her fingers to a hidden knife at her thigh. Alister, enjoying this a little too much, slips in another bladed weapon at the side of her corset for her to use. When they reach an empty hallway, he briskly locates a secluded room and commands a guard to stand outside of the door.

"We must not be bothered." He threatens the guard after Isa steps inside.

When he closes it, Isa whips out her bow from underneath her dress and aims an arrow towards Alister. He raises his hands and tiptoes towards the desk in the center of the room.

"Feisty, aren't you?"

"Stop!" Isa commands.

"Stop what?"

"Getting inside my head. You were the one who lured me into the throne room. It's why I ran."

"Not because you wanted to?" Alister leans his hip to the side of the desk.

"NO!" Isa releases an arrow. It hits the corner of a frame with a picture of the Vampire King staring intently.

"If you say so," Alister says, rolling his tongue over his polished fangs. "As A level four, you'll understand others. Their desires. Their dream. Their aspirations…"

He pauses, waiting for Isa to add to the list. She doesn't despite knowing.

"That half-elf of yours. Is he aware?" He opens one of the drawers from the desk and reveals a tinted flask. He pours the contents of the flask into a cup that had been perfectly placed on the side of the desk Alister is leaning on. He drinks the red liquid and when he finishes gulping it down, he gestures to her to take the cup.

She scrunches her nose in disgust and shoots the arrow at his foot. The glass shatters on the table, spreading crystalized pieces of it around the floorboard.

"Everything fine Prince Alister?" The guard calls outside of the door.

Isa reloads her bow and keeps her back to the walls of the room.

"Tremendous! Give us some privacy, will you? My lady friend here is impatient" Alister replies loudly, calling off his guard. He then advances at Isa with his hands in the pockets of his pants. Not a single drop of fear shone on his unscathed body.

Humanistic was not something Isa would ever describe this man. Everything about him, from when she entered the throne room to now was off. Anyone could say the same about him. His actions. His mannerisms. His appearance.

On his body, were layers of fine material. Difficult to obtain Isa would assume. Yet fabric alone, regardless of what is made of, can wilt if not handled with care. There at the ends of his ashed pants are a few loose threads.

These clothes aren't new. That Isa could confirm. Despite his attire, his charm was one of several qualities that allowed him to blend in with the nobles. No one knew if it was fake, or if he indeed bathed in the waters of his mother's womb to come out so graciously.

His widow peak antiquely contrasted his pale exterior as his sullen locks of thick black hair draped over the sides of his elevated cheekbones. Porcelain. Almost.

Isa wondered if his face had been fuller prior to his transformation. Perhaps that may be why she hadn't recognized him from Elder Arthur's pictures.

"Stop!" Isa commands him. "Unless you want another arrow in you.

Her hazel eyes briskly queued to the arrow lodged in his Tibia. He peers at the end of it and blatantly pulls the sharp tip out of him. He casts it aside and sits on top of the table where the glass shattered. He kicked his feet in the air like a child, enjoying Isa's bewilderment.

"Don't get me wrong Isa. It hurts, but one arrow won't kill me. Not where you aimed."

"Why doesn't anyone ever take me seriously?" Isa mutters.

"Because, in this form," his hand waves from top to bottom in her direction "You do not unleash your potential."

"What is that supposed to mean?" Isa's thumb runs along the bowstring. "Are you calling me weak?"

"Not completely." He flicks a small piece of glass off the table. "Only when you refuse to accept your level. Your level is your potential."

Isa held her tongue. He was right. In his own messed up way. It's why Vero wanted Isa to conceal her ability for tonight. Being a level four is an expense that comes too high of a cost.

"Does that soulmate of yours know your true level?" He asks, leaning his palms at the edge of the table, purposefully letting the glass sink into his fingerprints. The corner of his eyes crinkled slightly.

At the mention of Will, she immediately discovered his motive. It felt like talking to the Seer Slayer all over again. "Are you planning to expose my level?"

"I wouldn't do that to a fellow Seer." He replies swiftly, picking a specific shard of glass. "I'm not the enemy."

Truth.

"But your team might." He squishes the shard into dust. Isa mistakenly blinks, allowing him to appear right in front of her. His hands held Isa by her shoulders, pinning her to the wall. "Learn from me, Isa. It's always the ones who you hold close, that hurts you the most."

"They wouldn't." Angrily, Isa swiftly pulls a pin from her hair and points the tip of it towards Prince Alister's abdomen. Isa was confident the pin could hurt him given the potency of the poison Vero had laced it with.

"Then why haven't you told them? Afraid they'll gut you? They'll hate you? See you as a monster?" The prince presses unbothered by the weapon.

Isa's eyes wavered over his. He was trying to get her to listen. He could've killed her. Bit her right in the middle of the dance floor if he wished. But he didn't. He wouldn't. Not to a fellow level four. To the daughter of Perla and Baeu.

"Allow me to share a little secret with you." He leans closer to the tip of the weapon.

How do I keep finding myself in this situation? Isa thinks to herself.

She raises her eyebrow and cautiously leans closer to Alister holding the weapon still in place. With his free hand, he lightly tucks a loose strand of hair behind her ear. Doing so, the iris of his eyes glows like a sunset. His gaze signals to a window in which Isa caught sight of a hooded figure. The hood figure passes them and proceeds in the direction of the ballroom. When it was evident the figure had left, Alister whispered into Isa's ear.

"The relic your team and the Seer Slayer seek," With his free hand, he lifts Isa's mask and casts it aside. "Is not in the ballroom."

"Where is it now?" Isa stiffened.

"Don't worry about that. What you need to know is that I can protect you. I'll protect you, like how I protect my people. You are one of us, a Fourth."

"Us? As in the vampires?"

"Yes. We didn't have many options during The Disparagè. It's either to run, hide, or die. I tried to convince Beau and Perla to join me, but they declined."

"And?"

"And I meant my offer. You can stay here. You can keep your abilities as I do. Stay with our kind here. I couldn't save them, but I can save you."

"Alister,"

"Join me." His cold touch lingers.

She wasn't sure how to feel but it was something that sat in her gut. In a way, this did entice her to take his offer. She could see the potential as she would no longer need to fear for her life. Yet there was one thing stopping her. It was Will. He would die if she took his deal unless she said the vow. The vow would preserve his life if she were to lose hers.

"You need not to make your decision now. We will meet again." He makes a final bow and with his other hand, he slides an item in her hands. Behind them, an old clock strikes a quarter to midnight, and his body tenses.

"She'll be waiting for you in the forest." He warns her.

The two turn when the guard pounds vigorously on the door. When Alister opens it, a new set of horrors is unveiled. Like banshees, screams consumed the echoes of the halls, drowning out any of Alister's demands. One noise, in particular, caught Isa off guard as it made the sensation inside her stomach soar.

The blow of a whistle.

Negotiation with Hope

By the time Isa arrives inside the ballroom, the ring of the whistle disappears, and the ballroom floor barely becomes visible to the human eye. Isa feared she was going to suffocate, or worse, get trampled in the crowded room. She spotted a few victims as their spirits slipped out of her body.

"Ouch!" Isa flinches as a man with a monocle shoves her to the side. Luckily her hand caught the handle of a hanging torch. She glances at the exits, all of which are blocked. From the corner of her vision, she notices cracks along the windows leading to the outside of the forest.

"Bingo!" Isa punches the air.

Optimistic of her plan, Isa dives into the stampede of magical people until she hits the windows. With a singular swing of the blade Alister provided her, the glass shatters her free.

"Where are you guys?" Isa says aloud as she presses her broken watch to find her teammates' location. It flickered on it off, displaying hazy directions for her to follow.

She makes use out what little information it provides and smacks it a few times for a better signal. By some miracle, (given Isa's terrible navigational skills), she finds Jessie and Jack.

"Foxy, what are you doing here? Where's Will and the relic?"

"Wha-" Isa gasps when she turns to what is supposed to be changed. She knew something must've gone wrong as the result of her vision was far worse.

There in the dark corner of the castle walls, on the floor is Vero bleeding from her neck and Haru lying on the floor next to her. Jessie scurries with them pulling out vials and potions from her bag. All the needles coaxed in poison were nonexistent as Jessie's and Vero's hair fell past their shoulders. They were weaponless, bruised, and exhausted with the mayhem they fought through in the castle.

"What happened?" Isa gasps.

"Isa, where is Will?" Jack questions again, panicked. His mask was no longer on his face, revealing his bloodshot eyes.

"I don't know. I didn't see him after the dance. What happened to you guys?"

"When we got close enough to the relic, the Seer Slayer swooped in from the glass above and caused all the candles to go out. In the process, somewhere in the dark mess, Vero got bit after she stabbed a Vampiric guard." Jack reiterates. "What do you mean you didn't see him? We saw you leave with Will to the forest. We heard your voice."

"Haru, you need to do the unmatching vow otherwise you'll die!" Jessie wails over his body as she pours an elixir into his mouth. A pool of vital fluids continued to escape from Vero's neck despite the various regeneration salves Jessie applied to her.

His eyelids flutter open. He consciously shakes his head and uses his remaining strength to hold Vero's lifeless body.

"This is bad," Jessie circles to them. "Once Vero turns, she will go ballistic in her vampiric form. We need to leave this realm. There's enough time to make one portal for all of us."

"But what about Will?" Jack asks, turning to Isa clearly upset.

Isa looks at the sky and examines the curtains drawing at the sides of the moon. Once the lunar eclipse reaches its full color, all magic is lost until the red transitions away.

"I'll stay back. You guys leave and I'll find Will. The Seer Slayer is out there. She might have Will and the fake relic. I'll explain everything and get us out of here when it's over."

Jessie and Jack frowned. They knew what they had to do and frantically moved Vero and Haru out of the Vampiric Realm and into a portal they opened. Jessie gathered all her medicinal objects by tossing them into the pockets of her coat.

"Give the Seer Slayer no mercy!" Jessie shouts from the other side of the portal as it closes. The rage and anguish in her voice traveled to Isa as she ran inside the forest. She removed her overskirt and loaded an arrow into her bow. She only had two of them left. If she was going to use them, she needed to ensure one ends up inside the Seer Slayer's chest.

Running into the forest, Isa saw the world around her beginning to cast a redness to the trees and snowy floor beneath her. It was halfway until the moon had been completely covered. It felt as if she had been running into those dark red slides with no ending. She kept straight because she feared if she went in another direction, she might be going in circles. The only markings of her presence were those of her footsteps behind her.

At some point in her run, she found footprint paths, one of which was Will's. His mask was thrown to the ground into a bush leading deeper into the forest. Isa examines it for any hints or clues of what has happened to him. It was much too perfect in condition to signify any danger or harm towards him.

There had to be a way Isa could track them faster.

She revisits the potential of her abilities and holds his mask tightly. Pacing her breath, Isa closes her eyes. If she could transport herself to the Seer Slayer's dungeon, there's no reason why she couldn't mentally transport herself to wherever Will may be. Not to mention a possible method her grandmother must've used when she communicated with Isa.

"Relax yourself Isa," she tells herself.

She sits on the snowy ground with her cape providing little warmth to her body. This time when she closes her eyes the world around her goes dark. The door appeared right next to her, something that usually never happens. She leaves Will's mask on the floor and takes a step closer. The floor beneath her consumes his mask like a stone thrown into the ocean and a handle appears.

Isa grabs its cold golden handle and slams the door wide open. Standing near a cliff at the side of the forest is Will and a woman with Isa's face. Her clothes were entirely different from what Isa was wearing and both of her antlers were broken as if they had been sawed off.

The two were talking, most of the dialogue was Will asking her questions.

"Isa, what has gotten into you? Did Alister do something to you?" He moves his head up and down and shuffles away from her. The fake relic in his hand.

"You are so infuriating! I explained it before! Give me both of relics before the Seer Slayer finds us! The one you gave me is not enough!" she shouts angrily, stomping her foot. In comparison to the real Isa, her face lacked the scar above her cheek and frequently molded into harsh facial expressions.

Her eyes told a completely different story as if they had been genetically altered. They flicked in rapid motions as if she were part of a cyborg. Not to mention her clothes were far from close to what Will had made. Her black jumpsuit lacked the Seer Symbols and was ripped in various parts. She wore a waist belt and concealed an item within the backing of her dark cloak.

"We need to find our team. I'll hold on to the last piece in the meantime." He opens his watch and views the messages his team has left him. None of it made sense to Will and he didn't like the change in Isa's demeanor. He had his suspicions and wasn't going to give her both of the remaining relics too easily.

"Give. Me. The. Other. Relic." She snatches his shoulders.

"I don't understand what the members are saying-"

"Watch out!" Isa shouts from the forest behind them.

"Isa?"

The Seer Slayer captures Will in a chokehold and wrestles him. When she has enough, she grabs a hidden weapon and stabs it at Will's side. He immediately falls to the ground, letting the last relic piece slip out of his pocket. She gladly takes it and shoves Will towards Isa.

"You take him. I got something better." Smiling maliciously as she holds the bottom piece, the Seer Slayer assembles it onto the rest and waits for it to glow. To her disappointment, it doesn't.

Isa crouches next to Will's body checking his pulse and open wounds. Isa couldn't find a trace of blood on him nor any technical physical damage. This worried her as she didn't know what would cause him to roll into a fetal position.

"Isa?" He whispers her name touching her face. His eyes fought to stay open, and his mouth moved ever so subtly. He was shivering but not from the cold.

"It's me, Will. It's really me," she replies, scanning his body over and over. She presses his hand deeper into her face.

Little by little his grasp began to fade and so did she.

"No, no. I can't disappear now!" Isa panics grabbing Will tightly to hold up his body.

"Ugh! It's a fake! Stupid leech folk!" The Seer Slayer curses, ripping the faux part off her assembled lamp. She peers at the moon watching one-third of it covered in crimson. With her relics, she takes slow steps over to Will and Isa.

"Hello, Isa. Lovely, for you to join us. You and your little friends have been quite a nuisance. It is time for them to pay a bit of the price, don't you think?"

Isa could hear her steps in the snow and began to lift herself away from Will shuffling on the balls of her feet. The Seer Slayer stood a few feet away from them in all her glory. Her metal mask was gone, and she was done hiding.

Isa pulls her bow out along with one of the two arrows she has left. The Seer Slayer too pulls out a weapon. It was a replica of the sword Elder Arthur had the night he killed himself after his encounter with the Seer Slayer.

Isa recognizes her weapons and falls sick to her stomach grimacing.

"Give me one good reason I shouldn't shoot you, Seer Slayer." Isa points her arrow daring to let it go.

"I can give you more than one. If you call me by that name, I might make it one less." With her metallic hand, she holds a vial out and a needle pin Isa recognizes. "Thanks to your gullible team member, she was stupid enough to give me poison. Such a shame she got bit."

Isa shoots a steel arrow and watches it cut the corner of the Seer Slayer's ear. The Seer Slayer does not flinch and laughs at Isa.

"What a waste of an arrow." She comments, picking it up on the ground from behind. The tip of it was stained red like how the world was going to be.

"Now, do you want the vial or not?" She tilts her head, waving the vial.

"Fine, whoever or whatever your name is." Isa lowers her bow and tucks the second arrow into her boot.

"You're too easy, Isa. So sensitive. You wouldn't last where I'm from."

"And that is?"

"Dimension 105. There they call me Hope. Has a better ring to it." She retorts, crossing her arms.

"Ironic name. Figures."

"We may have different names, but you dare forget that you and I are the same." Hope counters. She swiftly moves close to Isa scratching the corner of her mouth with her index finger.

"D-Don't listen to he-ackh!" Will stops halfway in his sentence as he coughs a pile of blood. He tries to overcome it by attempting to stand tall, but in the process, his body sways unsteadily and his head throbbed.

"Will" Isa tries to reach him but is stopped by the Seer Slayer holding the vial. The only cure to his and Isa's demise.

"Give me the vial." Isa orders, stretching her hand.

"I don't think so." Hope swipes the vial away from Isa's sight and tucks it into the pocket of her black jacket. "You may have been used to everything being given to you, but not today sweetheart. If you want the precious vial, I need something in return. It's only fair."

"It's the relic. I know. I have it, but I need you to keep him alive or no deal," Isa grabs the bottom piece of the relic she tucked from her pocket and displays it to Hope.

Hope grins and retrieves the vial out of her pocket. She plays with it moving the liquid up and down like an hourglass reminding Isa of her limited time. She removes the lid and forcefully pours half of the blue liquid down Will's throat.

Relief sweeps over Isa when Will stops coughing and lays there with his chest rising and falling.

"Hurry, you shouldn't make him wait too long." Hope smirks, waiving the half-empty vial as Isa disappears.

"Hold on Will," Isa whispers watching him disappear into the darkness.

Isa takes a shaky breath of relief and rises from her original spot in the snow. She ran with all effort in her body, despite the side effects she felt sweeping underneath her. It was a reminder of Will's lifeline, and hers.

Final Piece

"Well, well well. Look who has finally arrived. About time. The moon isn't going to say red forever you know." Hope impatiently held her sword where she initially stabbed Will with the steel pin.

Isa grunted at her snarky remark, struggling to keep herself steady as she leaned her body on a tree truck. She needed to take quick breaths to recover from her run.

"The relic," Hope orders Isa as she approaches her rather than waiting for Isa to make her way to her.

"Demeaning and you lack manners. Such lovely traits." Isa gawks at her, keeping one hand on the tree for reinforcement. "Show me the antidote."

"Isa, don't!" Will musters, gasping on the snow-covered soil. There was rubble underneath him which stained his newly made attire brown. He could hardly keep his eyes open, for they stung potently, and his heart felt as though it would require an operation.

"Silence!" Hope kicks Will in the chest. In return, it earned a scowl from Isa.

"Don't hurt him you evil wen-"

"Nuh-ah. Best hold your tongue and play nice." Hope waves the vial in the air, gesturing to Isa of the power she holds. With great displeasure, Isa complies and exchanges with Hope begrudgingly.

"Much better." Hope examines the remaining relic carefully and disregards Will's body to the ground, tossing him away from her weapon. Her eyes widened with joy and the corners of her mouth lifted higher as she analyzed the bottom part of the lamp. It indeed was the real deal. There was weight to the relic, along with a certain sensation that comes when you hold it. The sensation itself is indescribable and can only be accentuated through the expressions of those who hold it. One can say it's enough to make a painting smile.

It was, in fact, the true remaining piece.

"I'm a little disappointed. I thought you would put up more of a fight." She snickers pridefully. With her sword, she angles it, spotting the moon's position. It felt as if she captured a pomegranate-soaked diamond onto her weapon. Admiring the coloration, she could lose herself had she been a commoner walking among the realm, capturing the scenery. But she wasn't.

She was here on a mission she needed to succeed. She had to be aware of attackers that may come after her. One being the two figures behind her underneath the trees. She could feel the weight of their presence despite the beautiful ghostly scenery of the Vampiric Realm as the snow chilled her feet.

If they were to plot something, she would be equipped for the occasion. In the belt of her waist were bombs she could throw at them, though it was a risk given the explosive would be strong enough to toss her off the edge of the cliff. They were enough for her to break into the castle, for she made the bombs extremely potent, each one with its own feature. She had regular bombs, sonic bombs, and one specific bomb of her creation, containing the poison of her pet basilisk back in her dimension.

All she needed to do was wait for the right moment to make her wish. The moon had to be in the right position.

"If you truly are me from another dimension, you'd know I'd protect my loved ones above anyone else," Isa replies, twisting her head to Hope, who was standing at the corner of the cliff raising the lamp to the sky. At the horizon past Hope, clouds ushered in their direction at an unsteady pace.

"You say we are different, but that is what I am trying to do." Hope whispers under her breath as she places the remaining piece into the lamp. The different colors of the gems glistened, and the lamp became stabilized under its unification. It would take a great deal of determination for someone to break it.

"For the people of my dimension." Hope raises the lamp to the sky with her two hands clasped tight against it.

Under the eclipse, the moon above turns the world into flames. Its crimson glow covered the land around them, spawning the lamp to shake in Hope's hands. Spewing out the tip of the lamp emerged portals covering the Vampiric Realm.

Out of one of them emerged a devilish giant with sparrow wings. Without hesitation, the monster sprinted straight to the castle, passing far from where they stood. Unstoned gargoyles flew from the skies with their widened wings, grabbing any victim off the ground.

As if on command, clouds in the sky thundered angrily, followed by heaps of rain pounding down on them.

Right on cue, Will and Isa wasted no time on their attack. As soon as the relic was assembled, Will ran straight to Hope before she could make a wish. In a rapid swing, he unsheathes his sword and yields the weapon straight to Hope's heart.

"You!" she seethes in between the words of her wish. If not said properly, it does not come true.

"Oh, fu-"Unfortunately for Will, Hope is prompt and poised to react as her sword clashes with his. She mistakenly allowed the lamp to slip from under her as she needed both hands to sustain the pressure of the sword.

The lamp remained intact on the cushion floor and continued to spout portals, one after another. A tidal wave of pressure knocks all of them to the ground, causing both Will and Hope to lose balance. She glances at the lamp and then back at Will with maddening eyes filled with gall.

"You half-breed mongrel! I am going to make you pay for that!" Hope thunders as she tries to slide closer to the lamp. Will blocks her, swinging his sword like a baseball bat, and hits the lamp further from them.

"I don't think so Ms. Slayer."

"I told you not to call me that!" In a flick of a second, the two bounce back into action, fighting one another over the lamp. This time, Hope no longer had the upper hand to use her ability to predict his attacks. She knew she had to bring in what she was taught.

Like the attack at the Celestial Facility, Hope moved with the grace of an acrobat as she contorted her body to stay out of Will's reach. She led with various acute strikes and calculated combative movements taught in her dimension. Will struggled as he was unfamiliar with her technique and how to defend himself against it. The fog closing in further hindered his combat skills, while Hope thrived in it.

As the two fought, Isa found herself hanging off the edge of the cliff. The impact of the lamp was stronger than she anticipated. Once she pulled herself up to the surface using her remaining arrow as leverage, Isa ran past them and scooped the lamp from the crystalized floor. She cups the lamp and threatens Hope while she seizes her blade on Will's chest.

Hope was never one to be reckoned with and sure as hell wasn't going to let Isa go without consequence. She held onto the hair of Will's head, digging her metallic gloved claws into his skull, encouraging him to lurch his body forward and deeper into her sword. It was enough to fracture a rib or two.

"Stop!" Isa yells from the cliff, dangling the lamp with her finger on its handle. She could feel its weight as if Will's life relied on it. "If you hurt him, I will toss it."

"That won't break the lamp," Hope scoffs, calling out her bluff.

"You're right," Isa replies, analyzing the relic. She forced herself not to stare at it for too long as it tempted her.

Physically.

Mentally.

Emotionally.

Like the quarts during her soulmate ceremony, she could hear a voice coming from the funnel of the lamp. It whispered half-hearted promises and unaccomplished dreams. Both of which the lamp could make come true.

Isa snaps her attention from it and maintains her focus on Hope. "The fall won't break it, but by the time you find it, you won't be able to make a wish."

The whites in Hope's eyes widened at the moon as the edges of it were returning to its natural pearly color.

"Ugh!" Hope protests, clutching Will like a rag doll. "I'm done playing games! You're not from my dimension. You haven't seen the things I have. Soon enough, you too will be a target once they find out what you are and the cycle will repeat all over again, that is, if they don't kill you!" Hope rattles, dragging Will and herself closer to Isa.

"Don't listen to her. She's speaking nonsense. Why in the realms would they kill you?" He justifies as he is on his knees in front of Isa with Hope tightening her grip on the blade.

"You didn't tell him?" Hope leerily hovers her blade on his body. Her eyebrows lift in surprise at the newfound information. For a minor moment, she saw something in Isa's expression that once reminded her of herself. A certain fear. The fear of rejection. Fear of being unlovable.

"I-" Isa stopped herself, unable to articulate her kept confession. The lamp heavily swayed back and forth, wavering on her shaking finger under the pouring rain. Below her, she could hear a stream somewhere in the abyss, or perhaps the abyss was the stream.

There was too much fog to know. All Isa could rely on was the drips filling her ears against the wind.

"You didn't know she's a level four?" she questions Will, turning the blade further away from him.

He stares at Isa, not saying a single word. He waits for Hope to return her intentness to Isa before quickly motioning his eyes to Isa's waist. With her other hand, Isa touches the spot he gestured to and understands his tactic.

"He didn't," Isa replies, solemnly. Hope angles her arm from its original place and leans her body farther from her.

With great satisfaction, the side of Isa's mouth pricks upward. "But he does now."

In the blink of an eye, Will yields the dagger Alister provided her with and whirls himself beneath Hope. He stabs her waist, activating the bombs. Hope retaliates as she sanctions her sword at Will, slicing his abdomen open. The two fall backward under the pressure of the explosives and collide on opposing sides of the cliff. Simultaneously, Isa snaps the lamp with her calloused hands using the force of the explosion.

Fragments of the shattered relic glistened around Isa, bursting into separate beams of light, shining as a sun inside the Vampiric Realm. A few hisses echoed in the forest, for it agitated the vampires in the neighboring village and fended off camouflaged poltergeists.

While the beam of light blinded those around it, Isa saw images of her family appear in front of her. For a brief moment, she lost recognition of the familiar faces as one by one vanished in front of her. Memories of her unrequited birthdays and special moments were swept from her fingers when she tried to touch them. They projected themselves around her like northern lights until there were none left.

With those memories, the light faded, and as promised, the dimensional portal closed, sparing a few more entities.

Isa falls on her knees, reconsidering if she has made the right choice.

39

Vows

There at the cliff, Isa couldn't recollect what had happened or what she saw in the blinding lights. She couldn't register why it had left her with such a hollow sensation or if it had something to do with her dying soulmate.

"No. No. No." Isa panicked as she called out Will's name amid the thick fog. "Will! Are you there? Answer me!"

Isa blows the whistle strapped at her thigh and blows into it several times. She waited a few seconds in silence, waiting for Will's reply. "Will. Please."

Answering her not-so-silent prayer, a whistle in the distance chirps loudly for Isa to hear.

"I'm here, Will. I'm here." Isa replies, snapping back into her consciousness. She breathlessly runs in the direction of the sound, pleading with optimism.

"I'm-"she gasps at his open wound. "Oh god. Oh god! Oh god!" Isa falls to her knees and tries to apply direct pressure to his abdomen. She tried hard not to let the texture of his intestines get to her.

"Red." Will weakly brightens. "Is it getting chill out here or is it me? AGH!"

Isa winces when more of his bodily fluids escape between her fingers. "Sorry! I am so sorry."

"Don't apologize. You didn't do this to me."

"Oh, but I did." Isa sobs, realizing her vision. It wasn't Varu and Haru who had paid the price. Instead, the vision came to life, but in exchange for another.

She changed it. But at what cost?

"I'll fix this. I'll make it right." Isa rips parts of the fabric of her clothes and wraps them around his disembodied waist.

There is so much redness.

It was everywhere.

She applied as much pressure as she could. But. It. Wouldn't. Stop.

With her other hand, she searched her pockets for her transporter. She recognized the wound as if it were a replica Jack had on in her vision. Frightening enough, Isa didn't have Jessie close by to heal Will. The only thing she could use was the remaining salve she saved in the pocket of her cloak. She pulled out the minuscule tub of the product and smeared it all on Will's wound. He groaned and clenched his jaw, fighting off the urge to push Isa off of him.

"Red," he panted, twisting his body back and forth like a worm. His cheeks drained of color as his mouth chattered against his chapped lips. Isa refused to acknowledge it as her eyes avoided him, in complete, utter denial. She refused to meet his defeat without trial.

"Ugh! If only we could get out of here- The portal! I can portal us out of here!" She pulls away her arms and pats herself down for the cube. "God, where is it!"

"Red," He breathes, blinking his eyes repetitively. Will didn't bother to examine his wound, as he knew it was futile.

"We'll be out of here in no time. Once you're all better, we can go on our trip, and everything will be perfectly fine." Isa rambles, rummaging through the pockets of her cloak and boots. She dunks all of her items to the floor, and searches for it.

"Red. You need to listen to me, we can't-"

"Don't worry. I will have us out in no time, now where is-"

"Isabel!" He trembles under her. Lifting both of his hands, he pulls Isa's face closer. The image of her vision flickered in her mind between Jack and him, comparing each other. Same expression of pain replaced with a different person.

"I've bled too much." He whispers. His skin was as pale as his hair. The light of which the sun blessed him was fading away.

Her sun. It was setting.

"There has to be something I can do to save us. To save you." Tears flooded her eyes and fell into his face. She too began to shake, but not from the snow falling on them.

She simply couldn't accept their fate. There has to be some loophole. Something magical and miraculous to happen. She read this exact scenario countless times yet, she didn't know what to do. She wanted to kick herself for disregarding the lamp too quickly. If she had granted a wish before breaking it, Will would be alive.

How could she be so stupid?

She should've killed the Seer at the cottage. She should've fought better in the cave and prevented Kate and George's death. She should've come with more weapons.

Every single flaw leading up to this moment swamped her head.

"You can stay." He cups his hand to her face, brushing his thumb over her lips.

"But-"

"I can't be saved, but you can. It's my dying wish."

"No." Isa shakes her head vigorously. "Hearing those words is a fate worse than death! If anyone should die, it should be me."

"Don't say that." The corner of his mouth fell. He wanted to console her. Cherish her. Tell her about the way she makes him feel.

"Yes, I should! You have so much more to live for-" He cuts her off, pressing his lips against hers as their foreheads touch. She could feel the roughness of his lips that weren't there before. "And so do you."

"You have a home, Isa. The Celestial Realm is where you belong. You have the cottage and our friends."

"They were yours before they were mine," she replies, clutching his icy hands. The hands that once were warm as a campfire.

"And I'd be happy to share that with you. Look around. You have so much love to share, and realms to explore. You gave me more than your heart, and I plan to do the same." He smiles, biting back the stabbing sensation in his abdomen. Blood tainted his mouth as he grimaced with every word he spoke. His efforts to hide his pain were far from perfect.

Isa cries harder, firming her grip on his body. Snow piled up around them and the forest howled in sounds of wind heading towards them.

"You don't owe me anything. It is I who owes you. I thought I couldn't possibly love again. You changed that, Will."

"And I hope you continue to love again without me."

"How can you say that? We're soulmates. That was the whole point." Isa grimaces at thought. "I don't want to let go. Not when I finally found you."

"Listen to me, Isa. I love you. I love you so much." He croaks, wavering from the blood loss. "I'm doing this because I cannot fathom the thought of not saving you when I am given the chance."

"And I refuse to let you." Isa stands away from Will's body with a transporter in hand. He grabs hold of her leg and swings the sword at his side. He hits the transporter enough for it to shatter into various pieces. Isa screams and freezes in place, eyes widened and mouth gaping. She falls to the floor, scurrying to collect the pieces.

"I hope you can forgive me." He whispers, his voice scarcely audible among the strong winds.

"Break apart the bind, with a heavy heart and mind."

"Stop!"

"Our hearts will no longer pair, for it will fall into despair."

"Please," Isa begs as the symbol burns bit by bit off her arm. She shouts his name, tears clouding her eyes, forming his silhouette.

"May this day be marked as the last,

"Don't do this to me. To US!"

"And keep everything in the past."

"What about our promise? Can't you keep it?" Isa weeps, holding fistfuls of rubble she wanted to throw at Will. The shards of the broken transporter cut the palm of her hands.

He succinctly pauses his chant, flinching at her cries. Analyzing his wound for the last time, he takes a heavy breath. If he didn't do it now, they would both be dead.

He was ready.

He lived his life and believed Isa should, too. It was a selfish choice, but he wouldn't have it any other way. He fulfilled everything he had ever wanted in his life. He found a home.

Family.

Friends.

Her.

He found *her.*

"I, William, separate my soul from thee, as yours is from mine." He peeks at Isa, her voice piercing through his ears. He consumed every detail he could capture and held onto them, knowing it would be all that he would have of her in the afterlife.

Feeling the bind of their souls loosening on the cutting board of their lives, Isa desperately attempts to cover his mouth, forcing him to pause the unbinding.

The two met in the silence, speaking with the windows behind their irises. Will lightly peels her hands, overlapping his with hers on his chest. Upon closer inspection, his eyes slowly fluttered to a closing.

In a delicate sweep, he brushes a tear on Isa's cheek and delivers the last line. *"Until we meet again, in our next life."* The corners of the fangs Isa everso adored pricked at her, knowing she had been saved.

Another blast of heated energy hits from the insides of their soulmate symbols, eradicating themselves until all had been left was the scar Hope had given Isa. Despite, the intensity of the barrage of her burns, Isa held onto Will's hand as her back hit the ground.

She lay there, shrieking with the banshees surrounding her body as she could not register what she had lost. Echoes of her cries reached the castle and woke the flesh eaters sleeping inside the corpses of the graveyard. She cursed the gods who had failed to fulfill their due diligence as they sat and watched her complete their bidding.

In the snow, her body wrangled as though she had been dumped into an active volcano and the lava was seeping from her heart and pouring out on the area where the symbol once took refuge.

For the longest time, she stayed that way, holding onto remnants of Will until the frostbite soothed her. When she had the strength, she hovered over Will, unable to peel away from his body. She feared if she blinked, his body too would vanish under the rising snowstorm approaching their direction.

She tucked her head in his chest, unable to hear the beating of his heart. The comfort of his gentle touch. She tried to find what was left of the sun she saw inside of him.

Nothing.

It was dark. So dark.

Much like her previous experiences with the dead, she saw a trail of his soul. It was as white as the snowflakes covering her crimson hair and floated like a cloud.

The visualization made her throat tight as if someone had wrapped a cord around her neck. Isa would've stayed in her fixation on her loss had it not been for the subtle sound of a soft moan coming from the opposing edge of the cliff.

Hope.

Isa peered at Will and then back at Hope. The entity inside her perked with curiosity, waiting for her approval to transpire.

Isa embraced it with open arms, allowing her eyes to flare a deep red as the vampires in the realm.

(Red. This. Red that. I know dear reader. You must be sick of the color by now.)

Isa swiftly removed her coat exposing an outline of her body and covered Will, as if she were tucking him into bed. Snatching the sword, he had used to break the transporter, she pointed it straight at Hope's rising and falling metal chest.

"Killing you would be too merciful," Isa reeled, scratching the tip of the sword on Hope's metal plate.

Mind Manipulation

When Hope woke, there stood Isa, hovering above her, staring down at her body with eyes of rage. There wasn't a spot of blood left to miss on her drenched clothes. It was as though she walked into a slaughterhouse. Smears covered her face, and his blood dirtied her hands with pieces of debris and remnants of shards replicating a broken transporter. The remains of the rain and clumps of the snow did little to nothing to clear up the mess on Isa, but she didn't care. All she wanted was for Hope to be six feet underground.

"Stand." She commands Hope calmly.

Hope shudders and blindly obeys.

She is a quick learner. Hope had to give Isa props for that, as it took her weeks of training to manipulate the entirety of the human body.

"Follow me."

Hope's legs stride next to Isa like a peasant, limping. The bombs left a number on her as they had blown off one of her mechanical arms.

The two stood there at the corner of the cliff. Hope was careful enough not to let herself slip under the wetness of the snow. Granted, if Isa would not let her escape that easily. Hope fought hard to break out of Isa's grasp but knew better. When the Enther is strong, it is impossible to break.

"The cliff is awfully beautiful, isn't it?" Isa asks with a deepening hoarse voice. There was a terror in her peace. One that Hope once wore in her dimension.

Hope nods her head, agreeing with Isa. "It is."

"Good."

Isa tilts her head to the sky, where the moon hid under clouds, afraid of her. She spins on her heels and grips Hope's face tightly as if she were to attempt to break Hope's jaw open.

"You should walk to the edge of it. Have more perspective." Isa insists, persuading Hope. She pulls her face closer to the edge, forcing her to peek into the void.

Hope nods her head and leans her body closer. Under the Enther, she could feel the pain of her master. Her anguish, Her loss. Her despair. Those are some of which surfaced most prominently. Of course, there were other emotions that Hope couldn't spell out, not without doing it justice. It was much far deeper than one could think. Empathy escaped Isa and numbed her from the inside out. Her demons, in turn, took over and replaced all sense of humanity from her. The Enther drives on it.

"It's dark." Hope comments, staring down, digging her boots firmly. Her master deepens her frown.

"No, it's not. Not dark enough." Her master corrects her, clamping a hand on Hope's shoulder.

"No, it's not." Hope says aloud, believing Isa. A memory of Will capturing the moonlight underneath a waterfall flickers Hope's vision. The waterfall roars at Hope and silences itself back to the present.

"Good," Isa affirms, hovering behind Hope.

She could push her, though she preferred mind control better. It brought Isa a certain satisfaction. She could see why Hope had abused this ability.

Isa peers once more below to study its depths. If Hope took her rising sun, she might as well pay her forward. Let her live in darkness.

Cold.

Isolated.

Darkness

All the things that Will defied. He brought warmth, companionship, and light. It's why she saw him as a sun. She didn't know it then, but it was because she spent all her life as the moon.

"Jump." Isa chasms from her sorrow and returns to her current drive.

Hope tugs at her feet and chews the inside of her mouth. She doesn't move or respond. It felt as though she was wrestling herself inside the casing of her flesh.

"Jump." Isa snaps, annoyed. She slices the air next to Hope.

Fighting her legs, Hope leans forward to the edge of the cliff, and, with her unbroken hand, she pulls out a small device.

"I SAID JUMP!" Isa commands, screaming at the top of her lungs. She slices at Hope's neck and harshly misses as her puppet falls forward into the depths.

Somehow, Hope unbinds from Isa's control and opens a dimensional portal before meeting the bottom of the cliff. Isa glowers from the edge and roars into the vast, as she undoubtedly had the one person she wanted dead, escape alive.

She tosses the sword at her feet and thrashes into the snow, bidding no mind to the stranger that had witnessed her from the woods. They ran as soon as Isa spotted them in between two bushes.

She didn't care who saw her, or what they would do with her secret.

None of it mattered. She did her job.

As a Seer.

As a Hue.

As a Dreamer.

41

Neither

Hours later, Alister came with a hoard of guards, approaching Isa with caution. He said her name, but she did not reply. She remained there clutching her dead soulmate overlooking the cliff with hatred in her eyes as they darkened. A single snowflake fell on her nose as if it had begged her to go home. It was very late, though Isa had barely noticed how much time had passed, as it meant nothing to her.

"We must hurry to the castle," he stands behind her. "Reports are out of your level. Someone has spotted you using your ability against the Seer Slayer."

He waited for her to correct him. For her to say Hope's name rather than the one this dimension had given her.

She didn't.

She kept in her dazed state, tightening her grip on her cloak around Will's body. She debated throwing herself off to the next life, asking herself if it would be worth it. A small voice in her head and a tug in her heart convinced her not to. It told her a hard truth. If she were to jump, his sacrifice might as well be pointless.

Isa would not taint his sacrifice. Rather, she will listen to the voice and stay where she is. The voice was her guidance.

It was Will's. At least she would like to think it was.

Peering at her blood-stained hands, Isa wipes them on a pile of snow, unbothered. With those same hands, she holds Will's body tighter. She didn't know how to part with it.

It.

"It's an empty shell. Will's not there." The voice in Isa's head murmurs.

Fresh scent as a meat factory, Alister sucks in a breath, fighting the temptation to lick off every drop of blood on them.

"Isa, we must hurry. If we do not leave, they will capture you and behead you. Let me help you-"

"Don't touch me!" Isa seethes, lifting herself away from his corpse, and points Will's sword at him.

Alister stays in place, retracting the hand he held out to her. "I'll allow you a few minutes."

He turns to his guards and shouts commands such as having them scour the perimeters and securing the castle.

As Alister does, Isa allows herself to fixate on Will for the last time. She wanted to make sure she could preserve all his small features in the back of her mind as she feared that with time, she would not remember him.

She whispers a silent prayer and flicks the retractable sword in her hand into a dagger. Warm to the touch, she allows Will to keep her cloak on his body, wrapping away the grotesque visualization of his severed abdomen. She couldn't risk a flesh eater getting to him.

"I should've let the Realms rot," Isa says to Alister. He hovers over her shoulder like a parrot.

The voice in her head does not respond. It knows she meant it. "I saved them. All of them. And my reward is to be hunted for using MY level. The level that had saved everyone but my soulmate."

Alister does not console Isa nor provide her with reassuring words. He knew better as someone who was once in her position.

With a heavy sigh, Isa hauls Will's body and drapes him over her shoulders as if she were giving him a piggyback ride. She then turns to Alister, grazing her eyes over to the lined-up guards who were holding their weapons in place, ready to unsheathe them. They each wore black with the Vampiric emblem on their uniforms, matching their individual noble steeds.

"Answer me this, and I'll follow you back to your castle."

A smile fixates on Alister's face. "Certainly."

She gawks at him, blowing a strand away from her face. "I broke the lamp."

"And?"

"And, you know what is going to happen to me, don't you? You know the price I have to pay?"

"Those are two questions."

"Indeed, they are," Isa admits.

"Which one would you like me to answer?"

"Neither."

"Neither?" he questions, flicking his tongue against his fangs. It was a game of cat and mouse.

"Yes, neither. Those aren't the questions I wanted to ask. They're too easy for you to answer with a simple yes or no."

"Well, what is it?"

"What is the price?" Isa eyes gleam, matching Alister's as he calls off his army. The two meet inside each other's mind as there, all will be unveiled.

42.

See You Next Time, or Not

Yes, yes, I know. I hate cliffhangers as much as the next person, but we will need to stop here.

As I mentioned, this story is not a merry one. If you've come all this way to be proven wrong, then clearly you are simply in denial. I know just the river for you to swim in.

Speaking of denial, Will is indeed dead. He will not be brought back to life or anything of that sort. Let that be known, Dreamer.

He's gone.

So is Haru.

I'll give you a moment to process this.

Ahem.

Are you back?

Really?

You're really back?

After that news? Huh. You must really like pain, or you didn't like them. It's hard to tell.

Perhaps, you may be quite stubborn, it is a common trait of a Dreamer as you have seen from Isa.

Anyhow, I am simply here to tell you, this is not entirely the end. The next part of the story will be just as painful and stressful as this one but with a twist.

Yes, you heard me correctly! There are more twists and turns in the future as you will see. Hope will come again, or should I say Isa will be the one coming to Hope…

I've said too much now. I must leave soon before I get punished. Look, I don't expect many of you to stick around for what is to come, but if you do, there's one thing I will say:

Good luck, dear Dreamer.

Bonus Chapter

The first time Vero woke up, she was hungry.

Really hungry.

Hunger took her over, as she unmistakably attacked a nurse and drained every last drop of his blood. His neck was close to nonexistent. The doctors had to tear his body away from Vero in an effort to salvage what was left of him and to prevent her from doing the same to the doctor.

Vero could hear the sound of his heartbeat as it pounded vigorously against his chest. The world was in disarray and smelled sweet. Sucking the life out of the nurse was the palette Vero thrived for. Though, it didn't last long. Right after they recovered his body, Vero was sedated.

The second time her eyes peeled open, Haru's name brushed her lips. A firm hand was on hers. One that she had been familiar with. She didn't need to sniff him to know who it was.

"Where's Haru?" Vero asks.

"We tried to hold back the ceremony- "

"Where the hell is he Jack!" she shouts, slamming her hand on the desk next to her. All the medical equipment fell to the floor, and the wood split in half.

"The Celestial cemetery." He answers in a low sullen voice.

Vero screamed slamming her hands over and over fighting against her restraints. The lights flickered on and off, dazing the room. Unbothered, Jack patiently sat there, as though he expected her reaction. He ordered the staff to avoid entering the room at all costs. He knew she wouldn't hurt him. She was ruthless, but never to anyone she cared.

"Vero,"

"GET OUT!" She screamed loudly, thrashing her head back and forth against a headpiece they strapped on her. It was supposed to prevent her from biting.

"I'm not going anywhere."

"OUT!" She shrieks, repeating the same words over and over. Eventually, one of the restraints in her hands broke. Using her nails, she rips the second restraint.

Jack climbs over to her bed and holds both of her wrists tightly together. Her head tilted downward as she pursed her lips together against her newfound fangs. Her body became frigid from his touch. It was human, unlike her.

"Let go of me," Vero demands. Jack ignores it and keeps her wrists in the same position.

Vero twists herself and digs her nails into Jack, expecting him to flinch. He didn't. He holds her wrists tighter and moves a strand of her hair away from her face.

Vero vigorously spins her head placing the hair back in its position, hiding herself away. She was much too embarrassed to let him, or anyone for that matter, see her cry. She attempted to shove him off, but he was much too persistent.

Jack takes a hold of Vero's hands and positions them to wrap around his waist. With a free hand, he unlatched Vero's muzzle and lightly cupped the back of her head. Her eyes widened and closed.

Vero didn't bother to struggle.

Instead, she wept like a child into his arms. Her moans carried the hallways, mimicking sounds one would assume would come from La Llorona herself. She repeatedly said Haru's name, hoping he would come to her. She wanted him to hold her and calm her demons the way she would calm his.

Jack stayed there by her side and patiently held her. When he felt her lightly tap his shoulder, he pulled away. He returned to his visitor chair and stared at Vero.

"Where's Will?"

"He's gone too," he murmurs.

Another tear fell from her eyes. She lost her soulmate and her best friend in one day.

Clenching her jaw, Vero felt her fangs pierce her upper lip. She expected them to bleed. It was a reminder for her. She isn't human anymore.

Unable to contain herself, Vero breaks out into a maniacal laugh. Her head swayed with the rest of her body. Jack scoots his chair, eying her with concern. He didn't expect her to have such a reaction.

"What's funny?" He asks carefully.

"Me. Everything. It's all a sick joke." she answers, as all her memories replayed in her head. She pushes the hospital blankets away from her and tears off any attached needles.

"You're not a joke-"

"I'm not saying I am." She cuts him off. "My life was."

"All my life I've imagined that Jessie would somehow create an elixir and Haru would be the first person I would see.

That's all I ever wanted. I didn't care to be blind to the world. I wanted to see Haru. MY Haru." she laughed some more.

"Oh, Vero," Jack said, sympathetically.

"Now I realize how silly it was of me to think that. Here I am dead as ever, and I am blind as a literal bat." Her laughter, hysterical. She blinked back at the pools tempting to spill.

"I'm so sorry."

"Don't be. You weren't the one that killed him," she answers bitterly.

"He died because he refused to do the unmatching vows. He loved you that much. Jessie tried to talk him out of it."

"How is she?" Vero changes the subject, her voice somber with a hint of gall.

"She's doing as good as she can be. She's somewhere around here." Jack lightly smiles.

"And Isa? Is she alive?" Vero's eyes move side to side, recalling the few details of the night it all happened.

Jack flinches in his seat. He anticipated this question and wasn't sure how or where to begin.

"They're after her. She's on the run." He replies, vaguely leaving out the details.

"What! Why?" Vero sits up in her bed. "How'd they find out?"

"What do you mean find out?"

Vero purses her lips, neglecting to answer his question. Jack scoffs, hurt. As usual, everyone knew something he didn't.

"She used her abilities." He answers her, twiddling his thumbs.

An expression flashes on her face. Her eyebrows knit together, deepening her internal anguish.

"Where are you going?" Jack stands up, following her to the door.

"To find her." Vero's eyes train in black with determination.

Not lifting a finger, the hospital door slams open under her heightened telekinetic abilities. She brushes her fangs with her tongue, sniffing the air. Bursting through the glass windows spouted her old staff. Vero catches it with ease and Jack follows behind her heels, meticulously typing on his watch.